Dear Reader,

The book you've just bought from my "Second Chances" series is truly evidence of the second chances God gives us. The books in this series have been published before, some by Dell, some by Harlequin, others by Silhouette and HarperCollins. I was a Christian when I entered the romance market in 1983, hoping to take the world by storm. What I found, instead, was that the world took me by storm. One compromise led to another, until my books did not read like books written by a Christian. Not only were they not pleasing to God, but they embraced a worldview that opposed Christ's teachings. In the interest of being success-ful, I had compartmentalized my faith. I trusted Christ for my sal-vation, but not much else. Like the Prodigal Son, I had taken my inheritance and left home to do things my own way.

I love that parable because it so reflects my life. My favorite part is when Jesus said, "But while he was still a long way off, his father saw him . . ." I can picture that father scanning the hori-zon every day, hoping for his son's return. God did that for me. While I was still a long way off, God saw me coming. Early in 1994, when I yearned to be closer to God and realized that my writing was a wall between us, that my way had not been the best way, I promised God that I would never write anything again that did not glorify him. At that moment, it was as if God came run-ning out to meet me. I gave up my secular career and began to write Christian books.

Shortly after I signed a contract for Zondervan to publish my suspense series, "The Sun Coast Chronicles," something extraor-dinary happened. The rights to some of my earlier romance nov-els were given back to me, and I was free to do whatever I wanted with them. At first, I thought of shelving them, but then, in God's gentle way, he reminded me that I was free to rewrite them, and this time, get them right. So I set about to rewrite these stories the way God originally intended them.

As you read these stories, keep in mind that they're not just about second chances, they are second chances. I hope you enjoy them.

In Christ,
Terri Blackstock

Books by Terri Blackstock

Cape Refuge (Book 1 in series)
Emerald Windows

Newpointe 911

Private Justice
Shadow of Doubt
Trial by Fire
Word of Honor

Sun Coast Chronicles

Evidence of Mercy
Justifiable Means
Ulterior Motives
Presumption of Guilt

Second Chances

Never Again Good-bye
When Dreams Cross
Blind Trust
Broken Wings

With Beverly LaHaye

Seasons Under Heaven
Showers in Season
Times and Seasons
Season of Blessing

Novellas

Seaside

BLIND TRUST

TERRI BLACKSTOCK

ZONDERVAN™

GRAND RAPIDS, MICHIGAN 49530

ZONDERVAN™

Blind Trust
Copyright © 1997 by Terri Blackstock

Requests for information should be addressed to:

Zondervan, *Grand Rapids, Michigan 49530*

Library of Congress Cataloging-in-Publication Data

Blackstock, Terri, 1957–
   Blind trust / Terri Blackstock.
      p.   cm. — (Second chances)
    ISBN: 0-310-20710-X (softcover)
    I. Title.   II. Series: Blackstock, Terri, 1957–   Second chances.
PS3552.L34285B57   1997
813'54.—dc21
                                                  97–2726

Published in association with the literary agency of Alive Communications, Inc., 7680 Goddard Street, Suite 200, Colorado Springs, CO 80920.

Interior design by Amy E. Langeler
Printed in the United States of America

---

05 06 / ❖ DC/ 20 19 18 17 16

This book is lovingly dedicated to the Nazarene.

Acknowledgments

I want to take a moment to tell you about Emily Kelly, my friend and biggest supporter, who recently went home to be with the Lord. Emily, a sister in Christ and a sister church member, has been reading my books for years, offering wonderful encouragement to me at times when I was certain no one in the world was reading my work. I never had to tell her I had a book out, because she was always looking and waiting for it to be placed on the shelves. I would plan to give her a free copy as soon as I saw her, only to find that she'd already bought it, read it, and recommended it to someone else.

In her last weeks, when cancer was ravaging her body and she was engaged in the toughest battle she'd ever fought in her life, she asked if my latest book was out. Reading it, she said, would help to get her mind off of her struggles. I hated the thought that she might not make it until my next book's release. I knew that the book itself would do nothing for her quality of life, but knowing she was there to read it did a great deal for mine.

She didn't make it until that next book, and I've felt that void so deeply. But I know that I am a better writer because of Emily, and that remains with me. I thank her more than words can say for the part she played in my life.

And I'm glad she finally won that battle.

Chapter One

The Bronco that had been riding Sherry Grayson's bumper since she'd left work was not the sole cause of her rising anger. But since it had been inappropriate to lash out at her roommate, Madeline, when she'd broken the news just fifteen minutes ago, she figured the Bronco was as good a target for her rancor as any.

Deliberately slowing to fifteen miles an hour in a forty-mile-an-hour zone, she crept along, hoping the driver behind her would get the message and pass her before she slammed her brakes to make him hit her from behind. It would serve him right. But wrecking her car wouldn't solve her problems, any more than bursting into tears would. And she didn't have the time nor the energy for either.

"Slow down," she muttered as tremors of anxiety coursed through her. She couldn't deal with a battle with a joyrider today. Yesterday, when life still had as much normalcy as it had had for the last eight months, she might have handled it better. But today . . .

"Get off my bumper!" Sherry blared, heat scoring her features when the Bronco almost bumped her. Heavy traffic detoured around them, but the driver would not pass her. It was an omen. An omen that she could no longer refuse to look back. After what she'd learned today, she would need strength from her past so that she could plunge forward.

According to her roommate, Clint Jessup was back from the black hole he'd vanished into without a trace eight months ago, and he intended to see her. The destructive driver behind her was a warning that life was going to be a bit rougher for a while. But she had braved rough times before; she could do it again.

Anxious to be rid of the vehicle that seemed bent on driving right through her, she made a sharp turn onto a quieter street and breathed a shaky sigh of relief that she could drive the rest of the way in peace.

But a quick glance in the rearview mirror told her the Bronco was still behind her. Her pulse accelerated as the first light of understanding dawned on her. The Bronco was following her.

Driving fast enough to keep a car's distance between them, Sherry strained to make out the driver. A man—no, two men—sat silhouetted against the sun descending at their backs. The driver's shoulders squared with determination as he drove, and the passenger sat slumped against the door in a pose of utter boredom.

Panic surged through her. Making another quick turn while she held her breath, Sherry watched in her mirror as the Bronco barreled around the corner after her, the sun no longer making opaque shadows out of her pursuers. The driver's hair flapped into his face from the hard wind at his window, and she watched a hand come up to push it back into place. It was dark hair, full and tapering back from his face, and against the light through his back window she could see the slightest hint of curl.

She made another turn as the panic coiling in her stomach became more pronounced. The sun was blazing toward her now, and without slowing her speed, she held up a hand to shade her eyes and glanced in the mirror again, hoping to mentally record his features and report him to the police. Sherry clutched the steering wheel more tightly and waited for the bright glare to slide off the windshield and give her a clear view of his face as they rounded a curve. The open collar of the driver's shirt flapped against his neck, and a ray of sunlight caught a strip of gold draping down from his throat, illuminating it like the razor edge of a knife. Some familiar pain stabbed her heart, and she released her breath in a rush. *The gold chain ... the engagement gift she had given him ...*

"No," she said aloud before her imagination carried her away. It wasn't him. It was just the knowledge that he was back that had made her heart conjure up images.

The sun descended behind the trees after its last blinding burst of orange, and suddenly the man came into full view through the mirror—the beckoning mane of soft, dark hair, the determined set of full lips on a tanned face, the chain glistening more subtly against his neck. And as her punctured heart sank to her stomach, her eyes rose to the dark, riveting eyes that refused to let her go.

Clint Jessup's eyes.

Oh, dear God, I'm not ready for this. Physical danger she could bear, but Clint Jessup threatened something far worse.

Suddenly her driving became uninhibited, and her foot pounded the accelerator to the floor.

As if he knew he'd been recognized, Clint's teeth flashed between tight lips, and he sped up as well. His shoulders hunched forward as he clutched the steering wheel. Searching for another turnoff in hopes of getting back into the flow and security of heavy traffic, Sherry forced her eyes to stay on the road and away from the rearview mirror. But no sooner had she spotted a turnoff a mile up the deserted road than the heavy hum of his engine loomed up beside her.

Sherry kept her eyes off the vehicle trying to stop her and remained intent on reaching the turnoff. But Clint had other plans. She heard his gears shift, heard the passenger in his car shouting at him, heard the squeal of his tires as he found a last burst of speed and screeched sideways in front of her. Stomping on her brakes, she steered to the shoulder of the road, skidding to a stop just short of hitting him.

The driver's door of the Bronco slammed, and in seconds Clint was at her car. Before the thought of locking her door occurred to her, he was reaching for the handle, opening it, leaning inside. Sherry shoved him away and pushed out of the car, her heart pounding. "You lunatic, are you trying to kill us?"

Clint leaned against her car door to close it. The suggestion of a smile softened his lips, but his black eyes were serious as they took in the sight of her. "Hi, Sherry," he said between labored breaths.

The mildness of his greeting rankled her, but somehow she couldn't make herself get back in the car and drive away just yet. "What do you want, Clint?"

A shrug and a sigh punctuated his slowing breaths. "I tried to call, but I didn't get very far with your roommate. I just wanted to see you."

Sherry slid her trembling fists into the pockets of her pants. "In the old days they used to knock on doors for that sort of thing, instead of running you down in the street."

"You would have just slammed the door in my face," Clint said. "I wanted to catch you before you got inside."

Sherry turned away from his probing eyes and peered up the street, wishing she could turn back time a half hour and prepare herself for this encounter. "Next time you want to follow someone, Superman, you might be less conspicuous if you kept a few inches between bumpers."

A slow, half-smile sauntered across Clint's face, casting an angular shadow on the new, deep lines in his bronze skin. "And next time you get followed, Lois, you might avoid taking the most deserted street in the city."

Sherry shrugged and reached past his hip to open her door. "Lesson learned. Now, if you'll excuse me."

Clint caught her shoulders and turned her to face him. "I wanted to see you, Sherry, not teach you a lesson."

Sherry stepped out of his hold and gave him a guarded assessment, fighting back the hope that told her to give him a chance. Reason left her for a fleeting moment, her eyes softened, and she mentally brushed his hair back as it eased over his face, mentally straightened the long, thin strand of gold as it looped from his neck where she had hung it months ago, mentally traced the tapering lines of his white shirt. His jeans were worn and faded, and he still wore the threadbare jogging shoes that he'd held on to—longer than he'd held on to her.

"Why did you move?" he asked.

Sherry glanced away long enough to tighten her grip on her unstable emotions, then brought her eyes back to his, unblinking, as if the simple movement would shatter them. "I was all packed up with no place to go."

His doleful gaze lowered to the pavement between them, and his throat convulsed. "I know I hurt you, running out like that before the wedding, but—"

"I survived," she cut in, desperately wanting to be spared the excuses that had taken him eight months to manufacture. She already knew the reason he had disappeared two weeks before their wedding. When Madeline, her roommate, had called her this afternoon to tell her that Clint was back and that he had called, she'd said something about his being away working on a book he was writing. The very idea had enraged Sherry. He wasn't a writer. He had never even mentioned a desire to write. He had been a youth minister before he'd skipped town. The flimsy, stupid excuse for his fleeing from commitment had added insult to injury.

"It was great to see you again, Clint," she said in a saccharine voice as she reached for her door again. "Next time you see me on the street feel free to run me off the road for a nice little chat." The door snapped open beneath her hand, but before she could step inside, Clint grabbed the door and blocked her entrance.

"We've got to talk, Sherry," he said in a firm, determined voice as he stepped closer behind her and set his other hand on her stiffening shoulder.

The touch shattered her facade and exposed the raw pain hidden beneath it. She clamped her teeth shut, grating out words that cut deeper with each syllable. "What do you want?"

"I want you back," he said simply.

An almost hysterical laugh came from deep in her throat to thicken the air around them. Slowly, she turned to face him, narrowing her blue eyes to hide the pain lurking there. "It's about eight months too late for that, Clint. I must admit, I didn't expect you to work the freedom bug out of your system quite so soon, but—"

"It wasn't the freedom bug, Sherry," Clint said. "You can't believe I would have skipped out on the wedding without a really good reason."

Sherry shook her head wearily and gazed off into the distance, the well of moisture in her eyes catching the light. "Clint, how should I put this? If you were kidnapped by savages and taken to some exotic island, and had to spend eight months swimming shark-infested waters to get back to me, it wouldn't make any difference. It's over. Dead. Can you understand that?"

His throat bobbed again, and he raised a finger to her chin, coaxing her face back to his in such a gentle way that she couldn't resist looking at him. "I don't believe you."

Swallowing back the emotion blocking her throat, Sherry steadied her voice. "Fine, then, let's test it. *Were* you kidnapped by savages and taken to some exotic island?" As she spoke, full tears sprang to her eyes, for she hadn't realized until now how much she wished it were true.

"No," he said before she could finish. A deep, jagged breath tore from his lungs. "I can't make you understand right now. I had to get away and—"

"Write?" The word was flung as a challenge.

The lines in Clint's face seemed etched deep with regret as he looked at the ground, then glanced toward the quiet man still sitting in the Bronco, the man Sherry had almost forgotten. The man leaned forward and nodded, as if giving him some silent signal. Clint's eyes glossed over with despair as he brought them back to her. "Yeah," he breathed out in a voice as dull as a twilit sky. "I had to get away and write."

Somehow the admission pierced her even more deeply than his disappearance had. "I'm sure the youth ministers of the world will appreciate the sacrifices you've made to record your amazing well of knowledge. Too bad you've lost all your credibility now that you've left your youth group high and dry and dumped your fiancée all in one moment of panic."

"Sherry, don't do this," he whispered, as though he didn't want the other man to hear. He touched her hair so lightly that she sensed more than felt it. "I've been through agony, and it's not over yet."

Sherry ducked her head away from his hand and slipped into the car. "Just think how much richer your writing will be after all that suffering," she said, her voice cracking. She cranked her engine, but he leaned inside the car door, still not letting her go.

"It's not over, Sherry," he said in a deep, desperate voice. "I'm not giving up on you. You're gonna have to do one major convincing job to make me believe that you don't care anymore."

Sherry stared at her trembling hands clutching the steering wheel as if it alone could anchor her to reality.

"I'm still crazy about you," he whispered, his hand slipping through her hair to settle on her neck. "An hour hasn't gone by that I haven't thought of you."

"That's very touching." Sherry knew that somewhere within her there must be a reserve of strength. But for the life of her, she could not find it. Her eyes fluttered shut. His fingers began to knead her neck, and she opened them again and shoved his hand away from her neck. "Now if you'll kindly move so I can shut my door . . ."

"I want to see you tonight."

"No."

"Why not?" he asked. "What are you afraid of?"

"My temper," she said.

"I know that temper. I can deal with it."

"I can't," she bit out, lips quivering. "It might land me in jail." Her face reddened to back up the words, seething blood and storming emotions threatening to implode, leaving her their only victim, if she didn't start driving.

"Then when can I see you?" The question was a pleading whisper against her face.

"Never. Now get away from my car."

Clint blew out a frustrated breath. "I'll let you go now, but it's not over by a long shot."

Sherry slipped her car into reverse. "It's your time, your energy. Waste it if you want."

Slowly, Clint stepped back and allowed her to pull her door closed. He stood watching as she backed away from the Bronco's barricade, then shifted into drive with a screech of rubber and went around it.

Sherry would have given all she owned for a little numbness at that moment, for her heart ached as she glanced back at him before making her turn. He was standing in the road, lean and forlorn, staring after her. Quickly, she turned, leaving him behind, though the sight of him was inexorably drafted on her mind.

The car seemed to drive her home instinctively, for her thoughts were caught in the eye of her raging emotions. The anger and bitterness she had carefully cultivated for her first meeting with Clint dwindled beside the bitter mingling of pain and attraction she still felt. It wasn't fair for him to come back now, she thought as she forced back her menacing tears. She had just begun to get her life in order, had just come close to happiness again after the nightmares of the last eight months.

Nightmares. She wiped at her eyes and thought how the whole eight months had been a series of nightmares. Memory settled over her like impending night as she remembered her first attempt to strike back at those nightmares . . .

<hr>

Something has happened to him!" she'd cried frantically to Gary Rivers, the police sergeant she had been involved with before Clint. It hadn't mattered that the police department had given up the search for Clint, deciding that they couldn't waste their time on someone who simply had premarital cold feet. So she had done something she'd sworn never to do. She had used her past relationship with Gary as a means to get help, even though she knew he had never really forgiven her for choosing Clint over him.

They had spent the morning going through Clint's house in a vain search for clues. "He wouldn't have just left!" she kept saying.

Gary had rubbed his blond beard and shaken his head dolefully. "I'm sorry, Sherry." He stepped over several boxes that Clint and Sherry had packed for their move into the house they were buying, the house they had lost because Clint had been gone for the closing. "But the man knew what he was doing. He didn't leave anything really important. He took everything he'd need."

"You're not listening to me!" she screamed. "He's hurt somewhere! Maybe dying! Maybe he's already—" The word had died in her throat. "If we give up on him we'll never find him. We've got to get to him!"

Gary had only shaken his head again, turning up the voltage on her fury. "We've done everything—"

"*Don't* say it!" she shrieked. "Don't tell me we've done everything we can. We haven't done anything! He's out there somewhere, and he needs me! Why don't you believe me?"

Gary had looked at her with sympathy she could simply not bear. "Sherry, it's never easy to admit that someone ran out on you. But it isn't all that uncommon for a man to get cold feet. Especially a man like Clint—"

Sherry had cut off his words by grabbing him by the collar and shoving him against the wall in a burst of raging adrenaline. "He was not afraid of marriage! He wouldn't do that!" she had gritted. "He wouldn't leave me like that! He loves me!"

Gary hadn't said another word, and she had let him go, muttering a quiet, hoarse, "Get out. You're no help."

She had spent the night among Clint's things, sleeping in his bed, wearing the clothes too old or too tattered for him to have taken, crying her soul out, praying that he'd walk through that door any minute and hold her.

But she hadn't seen him again.

Until today. And though she had come to terms with the ultimate rejection, she had never been able to hate him or give up on him completely, as long as the faint possibility existed that he'd left for some unavoidable reason. Not because he feared commitment. Not because he didn't love her. And certainly not so he could write.

But his reappearance today without a substantial excuse shattered those possibilities. More than ever, she had to face the fact that the commitment had been too much for him, that she had not been enough.

The crunch of rocks on the driveway of her house pulled her out of her reverie, and mechanically, she gathered the stack of papers on her seat and got out of the car. It was important to keep her routine, she told herself as she stooped to pick up the newspaper. If she just kept things normal, she would not lose control. If she kept the pain from her face, maybe she could exorcise it from her heart.

Slipping the rubber band off the paper, she used her free hand to shake it out of its roll. The front page told of the few small developments in the Givanti trial that her father's office was prosecuting. Givanti, the local businessman who had been indicted for murder and cocaine distribution, had been almost the sole focus of the U.S. attorney's life for the past few months, when he wasn't worrying about his daughter's emotional state. She walked out to her mailbox on the street and reached inside for the stack of mail. Her hand slipped beneath the weight, and the stack of papers anchored against her hip began to slide in a mini avalanche onto the hot May pavement. Muttering under her breath, Sherry squatted and began to reconstruct the stack, glancing from side to side, hoping no one had seen the clumsy performance. The only human in sight was someone in a black Pontiac parked several houses up the street—apparently waiting for someone—but he seemed more engrossed in the newspaper he read than in her. *Pull yourself together,* she ordered herself. *Madeline will take one look at you and see that you're falling apart. She'll have that prayer chain of hers activated within the hour, and everyone in town will know you're losing it.*

Madeline was waiting for her when she went in, her dark curls framing her concerned face. A cartoon animator affiliated with a Christian amusement park, Promised Land, Madeline had been her roommate and mainstay ever since the terrible day that she accepted that Clint was never going to return.

Trying to appear nonchalant, Madeline crossed her arms over the caricature of the mosquito, which her T-shirt declared to be the Louisiana state bird. Her curls fell into her eyes, and she blew them back as she rushed forward to help Sherry with her load. "Here, let me help." She took the stack of papers, then regarded Sherry carefully. "Feel okay?"

Sherry shrugged and tossed the mail onto the table. "Yeah, fine."

"Are you gonna call him?"

"Don't have to," Sherry said. "I just saw him."

Madeline gasped. "No way. How'd you know where to find him?"

"He found me," Sherry said. "He ran me off the road a few minutes ago."

"Ran you off the road? Are you hurt?"

Not physically, she wanted to say, but instead she shook her head and slumped onto the couch.

Madeline lowered herself onto the coffee table across from her. "Sherry, what happened? What did he say?"

"What difference does it make? I told him that I don't want to see him again."

"Did he say why he left? I mean other than that writing thing?"

Sherry felt the life draining from her face, leaving behind a hollow, expressionless shell. "No. That's his story and he's sticking to it."

Silence provided the response that Sherry expected. Madeline propped her elbows on her bare knees and pushed her curls out of her face. After a long while, the young woman's voice came quiet and uninflected. "I guess I really expected there to be more."

"Yeah. Guess I did too." The admission made Sherry's voice catch, and to avoid seeing the wave of sympathy washing across Madeline's face, she stood up and went into the kitchen. "What's to eat? I've got a ton of work to do tonight. I have to type four of Wes's bids."

"Anything I can do?" Madeline asked. She followed Sherry and leaned against the kitchen doorjamb. "Like listen?"

Sherry's hands fell limp on the package of sandwich meat she had reached into the refrigerator for. "Thanks, Madeline. I just don't want to talk about it right now."

Madeline slid up onto the kitchen table, for she rarely used chairs. "Good. At least you're not going to pretend it doesn't bother you."

Sherry abandoned the meat and closed the refrigerator door, letting her eyes rest on her hands gripped around the handle. "Yes, I am. As soon as I get over the shock, I plan to do just that."

"But not to me."

Sherry crossed her arms and leaned back against the refrigerator door. "No, not to you. I'm pretty transparent to you."

"And to Clint."

Sherry lifted her brows doubtfully. "Yeah. But if I was transparent today, he saw a whole barrage of conflicting signals, because I don't even know how I feel about seeing him again."

Sherry pulled out a chair and sat, combing a hand through her hair and trying not to renew her fury of the afternoon. "I told him I never want to see him again, but he swore it wasn't over." Her shoulders sagged, and she cradled her forehead in her hand and whispered a soft moan. "What am I going to do?"

Madeline slid off the table and disappeared into the living room, then returned with Sherry's load of papers and dropped them down with a thud on the kitchen table. "You're going to go on with life as if he never came back. You're going to bury yourself in your work until the shock wears off, and then you'll be fine. And I'm going to get our friends praying for you and for the situation, and then remind you that God is still in control . . ."

A wisp of a smile softened Sherry's face, and she pulled the papers in front of her. "You're very predictable, you know that?" Sherry asked.

Madeline grinned. "Good. You need a little certainty in your life."

Sherry's heart lightened at her friend's step-by-step approach to life's catastrophes. But as she sorted through her papers, she realized she was kidding herself if she thought the problem of Clint Jessup could be solved with a pat on the back and a stack of work. God was trying to teach her something, and for the life of her, she was tired of learning.

———◆———

Later that night, Sherry called her brother Wes to break the news. "Clint's back."

"Back?" Wes asked. "Just like that?" She knew he had given her fiancé up for dead. Like her, he couldn't believe that his friend had betrayed them, and had spent eight months filling in the blanks.

"Yeah."

"Have you seen him?"

"Yeah, today."

"And what did he say? What explanation did he give? Where has he been?"

She sighed. "Let's just say that the explanation left a lot to be desired. You know all those noble scenarios we came up with, about it all being out of his control, and his struggling all this time to get back to me?"

"Yeah."

"Fantasy. He just needed his space."

"That's what he *said?* That he needed his *space?*"

"No, but that's basically it."

Wes was quiet for a moment. "If I see him, I just might tear him apart with my bare hands. What kind of jerk would profess to be some called-of-God youth minister, then do something so selfish and hurt so many people? Abandoning my sister at the altar, lying to me about being a great guy and a wonderful future brother-in-law and uncle for my kids ..."

"He betrayed *me*, Wes, not you. And I wasn't left at the altar."

"Same thing. He betrayed a lot of us, Sherry. You, me, all those kids who trusted him and grieved over him. They're still praying for him."

"They need to," she said. "Look, I gotta go. I have to let Dad know."

"Right," Wes said. "He ought to relate, since he walked out on you, too."

Chagrined, she hung up, and stared at the phone for a moment. Wes, who she had once believed had no capacity for hate, truly hated their father.

For years, she and Wes had been estranged from him, after he had divorced their mother when they were both small children. For most of their lives, he had been a nonentity in their lives. In her, his absence had left a deep void, but in Wes, it had left deep bitterness. They had not known where he was or why he had abandoned them, until the day he'd come back to town and told them that he wanted to reestablish his relationship with them, now that their mother was dead. He was a lawyer now, and had money, something she and Wes had never had benefit of. And he told them that his life had changed when God had used a heart attack to bring him face to face with his mortality. He'd been convicted of his past mistakes and the pain he had inflicted on his children. The remorse and shame had brought him to his knees, forced him to ask forgiveness, and empowered him to make amends. Wes had not trusted the story and wanted nothing to do with him, despite his wife's insistence that their children needed at least one grandparent.

Sherry, on the other hand, had been more forgiving, and had embraced her father with an almost desperate love. When he had run for federal attorney this past year, she had been right there beside him, campaigning with him like a devoted daughter. He had won. Her father had proven that he loved her with his diligent attention and care for her, and even though Wes warned her that he'd lose interest eventually, as he had so many years ago, she had enjoyed her newfound relationship with him. She only wished Wes could understand how much her father had been there for her when Clint had disappeared. He had displayed startling bits of wisdom about forgiveness and patience, and had kept her hoping despite the fact that there seemed to be no hope.

Now, there was even less than no hope.

She dialed her father's number, got his machine, and said, "Dad, it's me. Are you there?"

He picked up immediately. "Hi, honey. I was avoiding the press. They're all over me with the Givanti case going on."

She didn't care about that. She only had the energy to deal with one thing at a time. "Dad, I thought you should know that Clint is back. I saw him today."

Silence. Then, "What did he say?"

"Oh, not much. That he wants to resume things. No real explanation. At least, not one that makes sense."

"Are you all right?"

"Yeah, I'm fine."

"You're not alone, are you? I could come over—"

"Madeline's here. I'm fine, Dad, really. I guess I should just be glad that he's not dead. The mystery's over. At least that part of it."

"Are you going to see him again?"

"Not if I can help it."

Silence again. "Honey, are you sure I can't come over?"

"Positive, Dad. I'll talk to you more tomorrow."

"All right, honey. Have faith, okay? All things work together for good . . ."

"Yeah, I know. Bye, Dad." She hung up, and sat wondering what good could come of this. Not for the first time, she wondered if she could even believe that Scripture anymore.

Chapter Two

If only I could explain, Clint thought dismally as he stepped into the new office building for Grayson Builders, where Sherry worked with her brother, Wes. It was the day after his disastrous encounter with Sherry, and he hoped Wes might help him get through to Sherry somehow.

Clint caught his breath as he saw Sherry standing with her back to him, staring down with unseeing eyes at the blueprint on the table in front of her. She was thinking about him. He felt it as strongly as he felt that she still loved him, but the knowledge was not enough for him as long as she fought those feelings.

Eight months without her, he thought with a shudder. Eight lonely, impatient months, wishing to God that one miserable night that changed his fate had never taken place. Eight months praying that someone else would not come along to replace him, that she would wait . . .

He watched her sweep her hair back from her face and hold it above her head, then let it fall in a helpless tumble. Her heavy sigh moved her shoulders, and she dropped her head. She was as tired as he was, he thought. The months had taxed her spirit, too. He wondered how many months it would take to get spirit back in either of them.

He had almost made her his wife. He had almost had the chance to begin a life with her. Instead, he was reduced to watching her from a distance, with the awestruck feelings of apprehension that he'd known when he'd first fallen in love with her. It had been a constant struggle to keep from voicing his feelings for her, when he'd met her at church and she had volunteered to help with the youth. But she had been involved with someone else—a cop who didn't seem worthy of her, at least in Clint's mind—so he had kept his feelings to himself. But when that relationship had ended, he felt the obstacles lifting, and he had lost the struggle with his heart . . .

It was the night of the youth Christmas production, and several volunteers had stayed behind to clean up. Sherry had been one of them, and he still remembered the sweet smiles she'd given him through the laughing faces, the bright blue twinkle of her eyes. Though he'd given no one any indication that he was interested in her, he felt that his interest was dreadfully obvious to everyone. When they had begun to leave one by one, he'd found other things to keep her busy so she would stay.

As soon as they were alone, he had scrounged up the courage to move their relationship to a different level.

"I really appreciate your help, Sherry," he said. "The kids enjoy having you around. So do I."

"Don't misread it," she'd said, and his soft smile had faded. "I think I'm doing it more for selfish reasons than any generosity."

"Selfish reasons? Like what?"

She couldn't make herself say it, and his heart had begun to burn as she'd turned away to close a box. He didn't know what had come over him just then, but something had told him that her admission was an invitation. And he'd accepted it. He touched her shoulder and she turned around. As she looked up at him, her eyes seemed to twinkle with anticipation.

"Sherry, I heard you and Gary Rivers weren't seeing each other anymore. Is that true?"

She nodded. "Absolutely."

"I'm sorry," he lied.

Her smile told him not to be. "We weren't right for each other, Clint. It had to happen sooner or later. God has better things for us."

Their eyes had locked, and he'd desperately tried to read what was going through her mind. "Maybe it's too soon," he said, "but I was thinking that maybe you'd let me take you to dinner sometime."

"I'd love to go to dinner with you. When?" The bold question had made him grin.

"How about tomorrow?"

"All right." That twinkle in her eyes was more pronounced. "I'll see you then. Seven o'clock?"

He thought about seven o'clock tomorrow night, and it seemed like an eternity away. "Okay. That's great. But right now I'd love to sit down over a cup of coffee. Do you have to get home?"

Something about her easy smile had made this feel so right. "No. Why don't we go to the coffee shop up the street?"

They had talked for hours, about his plans for his ministry, the kids they both loved, the dreams they shared . . .

And then he had walked her to her car.

He had always considered himself a strong man, a man who wasn't easily moved, a man who kept his head. But something in her face had made him kiss her that night. The moment their lips met, he knew this wasn't just an idle infatuation. There was something special about Sherry Grayson.

No other woman had ever made him want one moment to linger into eternity. No other woman had ever made him love so deeply that he would have given anything he owned to hold her for five more minutes ...

And there had not been another woman since that night. He had loved her mind, her beauty, and her loving ability to give. His absence had only made those feelings stronger. No, he thought as he watched her. For him, there would never be another woman.

He started toward her, the buzz of a power saw outside muffling the sound of his footsteps across the floor.

H*ad he left her for another woman?* The sickening thought crossed Sherry's mind as she stared, unfocused, at the blueprint Wes had asked her to make copies of. Had it been some idiotic, male desire that had wrenched him away? Hadn't the love she'd believed in been a little too good to be true?

An hour hasn't gone by that I haven't thought of you. His words echoed in her mind. *Then why?* she wanted to cry out. *Why did you leave me?*

As if in answer, the power saw outside cut off, and she heard footsteps behind her. She kept her head down, for she didn't want Wes or any of the others to see the tears in her eyes. But a familiar scent drifted to her nostrils, and she stiffened as his roughened fingers closed gently around her arm.

She swung around. "What are you doing here?"

"I was looking for you," Clint said softly. "Sherry, we've got to talk. You have to trust me. You have to believe in what we had, even if what I tell you doesn't make sense."

"Get out," she said.

"No, I won't. You have to listen to me."

"You haven't said anything to listen *to*, Clint. Some cockamamy stuff about writing a book. Do you really think I'm so stupid—?"

"It'll be clear soon, Sherry. Until then . . . I just want to see you. I've missed you. I would have risked almost anything to get back to you . . ."

"Risk?" she asked. "What kind of risk could it take? The risk of possible marital entrapment? Is that it?"

"No, Sherry. You know how much I wanted to marry you."

Her face reddened and tears sprang to her eyes, and her face twisted with the effort of holding them back. "You're a cruel man, Clint. I never would have believed that about you."

Clint took a step toward her. "Don't believe it now, Sherry. I never wanted to hurt you. I'm so sorry."

He touched her shoulder, and Sherry turned away, unable to trust herself to face him. A tear seeped through her lashes, but she kept her eyes closed.

Clint lowered his mouth to her hair, kissed it, then pressed his forehead against her crown. She felt his chest brush against her back, felt the fusion of their hearts telling her that she had a dreadful fight on her hands if she intended to forget him.

"Don't, Clint," she whispered desperately, but in answer he slid his arms around her waist and pulled her back against him.

"I still love you, Sherry," he whispered next to her ear.

Why couldn't she hate him? Why couldn't she summon enough anger to push him away and convince him that there was no feeling? "But I don't love you," she said, her voice as stiff and unyielding as her body.

As if her words had no meaning, he tightened his embrace. "It's so good to hold you again," he murmured against her neck.

"Let go of me, Clint." Her voice broke as she spoke, and she longed to extract herself from his embrace before her brimming emotions burst. Pulling herself together, she said it again more firmly. "Let go of me."

Clint turned her to face him, forcing her to look up into his pleading eyes. "Look me in the eye and tell me you don't love me," he challenged. "Your eyes don't lie. They never have."

Sherry's cheeks stung. "This is not a game, Clint."

"Look me in the eye and say it," he repeated.

A moment of silence rippled between them as Sherry looked up into his opaque black eyes and summoned all the strength she contained. "I don't love you anymore."

Clint's eyes bore into hers, searching, finding, measuring. "I still don't believe you."

"Fine, then," she said, her face burning. "Delude yourself. I don't care what you think."

"Then why are you crying?"

Sherry swatted at her tears and stepped backward. "It has to do with anger, Clint, and resentment. Nothing else. Play your games on someone else. I'm all used up."

"I know the feeling," he said, finally allowing her the distance she so desperately needed. "But I can make it up to you."

"No, you can't. Not when it was so easy for you to waltz out and waltz back in. I'll never trust you again."

He reached for her, but Sherry recoiled, stepping back into a model of a fourteen story building. The structure tumbled over and crashed on the floor. Suddenly, a man bolted through the double doors of the office, hand poised under his nylon windbreaker.

"It's okay," Clint yelled quickly, stopping him with a raised hand. "It was the model."

The man—the same one who'd been with Clint in the car yesterday—assessed the situation briefly, flashed Sherry an innocent, composed smile, then sauntered away as if going for a summer stroll.

Forgetting the collapsed model and the rush of emotion that caused her to back into it, Sherry brought her distrustful eyes back to Clint. "Is that the man who was with you in the Bronco yesterday?"

Clint stooped down and began to pick up the pieces. "Sam's a friend of mine."

Sherry wasn't satisfied. "What is he doing here? Why did he come running like that?"

"He's funny that way," Clint evaded. He stood up, and she noted the deep lines running like fissures between his eyebrows, lines that hadn't been there months ago. He brushed his hands off and set them on his hips. "Do you want to meet him?"

"No, I don't need to meet your new friend, thank you."

"But Sherry—"

Before he could detain her again, she was out the door, hurrying across the lawn as if her sanity depended on it.

For she was certain it did.

***

Sherry sat on the chaise lounge by the pool, letting the sun pour down on her. It had been too much for her to go home and continue feigning composure for the benefit of Madeline, who often came home to work when things at her Promised Land studio got too crazy. So she had come here, to her father's house, knowing he was in court and wouldn't be home.

If she could have cried, some of the soul-deep sadness might have been relieved, but suddenly her eyes were as dry as barren craters in godforsaken earth. Her despair found new levels, even beneath the agony that Clint's leaving had caused. What disturbed her now was that Clint had betrayed her in such a devastating way, then thought he could erase it all with a simple touch and some whispered words of regret.

The unfeelingness of it all ripped at her, leaving scars that she hoped would remind her the next time she was weak. She realized now that it had been weakness to delude herself while he was gone. New misery welled up as she remembered the letters she had written to him at first, a form of therapy that had helped her to cope. She had spilled her heart out in them, knowing he would never see them. And whether they had been packed with curses or lamentations, they had all ended with, *Clint, where are you, where are you, where are you?*

And today he could walk up behind her at work, slide his arms around her, and expect her to accept him as if the months of loneliness and humiliation had never occurred. Those presumptions hurt her almost as much as his leaving had.

A door closed in the house, and Sherry snapped her head up to see her father coming toward her.

"I didn't know you were coming by today," the stern-looking U.S. attorney said, although his handsome gray eyes twinkled with pleasure at the unexpected sight of his daughter. "Why aren't you at work?"

"I had a headache so I took off," she said. "I thought you were in court."

"We've recessed until this afternoon, so I came home for some peace and quiet. The media will probably be banging on the door any minute now."

"If you were going to get so involved in this case, why didn't you handle it yourself instead of giving it to Colin Breard? Isn't it too important for an assistant?"

Eric squinted in the sunlight and shrugged. "Breard deserved it. He wanted it. He'll probably be behind my desk in a few years, anyway."

The logic seemed misplaced somehow, but Sherry wrote it off to her father's fatigue. "So how's it going?"

"Slow," he said, running a hand along his gray temples. "Givanti's a weasel who had so many gambling debts that he started distributing cocaine to pay them off. Has mush for brains. It's a wonder he ever ran a business. Unfortunately, though, he has a shrewd attorney."

"But you guys are shrewder, right?" Sherry said with a smile.

"Let's hope." He sat down on the lounge chair next to hers, and clasped his hands between his knees. "So, how are things with you?" A look of concern gilded his gray eyes. "You looked a little upset when I came in."

That sympathetic look and tone had lost its comfort value, for while she knew her father loved her dearly and suffered with her, she couldn't bear the constant reminders of what had happened. Madeline's no-nonsense approach to heartbreak had been exactly what she'd needed. "I'm fine, Dad. Don't worry about me."

As if knowing when to quit after months of dealing with her hot-and-cold moods, Eric stood up and smiled. "Well, I'd better go fix myself a sandwich. Want one?"

The knots in Sherry's stomach had left her appetite dead. "No thanks."

He shrugged. "All right. Maybe another time." As if he couldn't think of anything else to say, he slid his hands into his pockets and started back toward the house. "Oh, by the way," he said as an afterthought, turning around. "Did you by any chance notice that black sedan parked in front of the Millers' house when you drove up?"

"No, why?" Sherry had been in such an emotionally explosive state when she'd come here today that a submarine could have been parked in front of his neighbor's house and she wouldn't have noticed.

A deep frown clefted his forehead, and he rubbed his jaw. "Just wondered. This trial has me paranoid. He's probably just waiting for the Millers to get home."

"Must be," Sherry said. "It wasn't Clint, was it?"

As if the question warranted his full attention now that she had broached the subject, her father came back to her. "No, not Clint. I suppose you've seen him by now, huh?"

Sherry nodded.

Her father turned to the blue water and focused on the sunlight reflecting from the surface. "Thought so. He seemed pretty intent on starting things up again when he was here yesterday."

Sherry looked up at him, surprised. "He was here?"

"Yeah. He said he'd seen you."

She let out a deflated sigh. "He thinks I should forgive him and run back into his arms."

Her father's unusual momentary silence was more eloquent than his words. "There are worse things you could do."

Sherry's eyes narrowed in amazement. "What did you say?"

Eric's eyebrows arched apologetically. "I just want to see you happy again, honey."

Sherry couldn't believe what she was hearing. "And you think I could be happy with a man who ran out on me? A man who humiliated me by practically leaving me at the altar? Have *you* forgiven him?"

"He isn't asking for my forgiveness," her father said in a wooden voice. "You're good at forgiving, honey. You've forgiven me. Maybe it won't be as hard as you think."

"That's right," Sherry snapped. "I'm the forgiving one, so people can kick me in the teeth and expect me to smile when they say they're sorry."

Her father's shoulders dropped as he exhaled. "I didn't mean to get you all—"

"I'm fine." She got up and started toward the house. "I'm going back to work. I don't have time to worry about Clint Jessup anymore. It seems he has enough people to do that already." She looked back as she reached the door, saw the look of pity on her father's face, and cursed Clint Jessup all the more for being the one who put it there. She didn't need her father's pity. And she sure didn't need Clint's brand of love.

Chapter Three

Wes saw the shadows of fatigue under Sherry's eyes when she came back to the office later that afternoon. He stopped what he was doing and pulled a chair up to her desk. "You okay, sis? I've been looking for you."

"Yeah," she said. "I'm fine. I was at Dad's."

He grew quiet for a moment, biting his tongue. Why she spent so much time with the man who hadn't given them a thought for most of their lives, was beyond him. He said he had changed, that the love of Christ had transformed him, but Wes was doubtful. Why now? If God was going to change a person, wouldn't it be while his children were young, when they desperately needed him? Would he really wait until they were older?

Something about the whole story rang false to him, and even though his wife, Laney, accused him of being too hard on the man, Wes couldn't seem to help himself.

"He said I should forgive Clint."

Again, he was surprised. "He did? Why?"

She shrugged. "I don't know."

Wes thought it over for a moment. "Maybe he can relate to him. Since he skipped out on you, too." The stung look on her face made him wish he hadn't said it.

"I really don't want to talk about this." She slid her chair back and struggled not to cry as she headed for the file cabinet.

"I'm sorry, sis. I didn't mean it."

"Yes, you did," she said, turning back to him. "You don't ever want me to forget that I was dumped by my father, and then by my fiancé, do you? Does it make you feel better to remind me, Wes?"

He slumped over and covered his face, wishing for once he had listened to his wife's advice and kept his mouth shut. "No, that's not true. I do want you to forget. I just have trouble with Eric, that's all."

"He's your father."

"We have the same DNA. That's about as far as it goes. Now, tell me about Clint. What has he said about why he was gone?"

Raking her hands through her roots, she sat back down at her desk. "Oh, it doesn't matter."

"Sure, it does."

She shook her head dolefully. "He wrote a book. Needed time. And space, I guess. Maybe I'm too much. Too overwhelming. Maybe I just smother the people I love."

"You've never smothered me, Sherry. You've been there when I've needed you, and I've needed you plenty. Don't buy into that stupid lie that the men in your life are weak because you've done something wrong."

"I know you're right," she said. "But I wanted so badly to believe—"

"That there was a good reason?"

She met his eyes as tears welled in her own. "Yeah."

Wes stared at her for a moment, thinking. He had liked Clint, had trusted him. He couldn't believe he had been so wrong. "Maybe there is a good reason, Sherry. Something more than that."

"Like what? Why won't he tell me?"

"I don't know. But I can't believe that Clint is capable of such a cruel thing as leaving his bride at the altar, if there wasn't some life or death reason behind it."

"I didn't want to think it. But I'm a crummy judge of character. You've said so yourself."

"Well, if you are, then I am, too. I thought the world of Clint. So did everybody who met him. Look what he did for his youth group. He took a handful of kids and grew them into a group of a hundred kids who came to church every time the doors opened. He never got tired of doing God's work. It just doesn't make sense that he'd skip town for eight months, then float back in with some explanation about writing a book. It's so disappointing. He's not the man we all thought he was."

Sherry's eyes took on a distant glaze, and he could see the wheels turning. "There's this guy who was with him yesterday and then again today. Sticks to him like glue. I knocked over that model, and the guy came running like he thought I'd shot Clint or something. It was so weird."

Wes frowned. "Sure is. Who does he say the guy is?"

"Just a friend. But yesterday when I asked him to explain where he'd been, for just a flicker of a second, I thought he was going to tell me the truth. But he looked at that guy, and then his whole countenance changed, and he gave me the song and dance about the book again."

"Something's not right."

"You said it. But I don't know if I'll ever get to the bottom of it."

"Maybe you shouldn't try. Maybe you should just steer clear of him."

"I'm trying," she said. "But he isn't making it easy."

———◆———

A little while later, as Sherry drove back to the office from the post office, she noticed that a black car like her father had described was tailing her.

Coincidence, she told herself without conviction. There must be hundreds of black sedans in Shreveport, and her imagination was making more of it than there was.

She parked her car in the private garage next to the office, and hurried in looking for Wes. Since he wasn't in his office, she stepped to his window and peered out toward the small parking lot. When nothing unusual caught her eye, she breathed out a long, shaky breath and set her bag on Wes's desk. She was getting jumpy. Clint Jessup's sudden return had distracted her in more ways than one. Stepping over, she glanced up the street to her right, and her stomach lurched at the sight of the waiting black Pontiac. Threading her fingers through her hair, she expelled a low, dreadful moan and realized the driver was waiting for her.

"What is it?"

The sound of Clint's voice made her swing around, and she caught her breath in a ragged gasp. "What are you doing here?"

"I was waiting for Wes. I want to talk to him." He glanced past her out the window. "What were you looking at?"

Sherry set her hand on her chest as if it could calm her constricted lungs, and turned back to the window, fighting the rebellious urge to tell him it was none of his business. She was becoming frightened, and he was the only one there at the moment. "It's just . . . that car. It's been following me."

Without questioning her suspicion, Clint stepped into the office and squinted up the street at the car she pointed to. When he saw it, his eyes closed and a long, tangled breath wound out of his lungs. "How long has this been going on?" he asked.

She didn't answer at first, because she wasn't sure.

"How long?" he asked more urgently.

"I don't know," she said. "I think he might have followed me to Dad's house today. I may have seen the car yesterday, too, but I can't say for sure."

"*God . . . please, no . . .*" The words came out as a craggy whisper. Clint took Sherry by the shoulders and turned her to face him. She felt a slight shiver in his hands, saw genuine fear and haunted despair in his eyes. "Listen to me, Sherry," he said, his hoarseness contradicting his steady monotone. "I have to go get Sam. He's down the hall. I'll be right back, and I'll take you home. Don't leave here until I get back. Do you understand me?"

"But . . . I have work to do."

"Forget work," he insisted. "Just give me your car keys."

"My keys?" The keys were at the top of her bag, and reluctantly, she surrendered them. "What are you—?"

"No questions now, Sherry. Just wait right here. Please."

Frightened at the adamant, admonishing look in his eyes, Sherry nodded acquiescence. She stood frozen, listening to the squeak of his rubber soles as he ran up the corridor, heard the exchange of muffled voices, heard Clint's athletic breathing as he ran back to her office. When he got there, he closed the door and leaned over her desk to catch his breath. "I'll drive you home, Sherry. And I want you to promise me that you won't go anywhere alone. Nowhere."

"Clint, you're scaring me."

"Good," he said. "Then maybe you'll listen to me. Come on." He straightened and reached for her arm, but she stepped back.

"Clint, I'm not going with you!"

"Yes, you are!" he rasped. "Now come on! And keep quiet."

Sherry suppressed her rising sense of panic as Clint reached for two white hard hats and handed one to her. "Stuff your hair up in this and pull it low over your face."

Nervously, she obeyed, then followed him down the dim corridor. She felt his hand trembling as it looped around her waist, heard the heavy, rhythmic sound of his breath, tasted apprehension rising like a lethal flood to drown her senses. Before they were out of the building, he stopped and pulled a pair of mirrored sunglasses out of his pocket, put them on, and set his hard hat on his head. "Now, walk fast," he told her. "And don't say anything until we're on our way."

She nodded. Swallowing the fear flooding her throat, she took temporary refuge in his arm as it wrapped protectively around her. They walked at a fast gait to the Bronco, and he let her in his side and slid in next to her. The engine rumbled to life, and Clint backed out of his space.

Five minutes had passed before Sherry found her voice. "Clint, you know you've just scared ten years off my life, don't you?"

Clint glanced in the rearview mirror. "I'm sorry, Sherry. I didn't think this would happen."

"You've got to tell me what's going on."

Clint only stared at the road ahead, swallowed, and glanced in the mirror again. In a voice racked with frustrated despair, he said, "I don't even know where you live now."

Sherry gave him her address on a street he was familiar with, then tried again. "Clint, are you in some kind of trouble?"

"First, let me get you home, Sherry,"

"Then you'll answer my questions?"

"Then you can ask them," he said.

Several more explosively silent moments passed as Clint wove through the streets leading to Sherry's house. "I'm going to park in that shopping center a couple of blocks behind your street. Do you have a back door?"

A cold, nauseous feeling began to take hold of her, and Sherry glanced through the back window. "Why do I have the feeling that any minute now a SWAT team is going to surround us and start shooting?"

"Do you have a back door or not?"

"Yes, I have a back door," she whispered.

"Then we'll have to come up through your backyard and go in that way so we won't be seen."

"Clint, people see me going in and out of my house all the time and nothing's ever happened before."

"Things have changed, Sherry," he said.

"Why?"

The heel of his hand landed violently on the steering wheel. "Because I came back to town!"

The Bronco whipped into the crowded parking lot at the shopping center, and threaded through the spaces until it stopped. But Sherry didn't care where they were, for her eyes were set on Clint, seeing the haze of truth for the first time since he'd come back. She had wished there were some deeper explanation for his leaving her, and now she was sure there was. And she wasn't sure she wanted to know it, after all.

When the engine was dead, Clint turned and gazed into her eyes. Through his mirrored glasses she saw only herself, blurry blue eyes full of fear and turmoil, a face growing paler by the moment. "If I'd just listened . . ." he began, but then he just shook his head helplessly and opened the door. "Come on. Take the hat off and we'll get you home."

They crossed streets like lovers on a stroll, stole through yards like prowlers in the night, and approached her back door like escaped convicts waiting to be caught. "Where are my keys?" she whispered when they reached the house.

"I gave them to—That was your house key too?" His impatient voice was rising in pitch.

"Don't worry," Sherry said, quelling his outburst with a trembling hand. "I have one here under the mat."

"Under the mat?" he whispered accusingly.

Ignoring his tone, Sherry opened the door and they slipped inside. Clint closed and locked it behind them, his eyes bright with disbelief. "You actually keep a key under your mat where any fool could find it?"

"It's a good thing," Sherry volleyed. "Considering you handed my keys over to some stranger."

"Sam is not a stranger," Clint said, taking off his glasses and bolting through the house to peer through the curtains.

"Then who is he?" she asked, following behind.

"A good friend."

"Is he in trouble, too?" Her voice shook as she posed the question, and Clint turned from the window.

"No." A hand mussed his hair distractedly. "Sherry, I gave Sam your keys so he could get in your car and distract the person in the Pontiac while we got away. Whoever's following you will think Sam's you, if he plays his cards right. I wish I could explain all this to you, but it's too soon."

"Too soon? Clint, you *have* to explain. You do intend to, don't you?"

Clint fell back on the sofa, covered his face with both hands, and slid them wearily down until he peered at the wall over his fingertips. "No. No, I don't. Not yet."

Sherry couldn't believe what she'd heard. "Do you mean to tell me that you've just scared me half to death and you don't think I deserve an explanation?"

Clint folded his sunglasses and put them in his pocket. His eyes sparkled with pain that went levels beyond what she had seen in them before. "You deserve one, Sherry. But I can't give it to you."

"Can't?" she repeated, aghast.

"The less you know, the better," he said. "It's for your own good."

She sprang off the couch. "My own good? Was your leaving eight months ago for my own good? Was it for my own good that you popped back into town yesterday, just when my life was going well again? Is it for my own good that you've managed to make me afraid to walk outside my door?"

His eyes held her with an embrace that reached right to her soul. "Yes," he said.

Sherry brought a hand to her forehead, beginning to ache with tension and clearer understanding. "I can't believe this. You've done something illegal, haven't you?"

Clint's face was a portrait of regret. He took her hands and pulled her back down beside him, held her shoulders, pressed his forehead against hers. "I should never have come back."

"But you did!" Sherry cried.

Clint slid his hands up through her hair, encasing her head in splayed fingers as he tipped her face to his. "I'm so sorry, Sherry. So sorry."

Sherry backed away, breaking his hold on her. "Don't touch me, Clint. I don't know you anymore."

"I'm the same man, Sherry."

"What am I supposed to do, Clint? Just accept what you tell me without asking questions? Why did you even come back?"

"There was reason to believe it was okay to come back," he said, leaning toward her. "I wanted to see you again, make it up to you. I was in too big a rush, but I'd waited so long already."

"And you didn't count on the cops noticing?"

"Sherry, I needed you—" He reached out with the words, but Sherry shook his hands off of her and stood up.

"And I needed you! Eight months ago when our wedding was planned! I needed you all those nights that I cried myself to sleep, pretending you were somewhere thinking of me, trying to get back to me—"

"I was."

"Yeah, right. You were off running from the law for doing who knows what! I only wish I knew what our life together was worth to you. What did you trade it for, Clint?"

A muscle in Clint's forehead twitched. "You're wrong, Sherry. It wasn't that way at all."

"Why should I believe you?"

"Because you know me better than anyone else ever has."

"The Clint I knew didn't commit crimes. He didn't run from his mistakes. He wouldn't have vanished off the face of the earth two weeks before his wedding."

"I'm the same man I've always been," Clint said wearily.

"Then I have a terrific flaw in judgment!" Sherry railed, her face burning with rage. A few moments went by, and Clint stood before her, hands hanging at his sides, as if he desperately wanted to touch her but wouldn't allow himself to again.

The spitting roar of Madeline's Volkswagen seemed to shake the house as it pulled into the driveway.

"Is that your roommate?" Clint asked, breaking the silence. Sherry nodded. "Madeline."

"Then I'll go," he said quietly. "I want you to promise me that you'll do your best not to be alone."

Sherry's eyes filled with unshed tears, and she dropped onto the couch. When Clint knelt in front of her, she looked down at him.

"You're going to disappear again, aren't you?" Her voice was so shaky that she could barely get out the words.

"I don't know," he said.

"Are ... are you really in that much danger?"

Clint only closed his eyes, but the answer was clear.

He stood up to leave, and she rose to face him, fighting the urge to throw her arms around him and beg him to tell her that when he left he would be safe, that she would see him again. But deep in her heart she knew it was not true.

"So," she said hoarsely, wrapping her arms around her own waist instead. The rest of the superficial words seemed to get clogged in her throat.

"So," he said, as if he, too, struggled for an appropriate departing line, but came up empty. "I hope you'll forgive me for messing up your life."

Sherry forced out a dry laugh. "No problem," she said with gentle sarcasm.

The front door opened, and Madeline, engrossed in the mail, didn't see them as she stepped inside. When she set her purse down and glanced up, she crossed her arms and nodded as if the sight of Clint didn't surprise her at all. "Well, well," she said. "The prodigal fiancé, I presume?" Glancing back at the mail, she began to open an envelope.

Clint's eyes remained fused with Sherry's. "It's nice to meet you too, Madeline."

Madeline cocked a perfectly arched brow and gave Sherry a questioning look.

But Sherry still stared at Clint, as if he would dissolve before her very eyes.

Madeline pulled the page out of the envelope. "What on earth?" she muttered. "Wait a minute. Is this some kind of threat?" She waved the letter at Sherry.

Sherry took the paper and saw clipped magazine letters glued to the page. Glancing at Clint with alarm, she saw deep dread smoldering in his eyes. Slowly, she lowered her eyes to the page clutched in her shaky hand, and read aloud:

"Tell him revenge is sweet, and falls on those we love."

Chapter Four

"Give me that!" Clint's face turned a deathly shade of gray as he snatched the page out of Sherry's hand and stared at the pasted letters. "It's even worse—"

Halting his thought midsentence, Clint reached for the envelope still clutched in Madeline's hand. "No postmark," he growled. He stormed to the window and peered through a crack in the curtain. "Someone hand delivered this."

"The man in the black car?" Sherry wasn't certain where the shaky voice came from, but she awaited Clint's answer—any answer—with a dimension of fear that seemed set apart from reality.

"What car?" Madeline demanded curiously, shoving her curly dark hair behind her ear.

Clint seemed lost in the world outside the curtain, and Sherry swallowed back a wave of panic and stepped behind him. Touching his arm with apprehension, she made him turn toward her. "Clint, it said 'revenge.' What does that mean?"

Clint looked at her as if she were stolen goods he had to find a hiding place for.

"Clint!" Her voice was becoming raspier as the fear in his eyes more closely mirrored hers.

Roughly, he grabbed the phone, punched out a number, waited long enough for an answer, then entered another group of digits.

"Clint, the mystery ends right now," Sherry said in a tremulous voice. "Tell me what they meant by 'revenge.'"

Clint slammed the phone down. "They meant that you're in danger, Sherry," he bit out, his eyes turning darker. "They're after you too."

"But I didn't do anything!"

"You're someone I care about," he explained in a vicious whisper. "They'll use you to get to me."

"*Who* will?" she shouted.

"I don't know!" he yelled back.

Incredulity sprang to Sherry's eyes. "You don't *know?* Well, what *do* you know? How much trouble are you in, Clint? How badly do they want you?"

Madeline clutched her forehead and stepped between them like a referee in a boxing match. "Wait a minute! This is beginning to sound dangerous!"

Clint swung toward her. "It *is* dangerous." He caught a ragged breath and gave a haunted look around the room, as if its very existence threatened them. "You can't stay here where they can get to you," he said in a more calculated voice. "You'll both have to come with me."

Sherry felt as if the tension in her shock-strained heart would cause it to collapse. "I'm not going anywhere with you!"

"Wait a minute!" Madeline shouted again, stemming Sherry's hysteria and forcing Clint to look at her directly. "What kind of danger are we talking about here? Getting eggs thrown at our cars, or our house blown up? Is this a matter of inconvenience or life and death?"

"Life and death," Clint said.

Sherry shook her head, every fiber in her body denying the danger that was becoming apparent to her. "I'm calling the police."

"No, the phone could be bugged," Clint said. "Besides, there's no time."

"Clint, I am calling the police!" she insisted. She reached for the phone, but he grabbed her wrist and stopped her.

"Go get your things, Sherry," he said. "We have to go." His breath was getting heavier, and she felt the slight tremor in his grip.

"No," she bit out. "Not until I've talked to—"

"Do what I say! Now!" Clint grated. "We have to get out of here! I promise you we'll call the police after we leave here, but right now we're getting out!"

Sherry jerked her arm away and stepped back, making a valiant attempt to assess this new version of Clint. "And what if I refuse to go?"

"I won't *let* you refuse," he warned, his face reddening as he set his hands on her shoulders. "You have no choice."

Sherry jutted her chin defiantly, and crossed her arms with a bravado she didn't feel. "How do I know that you aren't more dangerous than the person who sent that letter?"

"You *don't* know," he whispered harshly. "But I don't have time to convince you. You're gonna have to go with your instincts, Sherry, and I *know* they're telling you to trust me."

"That's not what they're telling me."

"Then you'll have to go with *my* instincts," he bit out. "I'm trying to save you, whether you cooperate or not. Madeline, get her things and yours. We might be gone for a while."

Madeline hesitated. "Like ... how long?"

He was growing desperately impatient. "Look. I don't care whether you even take a toothbrush! You have exactly sixty seconds to grab what you need or we're going without it. And don't try to use the phone in the bedroom. I'm telling you that if they find out where I am, we're all sitting ducks."

"Who's they?" Sherry demanded.

"Not now," he said again.

"This is kidnapping." She closed her eyes and struggled not to fall apart as Madeline disappeared into the back of the house.

Clint wrapped an arm around her waist and held her more like a lover cherishing his woman than a kidnapper clinging to his hostage. "Sherry, you have to trust me," he whispered against her ear. "You have to ..."

"Let go of me," she whispered. "I don't want you touching me. You're despicable, and dangerous, and—"

"Sherry, I'm not the threat. You don't understand." His pleading voice against her ear almost made her want to understand, almost made her trust him, almost made her unafraid.

Until the telephone rang, recreating her hope and shattering it at the same time.

"You can't answer it," Clint said, his arm tightening on her. "They could be checking—"

"It's probably my studio at Promised Land," Madeline said, rushing back in with two packed duffel bags as the phone continued to ring. "I told Justin to call me if—"

Clint hooked her arm as she reached for the phone, his eyes on the edge of violence. "I said to let it ring," he whispered slowly. "It's time to go." He swallowed and steadied his voice.

"We're going to go out the same way Sherry and I came in." He set an arm on each woman's shoulder in a brotherly gesture that could turn forceful instantly. "Open the door, Sherry. And move fast."

Sherry obeyed the order and pulled the door open. When they were outside, the three of them running through the backyard like soldiers expecting sniper fire, Sherry felt as if someone else occupied her body while she stood outside it, watching the man she had once loved turn into a quiet lunatic who treated her like an unexpected hostage, for that was exactly what she was.

Sherry tried to make eye contact with the strangers they passed on their way to the parking lot, but each seemed too caught up in his own life's worries to notice the cry for help in her eyes—a cry for help she was afraid to put voice to for fear that a worse danger awaited her if Clint was right. Clint opened the driver's door and shoved them in. "Get down on the floor," he ordered. He slid on his sunglasses and his hard hat. "And stay there no matter what happens."

"What . . . what are you expecting to happen?" Madeline asked in a carefully composed voice.

Clint didn't answer. Sherry hunched against the seat and stared up at the stern, gruff set of Clint's jaw, the glacial blackness of his eyes, the stiff set of his mouth, as he cranked the engine and set the car into motion. His eyes shifted back and forth from the rearview mirror to the side streets as he drove, as if he expected an attack at any moment. Hard, tense muscles bulged through his clothes, testimony to the newer, more defined strength she had felt when he'd held her. He was a different man, she thought with a shudder. The old Clint had been sensitive, gentle, selfless. There had been no hint that beneath it all were secrets and terror that could make him capable of . . . Sherry's heart sank as she imagined the things he could be capable of now.

But when he glanced down at her, hunched next to Madeline on the floorboard, that sharpness in his eyes vanished, and his eyes softened. For a moment a deep sadness surged through her. That glimmer of regret in his eyes cost her her strength and her hatred, and she felt only a deep, yawning void with no hope of being filled, and the fathomless need to see the Clint she loved in that hard, unyielding countenance again.

⸻

Clint didn't look at her again, for the fear and astonishment in her eyes tugged at his heart and distracted him from his purpose. He watched the trees as he whizzed past them, as if they were the enemy waiting for him. But somehow, in light of the things he had said and done to get the two women out of the house, he felt as if *he* were the enemy— theirs as well as his own.

Madeline's look of composure and patience disquieted him. Sherry was probably struggling to understand the image of a new, dangerous Clint, but Madeline was more objective. She was turning the few facts she knew over in her mind, trying to concoct an escape plan for the first opportunity that arose, and probably trying to gauge his love for Sherry.

Maybe, he decided with a dismal ache in his soul, it was time to reveal his pistol. Maybe then they'd both believe him capable of carrying out his threats.

He was sickened by the idea that it had come to this. Sherry was already afraid. The sight of a .357 Magnum would terrify her. When she'd known him—really known him—he hadn't even hunted. And now he stalked and hid like a predator, and she would see herself as his game. That almost made him want to turn the gun on himself. He'd rather do that than threaten her with it. Still, the sight of the gun might be threat enough to keep her and Madeline from trying some foolish escape that would get them all killed. What did he have to lose, after all? Her trust? His heart sank lower when he silently admitted that he'd lost that eight months ago.

His hand glided down his leg, and he pulled up his jeans, revealing the leather holster strapped to his leg. His hand closed over the small black gun. Sherry's heavy release of breath, as if she'd expected as much from him, almost made him leave it where it was. But it was for Madeline that he pulled it out and held it in his lap, aimed at his door. A deathly quiet, broken only by the sound of the engine, fell over them for a moment, but he kept his dull, lackluster eyes on the road.

Madeline wilted and dropped her head into her knees, as if a million plans had just been shelved, but Sherry's eyes grew colder and more determined *not* to wilt. "What have you turned into?" she asked beneath the roar of the engine.

Clint didn't allow himself to meet her eyes. "A survivor," he answered with metallic certainty. "And I've had lots of practice."

Clint tried to harden himself to the harsh pair of blue eyes boring into him with hatred as emphatic as the love he'd known harbored there. It seemed that time stood still as she made her chilling assessment of him, the fear in her eyes not as great as the despair. But until he had them all within the bounds of safety, he could do nothing to change those opinions.

"Where are you taking us?" Madeline asked wearily, as if she had nothing left to lose.

"We're meeting a friend who can get us safely out of town," he said. "I called him from your house and punched out a code on his beeper. He'll be waiting."

"Wonderful," Madeline mumbled. "Another one just like you?"

Clint shrugged. "I ought to warn you, Madeline. Sam'll see the two of you as just another problem to deal with. If I were you, I'd watch what I said when I met him."

Sherry's delicate nostrils flared a degree, and she seemed to sit up straighter in the small space allotted her. "If we're such a problem, then why didn't you just leave us?"

Clint turned off of the road and started a bumpy journey beneath a thick ceiling of pines that Sherry could see from the floorboard. "I've told you why," he said.

The Bronco stopped, stemming Sherry's comment, and Clint said, "You can get up now."

***

The scent of honeysuckle and magnolia blossoms filled the air, and the soft, comforting sound of rustling summer leaves and flitting birds played on her senses, calming her heart. Sherry inched up and saw that they had parked in a small clearing surrounded by walls of sweet gums and blossoming dogwood and a forest of towering pine trees. A navy blue van waited opposite them, and the brown-haired man Sherry had seen glimpses of for the past day and a half leaned idly beside it.

"Aw, man!" Sam blurted when he saw the two passengers. "Does this look like some kind of party to you? Nobody told you to bring guests."

Clint got out of the Bronco and leaned back wearily against it. "I had no choice."

"Like you had no choice but to leave her office when I told you to stay put?" Sam flared. "Like you had no choice but to play sitting duck without any safeguards at all while I was losing that guy? You pull that again, pal, and I may not show up to bail you out."

Clint frowned, ignoring the threat. "There was a letter in their mailbox. Cut-out letters that said, 'Revenge is sweet and falls on those we love.'"

"Terrific," the man muttered without surprise. Gray eyes focused disgustedly on a tree-mottled sky. "Not only do we have to pull a vanishing act in broad daylight, trying to keep ourselves intact, but we also have to worry about keeping *them* in one piece too. And they don't exactly look like willing participants. I told you it was a mistake to come back when you did. But what do I know, right?"

As if the man's ramblings were nothing new and therefore not worth acknowledging, Clint opened the van doors and looked inside, then dropped his head in a fatigued slump. "You could have at least gotten something with seats," he said. "It might be a long ride."

Sam made an up-and-down assessment of Sherry, then Madeline, his cool eyes telling them they were a burden that he did not welcome. "Who knew we'd have company? They can sit on the floor," he said.

Sherry opened her mouth to lash out, but Madeline beat her to it. "Look, Mister Whoever-you-are. This is no picnic for us, either. If you don't want any crashers in this little game of yours then just leave us and we'll walk home."

Sam uttered a low, dry laugh. "Lady, it sounds awfully tempting. But I'm not in the business of throwing pretty little appetizers to the wolves. It's my experience that it only makes them hungrier for what they're really after."

Clint clutched the roof of the van with both hands and glanced over his shoulder. "Come on. Get in."

Sherry planted her feet and refused to move, and Madeline did the same.

Sam stepped toward them, silver eyes conveying his impatience. "The man said to get in."

Still, Sherry didn't budge. Sam started toward her to meet the silent challenge in her eyes, but Clint stopped him. "I'll handle her." He looked at her for a moment, then scooped her up.

"Get your hands off me!" she railed, struggling to beat her way free of him. And Clint acquiesced, depositing her onto the bare metal floor of the van.

With a slight grin, Sam stepped toward Madeline, but her gritting, "Don't you dare touch me," warned him off, and she climbed into the vehicle of her own volition.

"You won't get away with this!" Sherry sputtered as they slammed them in and climbed into the front. "My father will have the entire police force looking for us before it even gets dark." The words were empty, she thought. He wasn't likely to realize she was gone at least until tomorrow. But the two men abducting them didn't know that.

"Yeah, yeah," Sam said, as if he'd heard it all before. Then he cranked up the van and started toward the highway.

Through eyes misty with fury and betrayal, Sherry watched Clint settle onto the floor where the passenger seat should have been and lean back against the door of the van, covering his face with a hand. The new lifestyle didn't come easily to him, she thought. There was at least some degree of suffering that went with it. She watched his chest heave, as if the weight of breath was too heavy. He leaned forward, hiked up the jeans on his right leg, and returned the gun to its holster.

Closing her eyes, Sherry fought the tears that would reveal her shock, her fear, and her rage. It was best to retain a neutral expression at times like these, she told herself, even if everyone knew she was faking.

Forcing her eyes to the world whizzing by outside the van, she wondered in anguish where the road had turned. What had happened to transform the man she would have spent the rest of her life with—the generous, kind, sharing man she had been head over heels in love with?

A fleeting memory came back to her of her last Christmas with Clint, when he had taken gifts at his own expense to the patients in the children's ward of the hospital. He'd told her that night of the younger brother he'd had who had died after a long hospitalized illness, and the way he had never been able to forget the loneliness and boredom that had laced those last few months for the little boy. He'd never gotten over the need to find that younger brother in someone and offer the comfort and sunshine his own brother hadn't been able to accept. So he tried to brighten the lives of the children confined during the holidays, as he brightened the daily lives of the youth who depended on him. She wondered now if he had remembered that ritual last Christmas—the one she'd suffered through alone—or if he'd been too caught up in his new troubles to think of anyone but himself. Was that man still there beneath the harsh, cold shell of the criminal with the gun strapped to his leg and the eight months of mystery in his eyes? Or was this all that remained?

Madeline nudged her out of her miserable reverie, and gestured toward Clint with a nod of her head. "What did he do? Why are we running?" she asked in the quietest whisper.

Sherry gave a helpless shrug. "I wish I knew," she sighed.

"If we just knew what we were up against . . ." Madeline's words trailed off as Clint opened his eyes. He stared at Sherry for a moment. Then he moved toward them, and sat before Sherry with his hands clasped between his bent knees.

"Sherry, I know you're afraid," he said in a soft voice that was barely audible over the road noise. "I'm afraid, too. But I want you to trust me."

"Famous last words," Sherry muttered. "Kidnapping me or my roommate is not the best way to win my trust, Clint."

Clint frowned. "Sherry, whether you can believe it or not, I'm doing this because I love you."

Something in his eyes when he uttered the words tugged at Sherry's heart, silencing her comeback, but Madeline was unaffected. "Give me a break," she moaned.

"Just tell me what you did, Clint." Sherry pleaded. "Make me understand what's going on here to make you kidnap us."

Clint kneaded his eyes, leaving them red. "Not yet. There's no telling what could happen before we get out of town. It's best if you don't know."

Sherry closed her eyes.

"Trust him," Madeline said sarcastically.

"The bottom line," Clint said in a bolder voice, "is that you *have* to trust me. Both of you. You just don't have a choice. At this point there is nothing else you can do for yourselves." Then, as if there was no point in continuing the conversation, he turned away and went back to the door.

"There's something we can do for ourselves, all right," Sherry whispered to Madeline when he was out of earshot. "And we're going to do it as soon as this van stops."

Chapter Five

The ordeal seemed to shift from frightening to downright intolerable when Sam began to sing "You Ain't Nothin' But a Hound Dog," butchering the Elvis tune.

"Please!" Madeline groaned. "This is enough of a nightmare without your singing."

Sam glanced over his shoulder, an amused half-grin working at his profile as he chanted the lyrics again, louder and even more off-key than before.

Sherry buried her face in her knees and wrapped her arms over her head, but still the wailing continued.

"Give up, Madeline," Clint moaned from his position on the floor. "I've been listening to it for months. He sings when he's nervous ... or bored ... or tired ... or happy ..."

Sam arched an undaunted brow and did a drumroll on his steering wheel, humming loudly.

"He would have been a rock singer," Clint explained, "except that he lacked one crucial element called talent, plus he can never remember the lyrics."

"Just for that," Sam said in a mock wounded tone, "I'm going to have to do my new and improved version of 'Peggy Sue.'"

"First they kidnap us, then they torture us," Madeline mumbled.

Sam cocked a brow. "Driving throws me off-key. I'll do better on the plane."

"What plane?" Clint perked up at the new development.

"The one I arranged for when I realized things had blown up in our faces. It should be waiting for us at the little airstrip not too far from here."

Sherry nudged Madeline. "This is the time," she whispered. "Pretend that we won't give them any trouble, then when they let us out we can tell them we have to go to the bathroom and make a run for it."

"Be serious," Madeline returned. "Don't you think these guys can outrun us?"

"Maybe they can," Sherry said. "But if we have a few minutes' head start we might get to safety before they can find us."

The road turned rocky, and the interior of the van darkened as they entered another wooded area and wound down a path that didn't seem at all suited for such a vehicle. Branches scraped against the sides of the van, and the sound of gravel under the wheels sent a shiver up her spine. How far into these woods would they take them? And how in the world would they ever get back out if they did escape?

Calm down, Sherry, she told herself. There must be a clearing somewhere, otherwise there couldn't be an airstrip. They could just hide in the woods until Clint and Sam gave up on them, and then follow the path. *Don't be ridiculous,* she reminded herself. Clint wasn't going to give up. Not unless his danger was so immediate that he couldn't risk wasted time.

The van came to an opening, and she saw a large field with a runway down the middle. A small single-engine plane idled there, waiting for them. Sam stopped the van, and the two men got out and slid open the side door. "Let's go," Clint said, holding out a hand for Sherry.

Sherry stepped down. The forest surrounding the airfield seemed rougher and more primitive, as if it was rarely visited by the human species. But there had to be a way out, she told herself, for they weren't far from the highway. "We . . . we need to go to the bathroom," she ventured.

"You'll have to wait," Clint said.

Madeline danced around impatiently. "Come on, have a heart."

"She won't make it," Sherry said. "She's got a small bladder."

Madeline blushed convincingly as Sherry pulled her to the trees. Clint started after them, but Sherry spun around, forcing her breath to function normally. "Look around you, Clint. Do you really see any possibility of escape? There are probably snakes in there, not to mention other rabid, hungry animals. Would I really be foolish enough to risk getting stuck here overnight? Let the woman go in peace."

Clint heaved an impertinent sigh. "All right," he said finally. "Hurry up."

Sherry led Madeline off in the direction that seemed least dangerous—an area of the woods with thick bushes and matted vines webbed between the trees.

"All right," Sherry whispered as they pushed limbs aside as fast as their arms would move. "As soon as we get far enough away that they can't hear, we're going to run."

"Where?" Madeline asked in a whisper. "I don't know where we are. Do you?"

"We'll figure it out," Sherry assured her.

"But it'll be dark in a couple of hours. What if we get caught in here overnight? What about those rabid, hungry animals you mentioned a minute ago? I'm not so sure I wouldn't rather be with Clint and Sam."

"How can you say that?" Sherry hissed. "They have guns. They're taking us on a plane to who knows where. They're making us accessories to whatever they've done."

"We're not accessories. We're victims," Madeline argued. "And a guy who sings 'Peggy Sue' couldn't be that dangerous."

Sherry had never wanted to strangle her roommate more. "Madeline, even if we could be sure they wouldn't hurt us, they are obviously not the only ones involved. There are others. Someone's in that plane. How do you know they aren't dangerous?" Sherry led Madeline at a brisk pace while they whispered, brush cracking underfoot. A branch scraped Sherry's arm, drawing blood, but she tried to ignore it. Her eyes darted from left to right, straining for some idea of an escape route. As if by miracle, she spotted a dry spring that cut a path of earth through the trees. She turned around and held a branch up for Madeline to duck under.

"Look, there's a clearing between those trees. Looks like a spring might have been here once. We could jump down in it and run as fast as we can that way until we reach the edge of the woods. Then we're safe."

Madeline eyed the beveled, leaf-filled ditch and brought troubled eyes back to Sherry.

"Madeline, are you with me or not? We have to go now."

"Okay," the woman finally agreed, though every nuance of her expression indicated fierce doubt. "Take off. I'm right behind you."

Sherry skidded down the incline to the dry spring and started to run as fast as her legs would carry her. Two years of jogging might have put her in shape for this sort of thing, she thought as she leapt over rocks and roots. But her sparse diet for the past two days, her sleepless night, and the strain that had been tearing at her muscles all day put her at a grave disadvantage.

Somewhere in the distance behind them, she heard her name being called in anger, and forced her legs to move faster. She heard Madeline stumble and fall, then begin to run again.

The sound of distant car engines caught her attention, telling her that the highway was not far away. She strained her ears and listened for the direction, but Clint's voice came threateningly behind her.

"Stop it, Sherry! You're going to get yourself killed!"

"This way," she whispered to Madeline. "I can hear the highway."

They scurried up the side of the ditch and tore out through the thick wall of trees, vaulting in the direction of the road sounds that seemed even closer. But progress was slow, for nature prohibited them from getting through without stopping every few minutes to make passage.

"Over there!" she heard Clint yell to Sam, too close behind them.

Sherry hurled her body through the brush, ignoring the way thorns clung to her clothes and snagged her skin. She came upon a drop-off and told Madeline to jump.

"But it's an eight-foot fall, at least," Madeline whispered.

Sherry ignored her and jumped, landing in a springing position that tested every muscle in her body. Madeline followed, but her landing was not as graceful. She fell, sprawled, her knee twisted beneath her. She yelled.

"Can you walk?" Sherry asked frantically. "Can you get up?"

Madeline pulled herself up and tried to take a step, but her knee gave way.

The sound of cracking branches, running feet, and mumbled expletives reminded them of their urgency. "Go ahead, Sherry," Madeline whispered. "You're almost to the highway. I'll be all right."

Sherry wrapped her arm around Madeline's waist and tried to help her. "No. I'm not going without you."

"For heaven's sake," Madeline pressed. "It won't do any good for us both to get caught. At least you can go somewhere and call the police."

The sound of the two running men grew closer, and Sherry hesitated.

"Sherry, use your head! Get out of here!"

She looked above her and saw Sam come into view. "There they are!" he shouted.

"Run, Sherry!" Madeline ordered.

Torn, Sherry saw Clint running toward the drop-off as if to jump, and she turned and bolted into the woods, running as fast as she could go. The highway sounded within feet of her. Perhaps she'd make it. But behind her she heard Madeline yelling and sobbing, and Clint's heavy footsteps gaining on her.

Twenty yards ahead she saw the trees thinning, heard the sound of an eighteen-wheeler rolling by, and felt the first bit of relief she'd known in hours. But suddenly Clint was behind her, his footsteps pounding the earth. A long arm reached out to grab her.

A scream tore from her throat, but he pressed his hand over her mouth and tackled her to the ground. She struggled with all her might and squirmed away, scrambled to her feet, and started to run again. But Clint caught her around the waist, clamping her arms to her sides. "Don't . . . even . . . think about moving."

Tears of helplessness burst into her eyes and spilled over her cheeks. She shut her eyes.

"I love you, Sherry," he whispered heavily. "I'm not gonna hurt you."

Tears ran down her cheeks, and a sob burst from her throat. "You already have," she whispered.

He turned her around and she stared up at Clint, watching a look of sympathy flash across his face, a look brought on by her tears and vulnerability. Still holding her with one arm, he wiped beneath her eye with a knuckle. She moved her face aside. "I'm going to keep trying to get away from you until I do."

"And I'll have to keep stopping you," he said.

"You might have to kill me to do it."

He didn't answer, but a look of both pain and anger twisted his face, and he started walking, pulling her along beside him.

Sam was waiting with Madeline when they reached the drop-off that had been their downfall.

"Oh, Sherry," Madeline moaned when she saw that she'd been caught. "You were so close."

Sam and Clint exchanged sober looks. "Get up, Madeline," Clint said. "We're going to the plane."

Sam shook his head with something nearing disgust in his eyes. "She twisted her knee. I'll have to carry her."

"We'll follow this drop-off until it's low enough to climb," Clint said, his bass voice deep and without inflection. He took Sherry's hand and pulled her behind him.

Sherry followed without a fight, though her eyes, now dry and alert, kept a constant lookout for some other escape route. Another one would arise soon enough. When it did, she would be ready. And no matter what the cost, she would risk it. For she had no intention of falling under the power and dominance of the dangerous criminal wearing the face of the man she had loved.

Chapter Six

The plane that waited for them was small and didn't seat more than eight people. Clint pulled Sherry on and made her sit in one of the back seats, hooked her in, and told her not to move. But he knew she would try again. He was all out of threats. Short of actually hurting her, he didn't know how he would protect her.

He went back to the front of the plane, where the pilot, a woman named Erin, busied herself with her checklist before taking off.

In the seats behind the pilot, Madeline sat with her pant-leg rolled up, checking out her knee. "So what do you think?" Clint asked. "Anything broken?"

"Like you really care," Madeline said. Then under her breath, she added, "I think it's sprained."

Sam closed the door and took the seat beside her. "Should keep her from pulling another stupid stunt for a while."

"Yeah," Clint mumbled. "But what's to keep Sherry from it?"

"That lock on the door, for one thing," Sam said. "And the fact that the first step out of here will be twenty thousand feet down."

Clint closed his eyes and rubbed them roughly. He hated the look he could still see in her eyes, the look that said, "I loathe you and I'm afraid of you and I'll do anything in my power to be away from you." He hated that she didn't trust him enough to believe him when he said they were in danger, not from each other, but from someone else. But how *could* she trust him?

"*I'm not gonna hurt you.*"

"*You already have.*"

Her words raged in his mind, until he wanted to throw in the towel and walk out into the line of fire and die. She was all that kept him from it, all that had for eight long, agonizing months.

"We need to keep them separated so they don't cook anything else up," Clint said in a distant voice. "I'll ride in the back with her."

Sam surveyed the pensive lines etching Clint's face. "All right, I'll stay with her."

Color rushed back into Madeline's cheeks. "I'm not riding with you. I want to stay with Sherry. We're not going to try anything."

"Of course you're not," Sam said. "You got it all out of your systems, and now you're just as happy as a lark to go along with us. You're staying where you are."

When Sam reached for her seat belt to hook her in, Madeline jerked it away from him and did it herself.

As Clint took his seat beside Sherry, Sam began humming the tune to "Let It Be."

———

The pilot began to pull down the small runway, and Sherry braced herself. She pulled her feet up onto the edge of her seat and wrapped her trembling arms around her knees. How long would they be in this plane? How far would it take them? She tried to calculate how long it might take for someone to realize she and Madeline were missing. Would Wes realize it today and call the police, or would it take several days? He was so busy with Laney and the kids these days, not to mention his demanding work schedule, that she feared her absence might take too long to notice. Would her father notice, or would he assume she was just busy or depressed, and leave her alone?

But someone at Promised Land would surely notice that Madeline hadn't shown up in the animation studio. Her managers—Andi or Justin—would surely report her disappearance. Wouldn't they?

Clint kept looking at her. Angry, she asked, "Why don't you sit someplace else?"

"There aren't that many other places to sit."

"You could sit with the pilot."

"She doesn't need my help," he said. "She's used to piloting a DC10. This one is a piece of cake."

"You could sit up there, anyway. I don't want you near me."

"Too bad."

The plane began to pick up speed, bumping and jerking over potholes and rocks.

"Brace yourselves, guys," Erin called out. "It's a rough runway." Finally, they lifted off.

Clint looked over at Sherry. "You okay?"

"Depends. Can she really fly?"

"Of course she can. She's a commercial pilot."

"Among other things, apparently. Looks like you've picked up a lot of new friends since you left me. Has Erin been with you all this time?"

"Only when I've needed a pilot."

She thought that over for a moment. "You must be making more money than you did as a youth minister."

"I'm not paying for this, Sherry."

"Then who is? Some drug lord?"

He gaped at her, hurt. "You really think I'd be on the payroll of a drug lord? You *really* believe that?"

"I'd believe anything about you, Clint. Nothing would surprise me anymore."

The admission stung him. Angry, he unhooked his belt and moved to the front seat next to Erin. Sherry said nothing as he settled in.

For a while, she watched out the window, trying desperately to gauge where they were going. But all she could see were clouds and small squares of land, and miles and miles of trees. After a while, the clouds grew thicker, and she wasn't able to see anything below them.

Her eyes drifted back to Clint, sitting next to Erin, staring dismally into space. Some irrational part of her wished he hadn't moved, that he had stayed here beside her. But that wish made her angry. Her memories tugged up tender feelings, but those memories had no basis in truth. Somehow, she had to keep remembering that.

She was surprised when she felt the plane descending, and she looked out again, expecting to see an airport. All she saw, instead, was a forest of trees below them.

They touched down, and she realized that they had landed on another airstrip out in the middle of nowhere. She closed her eyes and breathed a prayer that God would go with them and protect her from whatever Clint and his new friends had in store for them.

The plane rolled to a stop, and she watched as he and Sam opened the door to the plane and got off. Sherry quickly unhooked her belt and leaned up to Madeline. Erin shifted in her seat to watch them.

Madeline had her leg propped on the seat next to her, but she seemed more worried about Sherry. "Are you okay?"

Sherry shrugged. "Yeah, how about you?"

"Fine except for this," she said, pointing to her knee. "Sam actually seems like a decent guy."

Sherry started to protest, but Erin said, "He *is* a decent guy. They both are. The best."

Sherry and Madeline both looked up at her.

"Are you aware that they kidnapped us?" Madeline asked.

"It was for your own safety," Erin said. "Trust them."

"Don't listen to her," Sherry said. "She's in with them."

"Not really," Erin said. "I'm actually a full-time pilot for an airline. I only do these flights on a case-by-case basis. I've only flown them around a couple of times, but I can tell you that you have nothing to fear. They won't hurt you."

The door opened, and Clint and Sam came back in. "Okay, let's go. Madeline, can you walk okay?"

"Do I have a choice?" Madeline asked as she got up.

Erin winced as Madeline did. "Sam, isn't there something you can do for her?"

"I'll try to get her some ice," he said. "But we don't have a lot of time to kill."

"Wait." Erin reached for a flight bag tucked under one of the seats and withdrew a bottle of Tylenol. "It's not much, but it'll help some." She handed it to Madeline.

Madeline took it suspiciously. "Thanks."

"Try to keep it propped up if you can."

Madeline gave a perplexed glance back at Sherry, but Sherry shot her a don't-trust-any-of-them look.

They all filed off, and Sherry saw the truck and camper parked beside the airstrip, waiting for them. Clint took Sherry to the back of the camper, opened it, and told her to get in. She complied. He locked her in, but she went to the window and watched out as he and Sam made Madeline get in the pickup. Then Clint and Sam stepped aside, talking quietly for a moment.

Seizing the opportunity, she turned around and took a quick inventory of the "luxuries" in the camper. A sink, a small refrigerator, a cabinet. Attached to the wall was a small bed, and above her head was another fold-out bed. Across from the bed was a narrow closet. She opened it and found it empty. She opened the cabinet below the sink and found several cans of food, a loaf of bread, some peanut butter. A light dawned in her mind, and she pulled open the drawer. Among the forks, spoons, butter knives, and can opener lay a paring knife. Quickly, Sherry grabbed it and, following Clint's example, tucked it under her sock against her leg.

A shudder coursed through her at the thought of using it, and she sank onto the bed again. If it came down to it, would she be able to hurt Clint to get away from him? She leaned her head back against the wall and closed her eyes. She wanted to think she could, but for the life of her, she wasn't sure.

The door of the camper swung open, and she looked up to find Clint hunched in the doorway.

"Wh–where's Madeline?" she asked when he closed the door behind him.

"She's riding in front."

"Why?"

"Because I wanted to ride with you."

"That isn't necessary."

"Isn't it? Isn't it absolutely necessary to stop you from killing yourself trying to keep me from saving you?"

"Nobody asked for your protection, Superman."

Clint stepped further into the camper and reached into the refrigerator for a canned Coke. "You sound pretty sure of yourself for someone who's never taken a chance in her life until today."

Sherry lifted her chin at the barb. "I took a chance when I got tangled up with you."

"I don't recall that you had any reservations at all." Clint set one of the drinks on the table in front of her, then popped the top of his own and took a long drink.

Sherry shrugged and looked out the window as the camper started to move. "Who knew what you were underneath? Who had any idea?"

"And maybe I was wrong about you all this time," he said. "Maybe that heart I kept remembering was nothing but ice and bitterness. Maybe all that 'for the rest of our lives' stuff was just a line to get what you wanted at the time."

Some emotion seemed to show in her eyes, but instead of making them softer, it made them harder. "Maybe so," she agreed.

Clint gave an unconvinced grin. "Maybe you knew all along that you were tangled up with some sort of gangster, and you needed the excitement in your life." He set down the can, considered it. "There were clues, you know. All those ideas I used to be so engrossed in at church, they weren't really project plans for the youth group. They were blueprints of banks. You probably thought I didn't have much money, but the truth is that I have millions stashed away in a Swiss bank account." He shrugged and looked back at Sherry's cold eyes. "Remember all those plants I kept in my apartment? They weren't really plants. They were just clever props where I hid the money. It worked out real well for a while, and I only had to kill a few dozen people. You probably thought I was at home sleeping when I wasn't with you. In reality, I was flying to distant parts of the globe to launder my money."

Sherry bit the inside of her cheek in impatience with his outrageous story and looked out the window.

"Don't know why you never suspected anything," he said, shaking his head with exaggeration. "When criminal behavior is so deeply ingrained in someone, the way it is in me, it's really hard not to spot. Unless . . ." His eyes widened in feigned understanding, and Sherry couldn't help looking at him again. "Unless you're a female thug yourself!"

She rolled her eyes and looked out the window again.

"Of course," Clint said, clutching his head. "Why didn't I see it before? You and your brother are in this together! That's how he made his fortune! He didn't really get it from his wife. In reality, he probably sells used cars to third world nations! I knew there was something fishy about that guy!"

"If you think your flip attitude is going to lighten up this miserable situation, Clint, you're wrong," Sherry said. "I don't find anything about this funny. I think you and your stupid tone-deaf friend are disgusting. As far as I'm concerned, I am a hostage, and you are a kidnapper. And when the police find us after I'm reported missing, I'm going to help them put you away for the rest of your life."

Clint's eyes glittered with anger. "I'm not a criminal, Sherry. I'm a victim. And I can't tell you how good it feels to know the woman I planned to marry has such faith in me."

"Faith can die, Clint!" she returned. "And I take full responsibility for winding up where I have in this relationship. I should never have loved you, and I should never have believed in you. Sometimes faith is just a flimsy means of self-betrayal, an excuse for not having to depend on yourself. I learned a valuable lesson when you disappeared, Clint. I learned not to believe in much anymore!"

Clint's eyes were anguished as he tilted his head helplessly. "I did that to you?" he asked in a raw voice.

"I did that to myself," she said numbly. And then she closed her eyes and banded her arms tighter around her knees, constructing barriers that no one was likely to break down.

"There's something I should warn you about," Madeline told Sam as she watched the signs that whizzed past on the highway. She was pretty sure they were going south, but the knowledge did her no good at all. "I have a very low threshold for pain. Any minute now this throbbing in my knee is going to reach the unbearable point, and you'll hear some moaning like you've never heard before."

"A low threshold, huh?" Sam asked, raising a brow.

Madeline nodded. "Well, I could pretend to be brave. But under the circumstances, I don't see what good it would do me."

Sam winked at her. "Don't worry. If I decide to torture you, I'll go easy on the knee."

"That's reassuring," Madeline said. Somehow, the torture threat didn't pack much weight when it was delivered with a grin that told her Sam would rather tickle her any day. She wondered if her hunch was well-founded.

His eyes were the color of a winter storm with the first sparkling rays of sunlight warming through, and they made her smile against her will. "Ever had your portrait done?"

His brown eyebrow cropped further upward with the question. "My portrait? No, why?"

"Because I'm an artist. An animator, really, but I like to do portraits as a hobby. I've never drawn a criminal before."

Sam laughed aloud. "And now that the opportunity seems to have dropped into your lap, you might as well take advantage of it, right?"

Madeline shrugged and glanced out the window. "Something like that."

Sam considered the idea for a moment. "You could do it as a cartoon, since that's what you're used to. I'd probably fit that medium best, anyway."

The beeper on his belt sounded, and Sam reached down and retrieved it.

"The little Mrs.?" Madeline inquired.

"Yeah, sure," he said. "I told her never to call me when I'm working." He took the beeper and read the coded message coming across the tiny screen.

"Aw, no," he mumbled. "We've got to turn around."

Madeline sensed the sudden swing in his mood and thought it was best not to go on with the bantering. "Are we going home?"

He shook his head. "Just someplace different. I've got to find a phone."

———◆———

Sherry opened her eyes when she felt the camper stop, and a new wave of apprehension passed over her. "Are we there?" she asked Clint, who was sitting on the narrow counter looking out the window.

"No," he said. "I don't know why Sam stopped."

The back door opened, and Sam stuck his head in and gave Clint a quick, whispered explanation.

"He has to use the telephone," Clint said when he'd closed the door again. "He got a message on his beeper telling us to turn around."

She slid to the edge of the bed, her eyes suddenly more alert. "Are we going home?" she asked, just as Madeline had.

"I don't know where we're going," he said. "We'll have to wait until Sam makes the call."

"You mean you take orders from someone else?" she asked.

"Does that surprise you?"

"It frightens me," she admitted. "What if this other person doesn't like the idea of your taking hostages?"

Clint gave her a wan smile. "I can guarantee you that he won't."

Sherry swallowed hard and struggled with the fear drawing the blood from her face. "He doesn't even know us. What if he—?"

"He isn't going to let anything happen to you," he assured her. "He's as worried about your safety as I am."

"Well, that isn't exactly comforting, since you just chased me down in the woods," she snapped.

Clint turned back around to face her, his eyes slicing into her. "He has his own methods. I haven't always agreed with them at first, but he's been able to convince me so far."

Was it another threat? Sherry wondered miserably. Was he telling her that if the order was given, he'd kill her? Or was he saying something entirely different? Closing her eyes again, she tried to deal with the fear threatening to conquer her.

The door opened again, and Sam leaned inside. "We have to go north. It might be a three-hour drive or more. But we can't take the plane any further because Erin has to get it back."

"What happened? Why the change?" Clint asked.

"A little matter of a bomb," Sam said in a metallic voice. "The place was empty, so nobody was hurt. But the whole place is history. We think it was meant as a warning. So we've come up with another place we haven't used before. Just tap on the window if you need something, and I'll try to find a discreet place to stop."

The door closed again, and Sherry's piercing, fearful eyes locked with Clint's. "A bomb? What kind of hell are you taking me to?"

Clint sank down on the floor and leaned back against the door. "My hell," he said. "For the past eight months."

Chapter Seven

Sam's face was grim and pensive when he got back in the cabin. "We're going to be driving for about three hours," he told Madeline. "I'll try to find a place up ahead where I can get you some ice."

"I'd be deeply indebted," she said.

"It might be a little while, though. This station is closed, so we'll have to wait for the next town."

"I'll survive," she said. She studied his rugged profile, the pensive way he rubbed his beard, the deep lines around his mysterious eyes. His new mood scared her, and when she was scared, she talked. "So how is the Mrs.?"

"Dandy," he said. "She told me to pick up a loaf of bread and some milk."

"And did you tell her you were bringing guests home for dinner?"

"Yeah. I told her to get the dungeon ready and not to feed the alligators, that they were getting a special treat tonight."

Madeline's fears lightened a degree, and she looked out of the window. "Is there really a Mrs.?"

Sam grinned. "You mean are there really hungry alligators?" He glanced askance at her. "Do I look like the kind of guy who would throw a little beauty to the alligators?"

Madeline smiled faintly. "Then you are married?"

"Was once," he said, sobering. "It didn't work out."

Madeline studied the abrupt flash of vulnerability in his eyes, and suddenly she wasn't quite so afraid anymore. "Too many late hours and unexpected guests?"

"Something like that," he said seriously. "And the fact that she hated guns. Unfortunate, considering I practically sleep with mine." There was a note of regret in his voice, a flicker of bitterness, before he changed the subject. "Why haven't you been snapped up?"

She smiled at the choice of words, but quickly sobered. "Haven't wanted to be, I guess," she said. "I like being independent. No one to answer to, no one to depend on. If you get kidnapped or something, you don't have any explanations to make." She flashed him a quick look. "Not like Sherry. Her father and brother will be pulling their hair out worrying about her. Calling the FBI, the CIA, the PLO, the KGB ..."

"And you like knowing there's no one back home to worry about you?"

Madeline nodded. "It just makes things easier to deal with, you know?"

"I know," Sam said, nodding. "I know."

———◦•◦———

It wasn't long before Sam pulled into a 7-Eleven parking lot and stopped the camper. It wasn't much, Sherry thought, and she didn't know what town they were in, but it was a chance. The best one she'd had since this whole ordeal had started.

"I have to go to the bathroom," she told Clint.

"If you remember, I've heard that before."

"Well, it's true. It isn't like it's a new development in the human body."

Clint studied her for a moment, wondering if he could, indeed, trust her this time. Nothing in her attitude had changed since her last desperate escape attempt. "Sherry, you don't have to keep trying to get away. You'll understand this all soon enough. You know I'm not going to hurt you."

"I don't know that," she mumbled. "I don't even know who you are anymore. You've threatened to hurt me several times today. But that's not why I want to use the rest room."

Clint raked his hand through his hair and held her eyes in a searching embrace, then he gave a dull shrug and sighed.

"So are you going to let me go?"

The door to the camper opened, and Sam stuck his head in. "I'm getting Madeline some ice for her knee. Anybody need anything?"

"We could use something to eat," Clint said.

Sherry sat up rigid, realizing Clint was going to ignore her request. "Will you please tell him that I have to go to the bathroom?"

Sam laughed aloud and peered around Clint. "I've heard that before."

Sherry's face stung red. "Are you people aliens or something? Don't you have bladders?"

Sam flashed Clint a surrendering grin. "She does have a point there, you know."

Clint nodded wearily and took her arm. "All right, Sherry. But I'm going with you."

"Fine," she said, though she deflated inside. She'd worry about getting rid of him when she got there. Maybe there was a window, or some people . . .

Roughly, he held her arm and walked her across the dark parking lot. The store was flooded with bright lights that her eyes had to adjust to, and she tried to focus long enough to see if anyone was there who might help her. But she didn't have time. Before she had even made eye contact with the store clerk, Clint had hurried her into the corridor leading to the rest rooms. And there was no one there to think it odd that he followed her into the lady's room.

No windows, she thought, looking around the dirty room with a sinking heart. Jerking free of him, she went into the stall. She tried to close it, but Clint wouldn't let her. Amazed, she gaped up at him. "What do you think I'm going to do? Drown myself?"

Clint scanned the possibilities in the stall. When he was satisfied that there was nothing there that would help her, he stepped back and allowed her to slam the door. "All right, but you have exactly thirty seconds."

Thirty seconds! she thought frantically. She tore out the roll of tissue paper and searched for something, *anything,* that would give her an idea for escape. But there was nothing. *Nothing!*

Nothing except the knife tucked in her sock. With a trembling hand, she took it out and examined it. It shone with a gloss that twisted her soul. What would she do with it? Threaten him? He'd wrestle it away from her in a minute. No, if she used it, she would have to mean business. She would have to use it the moment she opened the door. She would have to hurt him.

"Fifteen seconds," Clint said.

Sherry closed her eyes and struggled with her choices. It might be her only one. And yet . . . she couldn't do it. As frightened as she was, she couldn't hurt Clint. Hating herself violently, she slipped the knife back into her sock and racked her brain for some other way. The person in the store was her only answer. She'd pretend to shop for something to eat, and somehow she would let the clerk know she was being held against her will. It was risky, and it might not work, but it was better than using the knife.

Just as Clint ticked off, "Five seconds," Sherry came out of the stall. Brushing past him, she washed her hands slowly, trying not to tremble.

Then she pushed out of the bathroom and back into the store area. "I want something to eat," she said, trying to make eye contact with the clerk, who seemed deeply engrossed in a book she was reading.

"Sam got us something," Clint said.

"But he doesn't know what I like. I need something salty. Some pistachios. Do you have pistachios?"

The woman looked up and shook her head. Sherry flashed her a desperate look, but the lady was undaunted. She merely looked back down at her book.

But Clint didn't miss it. "Come on, Sherry. It was a good try," he said. He set an intimidating arm around her shoulders and started her toward the door.

Sherry wasn't about to let it go that easily. "Lady, he's—"

Clint set his hand over her mouth, out of the lady's sight. "She gets feisty when she can't find any pistachios," he explained, though the woman didn't seem to care.

And with controlling force that had been worked into his muscular arms for months, he pushed her outside and into the camper. She landed on the bed with a bounce, and turned back to see his eyes burning into her with disgusted rage, but he didn't utter a word.

For some reason that she couldn't name, she felt unaccountably ashamed and deeply regretful.

O ver an hour later, from where she sat, curled up in her corner of the camper, Sherry watched Clint in his private torment, his head propped on the heel of his hands. Her heart ached, and she didn't want it to. "That place where we were going. Is it where you've been staying all this time?"

Clint dropped his hands and his eyes meshed with hers. "Yes."

"Did ... did they think you were still there? Is that why the bomb?"

"I doubt it," he said. "They obviously knew I'd gone home or they wouldn't have sent that letter to you. Like Sam said, it was probably just a warning."

"A warning about what?" Fear sprang to her eyes, and she looked out into the night, stellar lights and natural shadows dancing by the window.

Clint didn't answer. He simply stared at her with eyes as opaque and soulful as a cloudy sky at midnight.

"Okay," she said with resignation. "You won't tell me. But can't you take their warning? Can't you do whatever it is they want so they'll leave us alone?"

"No," he said.

Her balled fist came down on the thin mattress. "How could you have changed so much?" she blared. "How could I have been so wrong?"

His eyes held hers for a long moment, each looking to the other for the only balm that could soothe them. But neither could give.

"You weren't wrong, Sherry. I'm the same man I was the night of our engagement party, when Laney had her baby and we talked about what kind of aunt and uncle we would be. I'm the same man who had already made a list of names for our children. I'm the same man who had to call you three times every night after I left you, because I couldn't stand being awake and not having you with me."

Sherry swallowed the emotion blocking her throat and dropped her head to her knees. She heard Clint get off the floor, felt his weight move the mattress as he sat down next to her on the bed. A small light over the bed flicked on, lending just enough light for them to see each other clearly.

"Look at me, Sherry. The same man." Sherry reluctantly looked up again, and Clint's eyes were misty shards of midnight, cutting into her soul. Her own eyes filled, and she blinked back the evidence of her grief.

"Then what happened?" The question came in a raspy whisper.

"I can't tell you until we're out of danger. It's too risky."

Sherry's eyes blurred as she looked at him. "Too risky? Why? Are you afraid that if you tell me I'll see the real you even more clearly? Do you know that in all the time you were gone, it never once occurred to me that you had done anything criminal and could be hiding? The lowest thing I could come up with was that you'd been so overwhelmed with responsibility that you had to get away. But when you came back, it all came together, like whirling pieces of a horrible nightmare. Only I can't wake up. And it keeps getting worse!"

Clint lifted his hand to touch her hair, but stopped before it made contact. "It won't get worse, Sherry. I'm here now."

"But I don't want you here! Don't you understand that *you* are the nightmare? You're dangerous, and secretive, and unpredictable! I don't know who you are, and yes, I'm scared to death of you."

Clint touched her hair softly. "Baby, I'm not a criminal and you don't have to be afraid of me. You'll see that soon."

His touch sent currents of warmth seeping through her. More than anything she wanted to bury herself in his chest and feel the security of his arms around her, telling her it would be all right. But she couldn't.

"Don't touch me, Clint," she whispered.

But his other arm came around her, forcing her to lean against him, coaxing her into laying her head against his chest. The power and insistence in his embrace terrorized her. Where would it stop?

"You say you don't love me anymore," he whispered. "But I know how hard it is for you to let go of things. You don't replace things in your life, Sherry, and you never forget them. I know you still love me."

"You're wrong." Trembling, she tried to pull away.

Clint leaned toward her, his breath teasing her face. "I'm not wrong, Sherry. I'm not wrong."

His lips seemed to outline hers without touching, and she closed her eyes to escape the sight of them. "I love you," he whispered.

The moment of contact almost shattered her, for the kiss was so gentle, so sweet, that she found no trace of the violence she had sensed in him all day. But it was there, she told herself, lurking behind the tenderness, waiting to strike her when her guard was down. "Don't," she whispered through quivering lips. "Please, don't."

He let her go then, and pulled back, his brows knitted with pleading intensity. He slid his fingers down to her wrist, and she knew he could feel her pulse beating wildly. "You can lie to yourself, Sherry, but you can't lie to me. I've always been able to see right through those beautiful eyes. They've always given you away."

"You're seeing your own illusions," she whispered. "I can't help that."

His fingers laced through hers. "Do you know there were days when I wanted to die if I couldn't see you again?"

She closed her eyes, and his fingers tightened between hers.

"I kept thinking of how it felt to hold you." His hand left hers and traced the length of her leg. "The thought of holding you again was the only thing that kept me going. Without it, I would have—"

His eyes hardened as he touched what she had tucked inside her sock. Clint pulled up her pants leg and found the knife.

He held it up, and she snatched at it, fearing his wrath more than she had before. But he held it out of her reach. "What were you going to do with it, Sherry? Cut me? Kill me?"

"I was going to protect myself," she said, springing off the bed. "You had a weapon! I needed one too!"

His eyes scorched her, and Sherry faced off with him, her mind groping for a way to arm herself against the attack being launched in his eyes.

Behind her back, she reached to the sink for any potential weapon lying there, but Clint didn't miss the movement. In seconds he had grabbed her. She fought back, wrestling and kicking, but he became more forceful and crushing the more she fought. Holding her arms away from her, he shoved her back on the bed. Fury raged in her eyes, and her face washed crimson. "I'll fight you until I die," she declared. "I'll fight you until *you* die!"

Chapter Eight

She expected him to strike her, to shoot her, to throw her out. His face was crimson with rage, and he took a step back. "You're too late, anyway, Sherry," he said. "Want me to bleed? Been there, done that."

As he spoke, his hands worked furiously at the buttons of his denim shirt. She coiled up on the bed, fearing his wrath.

The heat in the camper suddenly seemed stifling.

He opened his shirt, and showed her a gruesome scar from his rib cage down to his waistline. "See, Sherry? Somebody beat you to it!"

She sat up slowly as she saw the long, crooked scar, and she inhaled sharply.

Clint heard the tiny gasp, and turned back to the sink. Self-consciously, he set his hand over the mark.

"It's a scar," Sherry said, the statement a question in itself.

Clint nodded.

She slid to the edge of the bed, her eyes suddenly lacking the disdain that had been there earlier. "Let me see."

Breathing a deep sigh of resignation, he dropped his hand.

Sherry muttered a groan as she examined the raw, red marking. "What . . . what happened?"

"It's a knife wound," he whispered wearily.

"Knife?" She choked on the word. "You . . you were stabbed?"

"Do you really care?" he asked with all the misery his soul contained. "You would have done it yourself if I hadn't found your knife."

Sherry gazed up at him, suddenly feeling the importance of making him believe she couldn't have used it. "No . . . I was just going to use it for self-defense if I had to."

His deep, unfathomable eyes misted, and he focused on the ceiling of the camper. "You know I'd rather die than hurt you."

Somewhere, deep within her, she did know that. She touched the scar with unsteady fingertips, and he held his breath and looked down at her. "When were you stabbed?"

"Right before I left." His eyes said more. They told her that was why he'd disappeared, that there *had* been a valid reason.

"Who?"

He shook his head, denying her that answer. "Not now. Not yet."

A sob was rising in her heart, waiting at the back of her throat for her to give it voice. "You could have died," she whispered.

"I didn't, though."

"Clint, tell me what happened. Please."

"I will, Sherry. When I can. But for now, you have to trust me."

———

D on't you ever get tired of driving?"
Madeline's question cut across the darkness and the road noise. Sam glanced over at her. With a deep sigh, he

said, "I get tired of a lot of things, but I still have to do them."

"But this has been a long day. And it's dark. And this road is so winding and eerie."

Sam smiled and patted her hand with bold familiarity. "Thanks for worrying, honey, but I can handle it."

"I'm not worrying about *you*," she said. "I'm worried about myself. If you fall asleep and drive off the road we'll all be killed. Why don't you let someone else drive for a while?"

A high-pitched laugh tumbled out of Sam's throat. "Someone like you?"

"No, I know you wouldn't trust me. But what about Clint? He could pull his own weight."

She could barely see him in the darkness, but she saw enough to know his face had sobered.

"Clint can't drive. It would make him an open target."

It took a moment for the words to penetrate, and suddenly Madeline's eyes darted to the side mirror that gave a view of what was behind them. "Target for what?"

Sam didn't answer. His fingers curled more tightly over the steering wheel, and his eyes narrowed.

"Are you a target? Am I?"

Sam's finger began to tap, slowly at first, then more rhythmically. When he opened his mouth, Madeline braced herself for an admission that she did not want to hear. But all that came out was a quiet, off-key, "Da doo ron ron ron, da doo ron ron."

Letting out an exaggerated sigh, Madeline leaned her head against the window and closed her eyes. She blocked out the worry she had for Sherry, trapped in the back of the camper with Clint. She blocked out the dread of where they were going and what would happen to her there. It was easy to do, for she had done it all her life, ever since she was a child and her parents had died in a car wreck. She had learned to turn away from pain and worry when she went to live with a distant aunt who saw her as another duty God had thrust on her. Long ago, as a curly-haired little girl, she had learned to concentrate on the present, and to take solace in whatever was at hand. And she had learned that God only put her in places that would make her the person he needed her to be.

Tonight she was in the presence of a man who represented a mixture of danger and security, so she took mental refuge in his presence and the soft, repetitive sound of his voice.

———◆———

Sherry was beginning to trust him. Clint knew it because she had fallen asleep, something she would never have allowed herself to do before she'd seen the scar and realized he, too, had been a victim. Now he moved to sit on the floor beside the bed, and studied the lines of her face in the dark confines of the camper.

A helpless feeling of loss overwhelmed him at the thought of the eight months that had separated them, when he had honestly believed that nothing ever would. But more than time had come between them, he thought, focusing on the ceiling.

Peace. Lying in this moving camper in the night with the woman he loved just out of his reach was as close to peace as he could hope to be. But it was enough for now.

Sherry's eyes fluttered open. She looked surprised to see him sitting on the floor beside her bed, watching her. "Hi," she whispered.

"Hi."

"I had a dream that we were married. That we were safe." She looked up at him, her blue eyes washing through him before they closed once more.

"Soon we will be," he whispered.

A nd she's cli-imb-ing the stair-way to heav-en . . ."
The soft, gravelly voice cut into Madeline's sleep,
pulling her out of her restless nightmare of running through
the woods away from an unknown pursuer. But it wasn't the
voice that had awakened her, for she suspected there hadn't
been much silence since she'd drifted off. It was the human
warmth surrounding and supporting her . . .

She opened her eyes, and found herself curled up against
Sam's shoulder. Startled, she bolted up.

"Well, if it isn't Sleeping Cutie," he rumbled.

"I . . . I didn't mean to . . ."

Sam chuckled under his breath. "Do I look like I have any
complaints?"

"But . . . I don't usually . . ."

"Fall into the arms of strange men?"

Her face tightened with sleepy indignation, and Sam
laughed again. "How's your knee?"

Thankful that he had the decency to change the subject,
she glanced down at it. "Hurts a little, but it's better." She
glanced out the window at the blackness. "I hope Sherry is
all right."

Sam laughed. "Well, it's so quiet back there that they're
bound to have either made up or killed each other."

"They haven't made up," Madeline said on a yawn. "So
they must be dead."

"Must be." Sam bit his grin as he glanced over at her.

A moment of quiet filled the truck's cab, and soberly,
Madeline studied his unshaven profile, the hard, angular line
of his nose, the sleepy flush of his cheeks, the ruffled disar-
ray of his brown hair. But his eyes were awake, bright, comforting. "So," she said after a moment. "What are you going
to sing for me now?"

A slow grin crept across Sam's face, and he gave her a wink. "Got any requests?" he asked.

※

The sound of gravel cracking under their wheels alerted Clint that they had reached their destination, and he peered out the camper window to the small cabin lit up in wait for them. Several cars lined the gravel drive, and a small crowd formed on the front porch at their approach. The chill hand of apprehension clutched him at the sight of so many more men than had been with him before.

The camper stopped, and he heard Sam's door slam. Several of the men approached him, exchanged words, and then the back door opened.

"You awake back here?" Sam whispered.

Clint rubbed his eyes and stepped outside so he wouldn't wake Sherry. "Yeah. What's going on? Who are all these people?"

Sam bit his lip distastefully. "He wanted us to beef up security since we brought our two guests with us."

"Security was tight before. It didn't need beefing up."

"Tell me about it," Sam said dryly. "But he's running this show."

"Terrific," Clint said.

"So how'd it go?" Sam's voice cut quietly across the darkness.

"Fine," Clint said. "She still thinks I'm some kind of criminal, but she's more afraid *for* me than *of* me now."

"She should be, pal," Sam said. "it's getting down to the wire now. Looks like we just have to hold out a few more days. Then it'll all be over."

The words left a hollow feeling in Clint's chest. Would it ever be over? Would he really ever be able to sleep at night without keeping one eye open for someone to spring at him out of the dark?

"Give me a minute to wake her up," Clint told his friend. "I'll be right there."

"Okay," Sam said. "But don't be too long. They have a lot of questions for us when we get inside. And I have a few for them."

———✦———

Madeline stirred when she felt the comfort of a bed beneath her, and a strong man's arms releasing her. The room was dark, but she looked up and saw the weary face of Sam, her captor, tucking her into bed. His silver eyes were shadowed, and the lines etched in his face seemed much more defined than they had earlier. He was bone tired, and yet he seemed to be concentrating all his efforts on covering her with the comforter he had pulled back. For a moment, she felt a jolt of fear that he'd crawl in next to her, take advantage of her now that they were alone.

His heavy hand rested on her shoulder when the comforter was in place, and she felt his pause and his warm eyes studying her. What was he thinking, she wondered, pretending to still be asleep. Was he considering what he was going to do with her? When his hand lifted, she heard him leave the room. No, Sam wasn't a threat. It was even possible that he was a nice guy.

Relaxing, she fell back to sleep. In her dreams, an off-key humming set a rhythm in her heart, a soft lullaby that made her smile.

Chapter Nine

Clint shook Sherry gently, waking her. Slowly, she became aware that the camper wasn't moving. She sat up. "Are ... are we there?"

"We're there," he said softly. He touched her warm cheek. "But before we go inside, I want to warn you. There are men with holsters strapped to their chests in there. But you don't have to be afraid. They're not here to hold you hostage. They're here to protect us both. Your father sent them."

Sherry bolted upright on the bed, her eyes rounded. "My father?"

"Yes. He knows where we are. He arranged for us to hide here."

"My father *knew* where you were?" The words came out on a shaky, disbelieving breath. "He's involved in this?"

"Yes." He silenced her with a fingertip to her lips. "I'll tell you every—"

"How long?" The question was uttered too loudly, and she grabbed Clint's arm and shook him. Her eyes blazed with fear and betrayal, and he knew he couldn't keep the truth from her any longer. "How long has my father been involved?"

"Since the beginning."

Sherry was mute with shock.

"He wanted to protect you," Clint said in a voice meant to be soothing.

"*Protect* me? He wanted to protect me?" She shook away from Clint and stood up. "I'm sick to death of being protected! And lied to! And afraid! Clint, why didn't you tell me this before?"

"I couldn't tell you everything when I didn't know if we'd make it here or not. I didn't want you just knowing that much, and thinking all the way that your father was some kind of criminal. You'll understand in a minute." He touched her face again, the gesture bestowing his promise to make things clear. "We'll go inside and get some coffee, and then I'll tell you everything."

Tears sprang to Sherry's eyes. Suddenly, she wasn't sure she wanted to know.

"Where's Madeline?" she asked, as if the change in subject could erase the reality.

"Sam took her in."

"She's probably scared to death," Sherry said. She wrapped her arms around herself, trying to stop the sudden shivering. "I want to see her."

"All right."

Clint stood up and took her hand, but she jerked it away. She had begun to trust him again, because she had wanted to so badly. But somehow the new development, all the lies and betrayals, confused her more than before.

"Sherry, when you understand, you'll forgive us all."

Unconvinced, Sherry turned away from him and started out of the camper. Two jean-clad men with pistols strapped to the left sides of their chests waited beside the camper door, and when she saw them, she gasped.

"It's okay," he said. He tried to dispel his own uncomfortable feeling at the new men Grayson had sent. "Let's just go on in."

The men followed them into the house, where at least ten others, including Sam, sat in a conference over coffee and cigarettes that filled the room with a haze. Sherry gave a dull glance over the men, one by one, wondering how dangerous they were and what they were all hiding from. Her breath caught when her eyes met those of Gary Rivers, the sergeant on the Shreveport police force, whom she had been involved with before Clint. Her mouth came open of its own accord. He had known, too. He, too, had been involved. And when she had begged for his help after Clint's disappearance, he had lied. He had even asked her out a few months ago, when he had *known* that Clint was hiding somewhere waiting to get back to her. "Gary?" The word in itself was an accusation.

Rivers stood up and reluctantly looked her in the eye. "How are you, Sherry?" The question came as calmly, as guilt-filled, as she expected. Out of the corner of her eye she saw Clint stiffen and take a step forward.

"I'm just great," she muttered sarcastically. Raising her chin, she turned to Sam, her eyes narrowed against any more surprises. "Where's Madeline?"

"In the first bedroom on the right," he said. "She was dead to the world."

Sherry shivered at the choice of words. "I want to see her."

"Go ahead," Sam said wearily, matching her defiant tone.

She looked at Clint, and with a brooding expression, he nodded that it was all right.

The room where Madeline slept, like the rest of the house, was decorated in rustic neglect. It smelled of dust and mold, and the oak floor was scuffed and scratched, dirty from years of muddy hunters' boots tromping over it. But the bed looked inviting, and Madeline lay curled up like a baby kitten.

Sherry wanted to kill her. Sitting on the edge of the mattress, she shook her. "Madeline, are you all right?"

Madeline pulled the covers up over her head. "Sherry, I'm asleep." She snuggled into a tighter ball.

Sherry tried to wrestle the covers away from her. "Madeline, wake up!"

"What is this?" Madeline snapped. "Boot camp?"

With a sigh of long-suffering irritation, Sherry shook her head. "Madeline, we were just abducted and driven to some dusty rundown house out in the middle of nowhere after a mysterious plane trip and driving for hours. Doesn't that make you the least bit curious?"

Madeline shook her head. "It makes me tired."

"Well, at least that aspect of my curiosity is satisfied. Obviously that man didn't hurt you."

"Sam's a pussycat," Madeline mumbled.

"A pussycat? Madeline, he packs a gun and he's dangerous."

Madeline struggled to open her eyes, but only managed two slits. "Read my lips, Sherry. He's a pussycat. The worst crime he's guilty of is singing off-key." She giggled into the pillow. "And you should hear how he slaughters perfectly good lyrics. There ought to be a law."

Sherry stared at her friend and wondered if Madeline was right. "Then you think they're on the right side of the law?"

"Could be."

Madeline's noncommittal assessment was exasperating, but for a moment Sherry turned the possibility over in her mind.

"My father's in on it," Sherry mumbled finally.

Madeline's head came up in a sudden exhibition of interest. "Your father?"

"All along," Sherry said. "Clint just told me."

Madeline threaded her fingers absently through her tousled dark hair. "Wow. What else did he tell you?"

"Nothing yet. I wanted to see you first."

"Well, go beat it out of him. What are you doing talking to me?"

Sherry twisted her fingers in her lap. "Gary Rivers is out there too."

"Gary?" Madeline sat all the way up this time, shaking her head as if to clear the fog. "Wait a minute. Gary was in on it?"

Sherry nodded. "It's all getting so big, and so complicated. I think I'm afraid to know."

"Well, it couldn't be as bad as it seems," Madeline said. "It never is." She yawned and gave Sherry her sleepy assessment. "So how'd it go back in that camper? I gave you up for dead when I quit hearing the yelling."

"We stopped yelling for a while," she said softly. "All it took was the reality of a knife scar on his side."

"A knife?" Madeline swallowed. She was fully awake now. "As in sharp pointed thing that does serious damage when thrust into flesh?"

Sherry nodded.

"Go get details, Sherry, before my imagination gets as carried away as yours."

Reluctantly, Sherry stood up and looked back down at her friend. "How's your knee? Need aspirin or anything?"

"It's okay. Sam got me ice," Madeline said. "Now, go. Get the story, then come tell me what's going on."

Sherry left her and headed back up the hall. Lowered voices from the living room beckoned her, and softening her footsteps, she stepped toward the door and listened.

"But he's dead." Clint's voice came clear and angry over the others.

"Did you tell anyone? Your pastor, or a friend?"

"Do you think I'm stupid?" Clint returned.

"Then obviously Paul told someone. Maybe that's why he died. Maybe they didn't think they could trust him because he waited so long to tell them."

"There was no way I could have known."

"You could have listened to us." She recognized Gary's voice—deep, accusing. "We told you it was too soon to go back there."

"What was I supposed to do? Just watch my life go by like it's some bad dream? For all I know it could have been eight more months before I was able to go back. These trials go on forever!"

"Well, your impatience brought Sherry into the line of fire, and nobody's happy about that."

"And you think I am? She's going to be my wife. I would never have dragged her into this intentionally."

"But you did, nonetheless."

She heard Clint's footsteps, heavy, irate.

"You're not fooling anybody, Rivers," Clint blurted, "with your sensitive concern for Sherry."

"Well, at least I *have* some semblance of concern! Not like you, dragging her into this mess just to satisfy your hormones."

Something fell over and crashed onto the floor, and the noise of a scuffle ensued.

"Stop it, Clint," Sam shouted. "This isn't helping anything. We've got to stand together. This guy was sent here to help protect you."

"Somebody'll need to protect *him* if he doesn't keep his filthy mouth shut!" Clint thundered. "Why did Grayson send him here, anyway?"

"He trusts him," Sam said. "There's no room here for grudges."

Tension seemed to float in the air like a lethal gas ready to explode with the lighting of a match.

Sherry heard Clint stalk across the room. "I want to make something clear to you, Rivers," Clint said in the low vibrato of fury. "I've had about as much of this as I can take. This is *my* life. I'm the pawn here, not you. None of this was my idea, and

I didn't ask for it. If it weren't for me, Grayson and Breard wouldn't even have a case. I've had it up to here with putting a hold on my life and waiting to be called to the stand and wondering who's going to jump out of the bushes next and who I can trust and if the woman I love is going to die because of something that I never even wanted to see!"

Sherry caught her breath and struggled to follow his words.

"I'll stay here with you for as long as it takes to get out of this, but I'm not going to take any more of your accusations. I could disappear right now and Givanti would go free, and you know it."

Givanti! Sherry stepped into the doorway and locked astonished eyes with Clint's black, piercing eyes. He relaxed his stance a bit at the sight of her. He was the mystery witness in the Givanti trial that her father's office had been prosecuting. He wasn't a criminal. He wasn't a kidnapper. He was *trying* to be a hero.

But one didn't have to know all the details to see that Givanti must have people after him. And it was her father's fault that Clint was the primary target for every thug in the area. *Her father's fault.* No wonder he wasn't trying the case himself. Her relationship with Clint presented a conflict of interest. Wes had been right. Her father couldn't be trusted.

"Now, if you'll excuse me, gentlemen," Clint said sarcastically, "I need to talk to my fiancée. I'm sure she has a lot of questions, and she's as entitled to answers as anyone. Is it all right for us to go outside?"

"Yeah, we've combed the woods. The place is secure."

Clint took her hand and started for the door. Two men got up to follow after Clint, and he ground his teeth together and shoved his hand through his hair. "I'd like to be alone."

"That's impossible," Rivers said with finality.

"Then keep your distance," Clint warned. "This is going to be a private conversation, not a group discussion."

He led her outside.

The midnight sky was star-studded, and the crescent moon hung overhead like a painting. Crickets chirped a deceitful song of peace, and wind whispered through the leaves and in her hair, cooling the burning feeling of horror shooting through her. The two men waited a few yards behind them, eyes alert and hands at their sides, as if they fully expected to be needed.

"You're the star witness in the Givanti case," Sherry said in a low murmur before Clint had the chance to begin. "I've figured that out. What I don't know is how."

Clint dropped wearily to a tall patch of grass and leaned back on his elbows. "Remember Paul Calloway?"

"The college student in your youth group," Sherry said. She recalled the handsome young man with blue eyes and shaggy brown hair, and the ambitious spirit they'd all admired. She hadn't seen him in months. He'd been at Louisiana State University this semester, she assumed.

"He borrowed my coat at a retreat we were on, when the temperature dropped and he hadn't prepared for it. The last day I saw you I found a vial of cocaine in that coat. I went to see him to confront him about it, and to try witnessing to him. Only it happened that I wound up witnessing a drug deal and a murder, instead."

Chapter Ten

"Paul Calloway killed somebody?" Sherry asked, amazed. "Paul Calloway tried to kill *me*," Clint said. The very name made his adrenaline surge, and he could feel his face reddening at the memories. "It's hard to believe that such a chain reaction could have started from one visit I paid to a mixed-up kid. If I'd only known when I knocked on that door ..."

There was no turning back. The knock on the door made it final, sealing the decision to confront Paul with his finding. Clint looked down at the vial in his hand and shook his head. It explained a lot of things. It explained Paul's sudden bursts of energy during the mission retreats Clint had taken the kids on. It explained the wild look in his eyes when he'd shown up late at special events. It explained his distant preoccupation at times when Clint was praying he'd get through to him. He would probably get angry for Clint's intrusion. But Clint could live with that.

Because it *was* his business. He had grown fond of the twenty-year-old kid who reminded him of himself at that age. He didn't want to see him ruin his chance at a good life before it even got started. Clint wasn't about to let him throw it away by getting drawn under the spell of cocaine abuse.

The door opened, and Paul caught his breath at the sight of Clint. "I . . . I thought you were someone else." Raking a distracted hand through his brown hair, the young man looked past him, his pale blue eyes darting up the street in front of his house.

"Can we talk?" Clint asked.

"No," Paul said quickly. "I'm expecting some people."

"Paul," Clint prodded. "It's important."

"Sorry, man. I'll call you later." The door started to close in Clint's face, but undaunted, he stopped it with his foot.

"I found something in the pocket of the coat I loaned to you last week, Paul," he said, "And I'm not leaving until I talk to you about it."

"My pocket? Wh—?" The word got caught in his throat as Clint brandished the vial. With a sigh that seemed more impatient than surprised, Paul stepped back and let Clint in. "I appreciate your returning it, but you can't stay."

Clint walked into the house that Paul had said he was taking care of while the owners were in Europe. In one look, he could see the disregard for property—clothes strewn over chairs and sprawled across the floor, dirty dishes cluttering the table, glasses with cigarette butts floating in rancid liquid. Briefly, he wondered if the owners had expected this when they'd asked Paul to house-sit. He turned back to Paul, who was at the window now, peering nervously out. "Man, I mean it. You have to *leave!*"

"Not until we talk," Clint insisted again. He sat down in a chair and leaned forward. "Paul, you don't need that stuff. You have a lot going for you, and I don't want to see you—"

"Okay, fine," Paul agreed, cutting him off. "I'll quit." He took the vial, rushed to the kitchen off the den, and poured it into the sink. Hurriedly, he ran some water down the drain, then came back to Clint. "See? It's gone. Now will you please go?"

"You expect me to believe that it's over just like that?"

Paul's face flushed crimson, and he banged his fist into a wall. "What do you want from me? An affidavit? I told you—" The sound of an approaching car outside stopped his words and he swung back to the window, cursing. "I knew this would happen. They'll see your car—"

"I'm on my ten-speed," Clint said. "Who are you expecting—?"

"You have to hide. Hurry up. Get upstairs! Now."

"What?"

"Hide upstairs, Clint! If these people see you, they'll kill us both. This is no joke. Get upstairs and hide in the bathroom. And don't come out under any circumstances."

"Paul, I'm not hiding anywhere—"

The rage in Paul's crimson face was urgent, desperate. "Listen to me, man! I'm trying to keep you from winding up just another unexplained stiff. Do what I say!"

The doorbell rang, and Clint began to believe the panic in Paul's eyes. "Please, Clint!"

Reluctantly, Clint started up the stairs, but he didn't hide in the bathroom. He got out of sight behind the rail overlooking the lower level. Paul was obviously nervous as he let several men in. Immediately, Clint recognized Tony Givanti, a local businessman, and Steve Anderson, recently named Teacher of the Year at the local high school. He strained to hear as the men filed into the house, arguing among themselves about the price of something for which they were negotiating.

Givanti ordered Paul to show them what they wanted, and as Clint watched from his hiding place, the young man produced several bags of cocaine.

"What's the street value?" one of the buyers asked.

"Over a million dollars," Givanti said. "You're getting a bargain."

"We can only pay half now," the buyer said.

Givanti bristled. "No way. We had an agreement."

"But things didn't work out like we planned. We had trouble coming up with the cash, but we'll have the rest by tomorrow."

Clint watched as Paul's eyes darted nervously upstairs to make sure he was out of sight, no doubt hoping that Clint hadn't seen or heard anything. Clint scooted back so the young man wouldn't see him. So this was how Paul had paid for his sports car. And this house was probably his. And the clothes and trips ...

"When you pay the other half, you get the other half," Givanti said. "I don't give credit. Tomorrow night, the warehouse on Fourth and Brine Street, you bring the money and we'll give you the rest of it."

"But we have buyers tonight, Givanti," Anderson said. "You know we'll pay you when we collect."

"I don't do business that way, gentlemen. You know that."

The men were red-faced as they made the exchange. One of them left, but Anderson lingered behind. Clint heard one of the cars drive away, and watched as the argument grew more heated. Givanti got angry and took a swing at him, and Anderson pulled a gun.

Fear coursed through him, and he thought of going into one of the bedrooms and calling the police. He got up quietly, staying in the shadows, and backed toward the bedroom.

The gunshot that cracked through the night stunned him, and he saw Anderson drop to the floor. He stood there, paralyzed, as Givanti ordered Paul to help him with the body. Clint watched as Paul helped the businessman carry Anderson's lifeless body out into the night. He went to a window and peered out, and saw them dump the body into the trunk of Paul's car.

He was drenched in sweat and trembling, trying to decide what to do when Paul came back in. Would Paul tell Givanti there had been a witness? If Givanti had so easily killed Anderson, what would he do to Clint?

He went into the bedroom, stepped over clothes and shoes, and tried to find the telephone in the dark. Through the window, he saw them closing the trunk. Paul and Givanti spoke for a moment, and then Paul got into the driver's seat of the car with the body. Givanti went to his own car and drove away.

That's it? Clint thought. Paul was going to leave, and allow Clint to get away? It didn't make sense, but he didn't take time to question it. When the two cars were out of sight, he rushed out to the ten-speed he had ridden over, hopped on it, and headed as fast as he could to Eric Grayson's house. This was too big for a phone call to the police, he thought, and he had to get to safety before Paul came to his senses and came back for Clint. Riding as fast as he could on the back roads, he headed to the home of Sherry's father, the U.S. attorney.

Eric Grayson listened earnestly to the news and contacted the police himself.

Mentally exhausted, Clint slipped out of the house while Eric was on the telephone, making plans for a major drug bust for the following night at the location Clint had given him. Looking back, Clint wasn't sure if it was simple fatigue or mental numbness in the wake of shock that had caused him to be so careless. But all he had wanted was to go home and sleep, and wake up to find it had all been a bad dream.

It smelled like rain, and the peaceful breeze sweeping through his hair had given him a false sense of security as he'd ridden his ten-speed up the driveway to his house. He pulled into the open carport and parked beside his car. Reaching for the keys in his jeans pocket, he began to see the scene again. *Murder*, he thought with a shudder. He had witnessed a murder.

He started toward his house, kicking at the pebbles lining the drive, and wondering if he'd handled it wrong. Perhaps it could have been stopped if he hadn't hidden, if he had let them know he was there. But then maybe he would have been killed instead. And maybe Paul too. How had the kid gotten himself into such a mess?

He flipped through his keys for the right one and stepped onto the dark porch. Feeling for the knob, he tried to insert the key, but a movement in the shadows caught his attention.

Paul was waiting for him, his dark, foreboding eyes angry and vengeful. "They can't know that you were there," he said through his teeth. "If he finds out, he'll kill me, too. No one can know that you were there."

"Paul, you've got to turn yourself—"

But before Clint could get the rest of the words out, Paul closed the distance between them, and a piercing pain—jaggedly rending and as hot as scalding metal inside torn flesh—coursed through him. He stumbled and clutched at Paul's jacket, the questions caught in his throat. He heard sirens, heard Paul cursing the fact that he didn't have time to hide Clint's body. And then he felt another stab, and darkness closed over him.

He woke sometime later in a trauma unit with Sam as his guard and a doctor at his side, and learned that Paul had left him for dead before he'd fled. Eric Grayson had sent the police to protect him the moment he'd discovered that Clint had left his house. It had been two days before Clint's mind was clear again ... clear enough to know that he was somewhere in south Texas with a battalion of stitches in his side, an IV running sustenance into his veins, and U.S. Attorney Eric Grayson standing over him with the news that everyone involved, except Paul, had been arrested as the drugs were changing hands the night following the murder. Paul was still out there somewhere, a lurking threat to Clint's life. And for that reason, Grayson said, there could be no communication between Clint and Sherry until after the trial. And that meant there would not be a wedding.

"I want her kept out of this," the older man told him with pain in his eyes, the only thing that kept Clint from ripping out of his bed and strangling him. "From what you've said about the way things happened, I don't think Paul Calloway is going to want anyone to know that he had anything to do with letting the cat out of the bag." Eric paced back and forth as he spoke, thinking it all through for what Clint knew was the thousandth time. "He must realize that if Givanti knew he'd allowed a witness to the murder, that Givanti would make sure someone took him out. The fact that he didn't warn them to change the location of the drug exchange after he knew you'd heard it, tells me that I'm right. He may even think he killed you, and he never confessed things to Givanti, because he's afraid of him, even in prison. When he hears there's a witness to the murder, Calloway might figure out that you're alive. He'll be interested in finishing the job he started with you, but I don't think anyone else will be looking for you. We have to keep you hidden until you can testify, or until we apprehend him. Meanwhile, everyone has to think you got cold feet. If every-

one thinks you just ran from the wedding, no one will con-
nect you with this, and we'll have the chance to convict
Givanti and catch Paul ..."

"But what about Sherry?" Clint demanded. "What will
she think?"

Grayson covered the uncertainty on his face with a trembling hand that betrayed his weariness. "We'll make her
think the same thing," he said quietly.

"That I didn't love her enough to marry her? That I had
to run?"

"It's better than letting her be used as a go-between. If she
knows the truth, it will be obvious. She'll even try to come
after you, or—"

The pain tore at Clint's side as he tried to sit up. "It won't
work," he said, as if the simple words could make it true.
"She'll never believe it. She knows how much I love her."

"Eventually she'll believe it," Grayson assured in a soul-
sad voice. "And then when the trial is over ..."

Clint dropped back onto the thin pillow beneath him, his
eyes pleading with the attorney's. "I was supposed to marry
her next Saturday," he whispered on the deepest note of
despair. "How can you take that away from us?"

"It's simple. If you love her, you'll see my logic. A heartbreak is easier to heal than a knife wound or a million other
dangers. She's my daughter, and I want her safe."

"She'll think I abandoned her just like you did."

It was a low blow, and it hit its mark. "I know she will.
But I'll be there for her. Maybe I can help her through it.
Clint, you have to understand. These men we're dealing
with, they're ruthless. If they had an inkling that you were
involved, they'd go after Sherry just for sport. They'd use her
to manipulate you."

"Then let her come into hiding, too."

"No," he said. "It's not necessary, because they don't
know. But if we tell her, if she even has a clue, someone

might figure things out. There are too many wild cards in this thing. The closer she is to you, the more danger she could be in."

Eventually, he had seen Grayson's logic and agreed with it. Sherry was safe, if nothing else. But he hadn't counted on it taking eight months for the case to get to court.

Chapter Eleven

Sherry's face was white as she stared at Clint, taking it all in. "I would rather have been with you in danger than where I was and safe," she said. "My father had no right to keep me in the dark, or to make that decision for me." She wiped the tears on her face, and asked, "So what is this? The Federal Witness Protection Program or something?"

"That's right. Your dad got the FBI involved since some of their activities had crossed state lines. Apparently Givanti's drug connections were pretty far-reaching."

She shook her head, trying to sort it all out. "But what made you come back when you did? You haven't testified yet."

"No, but the trial is taking forever, so there was no telling when they'd get me on the stand. And last week the police found Paul . . . dead. He was in an explosion in an abandoned factory." He swallowed hard. "As much trouble as he's caused me, I didn't want him dead. I prayed for him every day, that he'd repent and find God, that something he heard all those times at church would penetrate. But I guess I didn't have the impact I thought I had. I had no business in youth ministry, if I couldn't get through to someone who needed Christ so much."

"Clint, no one could get through to Paul if he was in that deep. It's not a reflection on your ministry. Think how many kids *did* listen. How many lives you changed. They all grieved over you, right along with me."

He blinked back the mist in his eyes and drew in a deep breath. "Anyway, I was convinced that he was the only one who knew where I was, and that I was out of danger, so I threatened not to testify if they didn't let me go home. But I was wrong. Paul must have told someone. And now you've been threatened."

She dropped to her knees on the ground and riveted her eyes on a blade of grass. "So who sent me that letter?"

"I don't know."

Sherry turned toward the wind and set her hand on her forehead. She was beginning to feel sick. Sick with the terror that Clint had faced for so long. Sick with the months of emptiness that shouldn't have occurred. Sick with fatigue and hunger and a fear that was beginning to be chronic. "So what now?" she asked in a dull voice. "Does Dad intend to hide us out here forever?"

"No. Just until I testify."

Fury rose, burning her throat. "And then what? Doesn't he think they'll get revenge? Doesn't he know that they won't let you just walk out of that courtroom, if they let you walk in in the first place?"

"Givanti wasn't The Godfather, Sherry. He was just a greedy businessman who got in trouble with his gambling debts and figured this was an easy way to get himself in the black. His cohorts weren't even that loyal to him, because they've made all kinds of deals with Eric in exchange for information on how they got the cocaine into the country and things like that. If I can get him put away, I really believe we'll be safe."

A gust of wind whipped Sherry's hair into her face, and she slapped it away. "What about the note, Clint? What about the bomb at the place you were staying? Obviously he's not going to sit still and let you do this!"

Clint didn't answer. Instead, he looked at her as if the instances she'd named were small events he'd chosen to forget. Sherry wanted to scream. "I can't believe my father would put you in this position. I can't believe he'd use your life to buy a conviction!"

"He isn't using me, Sherry," Clint said. "He's kept me alive when I couldn't have myself."

Her lips compressed into taut lines, full of contempt and despair. "And he made me think you just didn't love me, that you got cold feet, that I wasn't enough for you. All the time I was seeing guilt in his eyes when I thought it was sympathy. It just makes me sick!"

Clint's expression was soft now, devoid of the bitterness she'd witnessed earlier.

"He did the best thing for you. If you'd known, you would have run after me. Everything would have started to look suspicious, and what Givanti and his men didn't know, they would have figured out. I disappeared, and then Paul did, and then if you had, it wouldn't have taken a genius—"

"That's no excuse!" Sherry bellowed. "That's absolutely no excuse for lying to me! Or putting your life in jeopardy. I'll never forgive him for that!" She caught her breath on a sob and fought back tears. "Wes was right. He said our father didn't care about us. It was true."

Clint tore a weed out of the ground and looked down at it. "Sherry, I know it's hard for you. But you'll get past this confusion and you'll see that neither your dad nor I had a choice. We did exactly what we had to do. We betrayed you, but you know that you would have done the same thing in our place."

Sherry swung around, her hair lashing into her face with the force. "How do you know that?"

"Because you're as strong as I am."

Sherry threw up her hands, then let them fall heavily to her sides in helpless denial. "You and Madeline, you both think I'm some kind of rock. You both keep talking about how strong I am." She tapped her chest. "Look at me, Clint. I've been shaking since you ran me down two days ago. I'm inside out. I'm numb. You call that strength?"

"You're dealing with it, Sherry."

"Dealing with it? If you think I'm dealing with anything you don't know me very well. I'm tired of coping, Clint. I'm tired of trying to hold myself together by a thread. I feel like I'm hanging onto the side of a building, about to fall."

Clint's voice cut across the night and into Sherry's heart. "I know the feeling."

Sherry leaned toward him, her blue eyes wide and desperate, full of unshed tears. "Then let's leave. Let's just blow it all off and go somewhere else. You don't have to go through with this. My father cannot make you risk your life."

"I'm not doing this for your father. I'm doing it because it's the right thing."

"And what about me? I lose the one man I love because some stupid kid got into the wrong crowd? Does that make sense, Clint?" When he didn't answer, she closed her eyes and tried to massage the pain from her temples. "Why did you have to go there, Clint? Why did you get involved with Paul? It was none of your business!"

"You liked him too, Sherry. We thought he was our friend. He needed guidance and help. How could I have known I was going at the wrong time?"

"The wrong time? That's like saying Hiroshima was the wrong city. It changed our *lives*, Clint. It might have *cost* our lives, and it's not over yet." She took his face in her hands, and pleaded, "Don't testify, Clint."

"I have to." His voice cracked, and she heard the catch in his breath.

"Not if you love me," she said. "If you really love me, you won't be a hero. You'll give it up and let the professionals worry about it."

Clint took her arms, and his eyebrows arched, emphasizing the new lines on his forehead that spoke of the hard life he'd been leading since he left her. "Baby, you know I love you. But I have to do this. Otherwise this whole eight months was a waste."

"It's a waste, anyway, Clint!" she shouted. "And it's going to keep being a waste until you put an end to it."

"There won't be an end until I testify."

"There won't be an end until they *kill* you!" she shouted, shaking away from him. "And me too. If you loved me, you wouldn't drag me through this. You'd see that there are other ways."

"There isn't another way, Sherry. If there was, don't you think I'd have found it by now?"

She bit her lip and swallowed back a sob. "I can't stand it. I've mourned for you once. I don't want to do it again."

"You won't have to. All these men are watching over us, Sherry. And God is still in control."

"Then why does it feel like I'm right in the center of chaos?" With that, she ran back into the house, to seek the only refuge she could find—sleep.

Chapter Twelve

The telephone rang twelve times before Laney gave up. "Sherry's still not answering, Wes. It's after midnight. Where could they be?"

"Maybe they just turned the ringer off," Wes said, throwing a reassuring look at his wife. "Sherry was so dead set on avoiding Clint."

Laney leaned back in the bed and brought her knees to her chest. "It just doesn't feel right. I think we need to go over there and check on them."

"Yeah, you're right." He sighed and got up. "Neither of us will be able to sleep until we've seen that they're okay."

Laney looked up at him. "Wes, shouldn't you call your father first? See if he's heard from Sherry? Ask him if she told him where she was going."

Wes's jaw popped as he shrugged on the shirt he'd left hanging over a chair. "I don't have to call the U.S. attorney to find out where my sister is. There's nothing wrong. She's probably sleeping and forgot she left the phone unplugged."

"I wasn't suggesting him because he's the prosecutor, Wes. I suggested him because he's your father. She spends a lot of time with him. She might have told him something."

"I'll take my chances."

"You won't even call him?"

"No, I won't."

"Wes, don't you think that's a little stubborn? You should be putting your sister above your own pride!"

"Pride?" He swung around to his wife. "Are you kidding me? This doesn't have anything to do with pride. I don't even know that man, and I'm supposed to pretend that he's a part of my family?"

Laney got up, her long white gown pooling around her feet. "Wes, he *is* part of your family. You can't change that."

"I don't have to acknowledge it." He grabbed his keys off of the dresser, and headed out of the bedroom.

Wes pulled into Sherry and Madeline's driveway and saw that Madeline's car was there. He relaxed somewhat, and told himself that the scenario he had envisioned was accurate. At least one of them was home—they just weren't answering the phone.

Since it was so late, he started to drive on home, instead of waking them if they were asleep, but something compelled him to go in and talk to Sherry himself. If she'd been disturbed enough to unplug the phones, then maybe she could use her brother's ear.

He trotted up the front steps to the door and rang the bell. There was no answer, so he knocked hard, and went to the living room window to peer in. There was one light on in the living room, but no evidence that anyone was home.

He went around to the side of the house and peered into Sherry's bedroom window. A night-light cast a pale glow throughout the room, and he could see that the bed was still made. No one was there.

A prayer started to form in his mind as he hurried to the other bedroom and looked into Madeline's room. Still no one.

Frantic now, he went to the back of the house and checked under the mat for the extra key. When it wasn't there, he tried the storage room where he knew they kept another one. He took it and hurried back to the door to open it. The door opened easily, and he stepped inside.

"Sherry?" he called. "Madeline? Are you here?"

The silence screamed out at him. He closed the door behind him, locked it, then went through the house, searching each room. He saw a drawer open in Madeline's room, and some of the clothes had dropped onto the floor, as if someone had hastily grabbed something out. He went back into the living room and saw a stack of mail tossed down, unopened, next to Madeline's car keys.

He turned around slowly, trying to find some clue, anything, that would tell him where his sister may have gone. On the couch was an opened envelope, and next to it a paper lying face down. He picked it up.

In cut-out magazine letters, he read the words, *"Tell him revenge is sweet, and falls on those we love."*

He took in a sharp breath as the first talons of fear gripped him. He grabbed the phone and started to dial 911, then changed his mind and called Laney instead.

"Hello?"

"Laney, there's something wrong! They're not here, but there's a note. I need to call him—Eric. His number's probably unlisted. Do you have it anywhere?"

"Yes," Laney said. "I have it right here. But Wes, what did Sherry say in the note?"

"It wasn't from Sherry. It was from someone else. Look, I'll call you back as soon as I know something, okay?"

"Wes, please be careful!"

"I will." He dropped the phone back in its cradle and said a quick prayer. What had happened to his sister? He dialed the number, and waited as it rang two, three, four times. Finally, his father answered in a raspy, groggy voice.

"Eric Grayson."

His stomach tightened. "This is Wes Grayson," he said coldly. "I'm looking for my sister. Do you know where she is?"

There was a slight hesitation, and finally, Eric said, "Wes, we need to talk."

"Then you know where she is?"

"I didn't say that."

"Well, say it! Do you or don't you?"

"Wes, where are you?"

"In Sherry's living room." His lips were taut, and his words were clipped, angry. "I'm holding a note from some lunatic talking about revenge, and it's obvious that something's wrong. *Now do you know where she is or not?*"

"Just wait there, Wes. I'll be over in ten minutes."

"I just want an answer!" he shouted. *"Yes or no. Do you know or don't you?"*

But the phone clicked in his ear. Wes jammed it into its cradle. Where was she? And what was so important that Eric couldn't tell him over the phone?

Chapter Thirteen

It's never as bad as it looks, pal," Sam said to Clint. It was nearing two in the morning, and Clint felt as if this day had lasted a year. He sat alone on the grass, forearms propped on his knees, and Sam came to join him, a folded lawn chair in each hand.

Clint didn't answer. As close as he was to Sam, he didn't want to talk. But that had never swayed Sam before.

"The grass is always greener on the other side," Sam said, slumping into his chair and offering Clint the other. Clint reluctantly got up, dusted off his jeans, and plopped down.

"One in the hand is worth two in the bush." The line was delivered with great somberness. Clint gave Sam an annoyed glance, but still chose not to speak.

"Yeah," Sam said on a yawn. "Every cloud has a silver lining. That's the kind of guy I am."

Clint issued a barely audible moan. "I guess I should feel lucky that you didn't put a tune to those little nuggets of wisdom."

Sam laughed. "I figured you were miserable enough."

Clint shrugged. "Miserable. Is that what they call it?" He looked into the wind, letting it ruffle his hair. "You know,

Sam, life was no bed of roses when I was a kid. But it was okay. You feel better about yourself when you make it, with obstacles behind you that most people never have to face." He stopped and swallowed, and contemplated the stars. "Adversity always makes us stronger, and I keep telling myself that. But lately it seems that I've run out of positive sides. Everything keeps blowing up in my face. The rules of the game seem to keep changing, and I can't keep up with them."

Sam cocked his head, listening. That was the thing about Sam. He could listen like no one else.

"I don't know if I ever told you," Clint went on, "but my dad was a construction worker. Died when I was five. Fell from a building he was working on. My mother had to support my kid brother and me after that, and it wasn't easy. And then when my brother got sick . . ." His voice trailed off at the helpless memory of the little boy dying, and his mother's grief. Swallowing, he continued, his soft voice doing battle with the rustle of the warm wind. "Well, things were never the same after that. But we did the very best that we could. She always taught that there is one plumb line to discern right and wrong. Everything has to be lined up against it, and if it doesn't line up, then it's probably wrong."

"And what's that plumb line?"

"The Word of God," Clint said. "And there have been days when I've wanted to bail—just throw up my hands and run away. I fantasized about getting Sherry to meet me in Costa Rica or somewhere, but it was no good. God put me in that house on that night to witness that murder for a reason. And I have to play this out."

"I'm sold, buddy."

"Yeah, but Sherry isn't." He stopped and sighed. "Ah, Sam. Am I doing the right thing, or am I reading the plumb line wrong?"

"What do you think?" As usual, Sam's answer was non-judgmental, noncommittal.

"I think it's tearing Sherry up. And it's tearing me up. I never expected it to hurt quite this much."

"What did you expect? For it to be easy?"

"No." Clint leaned forward, propping his elbows on his knees and staring up toward the house. Was Sherry sleeping, or was she lying awake in torment like he was? Was she crying? "I just never expected to have to make such a sacrifice. My whole life is just dangling. I thought going back for Sherry would get it back into focus. I thought . . ."

"That she'd understand? Give her a break. She's probably scared to death. She'll come around."

"Will she?" Clint held Sam's eyes for an eternal moment, seeing ghosts instead of a friend's concern. "What if she's changed? What if eight months has dulled some of her feeling? What if we can't get it back? What if that Rivers jerk in there thinks he's going to win her back on his mission of mercy? Her champion, her . . ."

"And what if you're nuts? Anybody can look at that woman and tell she's still crazy over you. What if all this has made it stronger? That's the thing about living on the edge. You don't take things for granted. If anybody knows that, I do."

Clint heaved a sigh. "All I want is my job, a family, a home where the most exciting thing that ever happens is that the washing machine breaks down. I'm not like you. I don't thrive on adventure."

Sam uttered a high, disbelieving laugh. An owl hooted in the distance, joining in the mirthless exchange. "Is that how you see me? As some clown who thrives on adrenaline? Forget it, Jessup. That picture you just painted looks pretty good to me too. Danger is not all it's cracked up to be."

"It's the sacrifices, Sam," Clint sighed. "The awful sacrifices. And the wondering . . . wondering whether it's worth it. Whether you've sacrificed more than you intended. Whether you should run like crazy while you still can." He looked at Sam, bracing himself for an argument, hating himself for needing one.

But Sam didn't argue. "Nobody can tell you what to do, buddy. It's your life and your choice. I don't know what to tell you. I don't even know what I'd do in your place. All I know is that you have enough sense and enough courage to do the right thing, whatever that is. Maybe it's running off and taking Sherry with you, so you can start that family without constantly looking over your shoulder. Maybe it's seeing this through to the end. I don't know."

Clint looked at his hands. "Either way, a lot of people get hurt. If I do what Sherry wants and skip out, I've wasted eight months of your life, and the time Eric Grayson and Breard have put in . . ."

"Hey, pal. Stop right there," Sam said, pointing at him. "I was doing my job. If I hadn't been doing it for you, I'd have been doing it for someone else. Don't hang this on me or Grayson. It's your ball game. If you want to declare it a forfeit, it's your choice."

Clint leaned back in his chair, his neck on the aluminum back. Was it really his choice? If he abandoned that plumb line now, how would he live his life? If God had put him where he was for a reason, who was he to buck God's sovereignty? God had the power to take care of the Givanti trial and protect them all. And he had the power to use all of this for good. Clint couldn't let Sherry's damaged faith damage his own. Maybe, instead, God meant for him to help her rebuild it.

That is, if he could keep her from bolting, herself, after it was all over. If it came to it, could he bear to live without her?

Even if she could live without him. After all, she had done well enough for the past eight months. *What do you want, Jessup?* he asked himself. Did he want to know that she had shriveled up and nearly died with grief? Or did he simply want to know that there hadn't been a moment when she'd turned to someone else. Someone like Gary Rivers.

Someone she might turn to again.

Chapter Fourteen

Madeline slept like the dead, but that luxury didn't come easily for Sherry. She lay on top of the covers in the big bed next to her friend and stared at the high ceiling, wishing for privacy so she could weep without being heard. She couldn't get over what she'd learned tonight. The danger, the lies, the betrayal . . .

And she had believed Gary Rivers was her friend. He seemed to care months ago when she had begged him to help her find Clint. With sympathy and a listening ear, he had pretended to "pull strings" to find Clint. And when he had come to her, backing up everyone else's story about Clint's cold feet, he had seemed honestly sorry. Why hadn't she seen it? Why hadn't she suspected him of knowing where Clint was all along? She remembered the night he had shown up on her doorstep, summoning all his charm when he'd asked her to have dinner with him. He'd played on her memories of their past relationship, but he hadn't been able to get past her memories of Clint. She had turned him down gently, despite Madeline's protests. Had Madeline been in on it too? Had everyone in her life betrayed her? Had that entire chapter of her life been nothing more than a sadistic lie, a lie supervised by her father?

She closed her eyes and cursed herself. Wes told her that Eric had always been good at manufacturing lies, and that a man who was cold enough to abandon his wife and children could never change. She had wanted to believe differently, to prove to Wes that he was wrong. But he wasn't.

Had her father sent Gary to her to get her mind off Clint, whose life he counted as over? Her father had thought it better to make her believe that Clint had simply stopped loving her than to tell her that he was sending him into hiding and that he might never make it out. *Might never make it out!* The thought played over and over in her mind, making her stomach cramp and her head throb.

She sat up on the bed and looked helplessly around the dark room. She wasn't going to sleep until this tension found an outlet. She needed some air, some peace, some release. She turned her watch until she could see its face in the hall light. Three-thirty.

Quietly, she got up and put on her shoes. Despite the darkness, she would go out, she decided. She would slip out of the house and try to breathe. And if she could find a place, she would try to jog off some of the knots in her muscles.

She saw some guards sitting at the table in the kitchen. Quietly, she slipped past them. Outside, the air was hot and muggy, and the wind skipping across the ground was unsympathetic. It was the kind of night that forebode disaster. Sherry looked up into the opaque sky and wondered if anyone up there really cared about the sufferings of Clint or her. She searched herself and found that she still believed there was. *Faith is just a flimsy means of self-betrayal,* she had told Clint. But had she really believed it? Hadn't she always had faith in him, deep down inside her somewhere?

She started to walk aimlessly, then broke into a run, despite the fact that she still wore jeans and shoes not meant for the sport. Her feet pounded the dust and dirt beneath her, and humidity encompassed her, but she ran the length of the house, and her breathing came in dry, sobbing gulps.

Suddenly, as she rounded the side of the house, she heard a clicking sound. "Freeze!" a voice commanded.

She did as she was told. Before she could protest she was slung against the house, and a man's hands were sliding over her body, searching deftly for a weapon. "Please," she said, cursing herself for being careless when she'd known better. "Please . . ."

Immediately the frisking stopped, and she turned around to look into Sam's steely eyes. "Lady, are you crazy?" he grated. "I could have killed you! I thought you were . . ."

"I'm sorry. I wasn't thinking."

"You have to think, Sherry. We're not playing here." He let her go, and she tried to catch her breath.

"I never said we were playing. Nobody's having fun. And you can point that gun somewhere else!"

Sam dropped it to his side. "Where were you going, anyway? Trying to pull another vanishing act?"

"No," she answered. "I was tense. Frustrated. I couldn't sleep, so I was trying to run some of it off. I didn't expect anybody to jump out of the shadows and pull a gun on me. Don't you ever sleep?"

"Not much," he said. "I was in the kitchen, and I heard you out here sneaking around. You're just lucky it was me."

"Excuse me while I go count my blessings."

She started to walk away. "You want to count your blessings?" he asked, stopping her. "Let me help you. Clint Jessup is alive. He's healthy. He loves you. And he's finally reached a point where there may be an end to this mess. You need more blessings?" he went on, keeping his voice low. "How about this? You're alive, and other than a little 'frustration' that sends you flying out in the night like you're invincible, you're unscathed. I'd say you have a lot to feel lucky about."

Sherry lifted her chin defiantly. He looked down at her, frowning. "Clint has enough on his shoulders without having to stop everything and mourn for his fiancée," he told her.

"I'm deeply moved."

"Don't be," he said, getting angrier. "It's Clint's need for you I care about. I feel compelled to keep you alive for his sake."

The words were cold, stinging, and she glared back at him. Then, starting back to the house, she mumbled, "Madeline couldn't be more wrong about you."

Sam caught up to her in two steps. "What did you say?"

"She called you a pussycat. Said singing off-key was your only offense. I'll tell her she was mistaken."

A wistful look passed over Sam's gray eyes, and he swallowed. "Yeah. You do that."

And then he passed her and went into the house, as if he was the one who had been wronged.

Sherry stood staring at the door for a moment. Finally, out of fear instead of fatigue, she stepped inside the screened porch and started for her room.

Gary Rivers was leaning against the door that led from the porch into the house. Sherry ignored him and brushed past him, for they had nothing to say to each other. She'd had as much machismo as she could stomach for one night.

Chapter Fifteen

True to his word, Eric Grayson showed up at Sherry's house with police escorts. Though their sirens were off and their lights were dark due to the fact that it was the wee hours of the morning, their very presence put Wes on the alert. He was standing when his father came into the house.

"What's going on?" he asked in greeting.

Eric, who looked so much like Wes that it was eerie, only stared at him for a moment. "It's good to see you, son."

"My name is Wes. Where is my sister?"

"Sit down," Eric said. He lowered to a chair himself, and hung his hands limply between his knees. "Sherry's all right. She's in good hands."

"Whose hands?" Wes demanded.

"Mine, sort of. And Clint's. And a dozen cops who will protect her with their lives."

Wes began to feel sick, but he kept his eyes riveted on his father. "I'm going to ask you one more time. What's going on?"

"Clint's our witness in the Givanti trial," Eric confessed. "He's been in our custody since it happened."

Wes came to his feet. "You mean you knew where he was, and you let Sherry suffer? You could have explained things to her and you *didn't?*"

"It was for her own protection. Knowing would have jeopardized her life."

Wes's teeth came together. *"Where is my sister?"*

"Just listen, Wes," Eric said. "Sit down and listen!"

Wes wouldn't sit down, so Eric just looked up at him and tried to go on. "We thought there was only one person who knew Clint was the witness. If he'd told anyone else, it would have pointed to his own irresponsibility, and his life would have been in danger. We didn't think he'd tell anyone, and when we found him dead a few days ago, Clint convinced us to let him come back until he was called to the stand. He was desperate to see Sherry, and he thought the trial might drag on for months. He couldn't stand the thought of going any longer without seeing her. But it was a mistake, Wes. Apparently, someone else knew about Clint, and when they sent Sherry that note, we knew that Clint had to go back into hiding, and he had to take Sherry with him this time or she might be the object of revenge. Madeline had to go, too, because she was here when the letter came, and Clint didn't think it was safe to leave her behind."

Wes's face reddened. "Are you telling me that some murderer is out to get my sister?"

"She's safe, Wes. She's protected. I'm seeing to it that she's taken care of."

Wes stared at him for a long moment, then raised an arm and sent a lamp crashing to the floor. *"You're* taking care of her? The man who abandoned her when she was just a little baby? I'm supposed to trust you to do the right thing for her?"

"You don't have any choice, Wes. You *have* to trust me."

"I want to go to her. I want to make sure she's all right."

"You can't do that. In fact, I've posted people to guard your house, just to protect you and Laney and the kids. You have to take this seriously, Wes. You have to be careful. People might come after you to get to me."

"Why? I'm not anything to you. There's no connection here at all." His mouth trembled as he got the words out, and he slowly bent forward. "So help me, if anything happens to my family or my sister, you'll have me to answer to!"

"I understand that," Eric said.

"You think you're a big shot, don't you? Playing with other people's lives!"

"No, son, I don't. God's still in control."

Wes breathed an incredulous laugh. "Give me a break. Don't use that God talk on me!"

"Sherry told me you're a Christian."

"That's true, I am," Wes said. "But I don't believe you are."

"God forgives, Wes."

"Not everybody," he said.

"Everybody who asks. I've asked him, and I've asked Sherry. And Wes, I've asked you."

"Too late," Wes said. He stormed out the door, pushing aside the cops guarding the house, and headed to his car.

Chapter Sixteen

W ake up, Sherry!".
Sherry cracked open her eyes and saw that the sun had come up to paint pink-orange hues on the warped walls of the old structure. "What is it?" It seemed as if she had just closed her eyes and her run-in with Sam had been only a moment ago.

Madeline was sitting up straight in bed, her eyes flashing with exuberance and excitement. "I want to know what happened last night. Did Clint tell you what's going on?"

Sherry pulled upright and shook her head, trying to allay the hung-over feeling after her horrific night. "Yeah."

"Well, don't keep me in suspense."

Rolling her eyes, Sherry slid off the bed and stumbled toward the bag that Madeline had packed hastily when Clint had decided to take them. If she just had a cup of coffee, she thought. No, forget coffee. A toothbrush and a hairbrush ought to do for now. Then she could tell Madeline what she had learned. "I need my toothbrush," she mumbled.

She unzipped the bag and reached inside. Her hand closed around something small and rectangular, and she pulled it out. "A novel?" she asked with disbelief. "Clint told you to pack absolute necessities, and you packed *a novel*?"

Madeline shrugged. "I couldn't think. I just grabbed what I thought was important. I didn't know how long we'd be gone, or if we'd have a TV ..."

Sherry reached in again. "Dental floss?"

"I hate getting food stuck in my teeth."

"Well, I certainly see how that could be at the top of your critical list." Dreading what she'd find next, she grabbed the next thing out. "Your leotard? Madeline, what did you think they were going to do with us? Aerobics?"

Madeline moaned. "I'm sorry. I just grabbed whatever I could find. I got some of your stuff too. There really are toothbrushes in there. And a change of clothes for each of us. And a little mascara in case the need arises."

"Why would the need arise?"

"Don't you want to look your best for Clint?"

Sherry propped her elbows on her knees and covered her face. "Madeline, Clint's in a lot of danger. He's the witness for the Givanti trial, and all these men are here to keep him alive until he testifies."

Madeline gaped at her as the news sunk in. "Keep him alive? That doesn't sound good."

Under different circumstances, Sherry might have laughed at the understatement, but it wasn't at all funny.

"Yes." Her voice was raw. "We're all in danger, but Clint is the one they're after. They want to stop him, and I'm afraid they will."

"Wow." Madeline lifted her chin and swallowed, looking at the wall with rounded eyes. "Then there was a reason he left." She shook her head, as if trying to put all the pieces into place, then focused on Sherry again. "How did he get to be a witness?"

"Long story," she said. "He saw a drug deal and a murder, and he got stabbed, and they've been hiding him ever since."

"And Sam . . . what is he? Some kind of bodyguard?"

"He works for the Witness Protection Program. He's been with Clint the whole time."

"And that bomb they mentioned last night . . . the reason they changed our destination . . . someone was really trying to kill them?"

"That's right."

Madeline wilted in disbelief. "As amazing as all this is, I'm not that surprised. Sam seemed like a decent guy—not some crazed criminal. He's hard not to like."

Sherry refrained from telling her that her impression of Sam wasn't as favorable since the confrontation she had had with him last night. "He's liable to get hurt, too, if Clint does," she said. "And so are we."

A distant look glossed Madeline's eyes. "Wouldn't you know it?"

"What?" Sherry asked.

"I finally meet a nice guy, and I might not live to tell about it."

Sherry shuddered. "Madeline, I've got to convince Clint not to testify. That's the only answer."

"How would that help? For there to be an end to this, I would think he would have to testify. Then he could get on with his life."

"Until Givanti has him killed for revenge. The FBI won't protect him forever. Sam's job guarding Clint can't go on much past the trial."

Madeline shoved back her curls and tried to think. "But until then, if someone shoots at Clint, it's Sam's job to take the bullet?"

"Something like that, I guess."

Tears of compassion and worry sprang to Madeline's big eyes. "Well, is he a Christian?"

The question surprised Sherry. "I don't know."

"Well, we have to find out, don't we? If he's looking mortality in the face, he needs to know Christ."

"He's been with Clint for eight months. I'd imagine Clint's done some witnessing."

"Probably. But it won't hurt to make sure, will it?"

Sherry felt ashamed that she'd had such bitter thoughts toward Sam, and hadn't given his soul a moment's thought. She looked up at Madeline and saw her staring blankly into the mirror, her face pale and haunted.

"What is it, Madeline?"

She swallowed hard and shook her head. "I was just thinking. Wouldn't it have been cool if Sam had been an accountant or something, and we'd met on an ordinary day without bombs and guns and hideouts . . . I might have fallen for a guy like him."

Sherry looked down at her feet, wishing for a response. But sometimes there just wasn't one.

Madeline sighed and started for the door. "I'll see if they have coffee," she said quietly.

<hr />

"Do you always look like this in the mornings?" Sam's voice, gravelly from too little sleep, came from behind Madeline as she poured herself some coffee.

Madeline wasn't sure where her smile came from, but when she turned around she couldn't dismiss the one wreathing her face. "Is that a compliment or an insult?"

He gave a lopsided grin. "Don't want to commit myself," he said.

She sipped her coffee and looked at his sleepy eyes and the blue LSU T-shirt he wore. A holster was strapped across his chest as if it were a part of him. "So you're a cop, huh?"

"Yeah, but you aren't really surprised, are you?"

Madeline gave a slight shrug. "I don't know. I sort of had you figured for an underworld spy of some sort."

"Did you really? And did you think that your abduction was a matter of international security?"

Madeline raised her brows and pushed her black curls behind her ears. "It might have been. I thought maybe one of my *Khaki's Krewe* cartoons had been discovered to have encoded messages to third-world regimes, and I was being chased so they could debrief me about what I know."

His chuckle came from deep in his throat. "You watch a lot of television, do you?"

Her eyes widened flirtatiously, conveying that he was right, as she sipped her coffee.

"So where's the tape of this alleged cartoon?" he asked.

Madeline frowned. "That was the only catch to my theory. There isn't one."

She surveyed the laugh lines crinkling his eyes, eyes that had lived hard and fast and told her things about him that she doubted he would ever have said himself. As he stood before her they were waking up, becoming brighter, more alert. "You must not need much sleep."

"Not as much as you, obviously."

She looked at the swirl of her coffee, remembering the gentle way he had tucked her in the night before.

"How's your knee?"

She bent it for him. "Fine. A little sore, but I'll survive. I may limp for the rest of my life, but—"

The screen door slammed, and Sam swung around to see Clint leaving the house. "I have to follow him," he said, cutting her off.

Madeline followed Sam to the door and looked out over his shoulder. "There are guards out there with him."

"Yeah," Sam said distantly. "I like to stick close, though, just in case."

Madeline gave a heavy sigh and stepped off the porch. Sam ambled ahead of her to a fallen log, just slowly enough to offer her an invitation. "It's big enough for two," he said.

Madeline cupped her coffee in her hands and sat down next to him, where they had a clear view of Clint walking aimlessly across the ungroomed grounds. "So you've been guarding him like this for all these months?"

"Eight months."

"Don't you get tired of it?"

"Not as tired as he does," he said. "Besides, we've gotten to be tight friends, and I don't have many of those."

Madeline looked across the lawn to Clint. "I don't know him that well. I've heard he's a good man—a strong Christian. Is that still true?"

Sam smiled. "Even more now than before. This whole time he's been like Daniel, devoting himself to prayer, trusting in God, even finding things to be thankful for. Some of our guards think he's a lunatic."

"And you? What do you think?"

"I think he's walking proof of the Holy Spirit."

They both grew quiet for a moment, and Madeline realized that a statement like he'd just made was not likely to come from an unbeliever. But she had to know for sure.

"Sam, do you—"

"Madeline, I wonder—"

They spoke simultaneously, then stopped. She deferred to him.

"I was just going to ask you about your spiritual life. If you know Christ."

She couldn't hold her laughter back. "Are you witnessing to me? Because I was about to ask you the same thing."

He grinned. "I take it that means yes?"

"Yes," she said. "And you?"

He chuckled. "Yes, I'm a Christian. As of six months ago, when Clint finally got through to me."

"I'm glad," she said.

He nodded. "Yeah, me, too. It's made things so much better. I owe Clint big-time. I just wish Sherry wouldn't give him such a hard time. He doesn't need that."

The wind whipped Madeline's hair away from her face, and she looked at Clint. "Sherry has been through it too. If anyone's seen that, I have."

"So you've sort of been doing for her what I've been doing for Clint all this time," Sam said. "Protecting her."

Madeline considered the comparison a moment. "Not really. Protection is not my forte. I'm a believer in moving on. If I've done anything for Sherry, I've kept her from dwelling on things."

She watched Clint start toward an old building on the property, a barn or garage of some sort. The two guards followed at a good distance behind him.

"Well, she needs to dwell on this," Sam said. "Clint needs her right now. That's why we took the chance of letting him go back in the first place. It was a mistake, but at least it got her here. And now she's pulling this self-righteous stuff on him."

"She's not self-righteous," Madeline quipped. "She's scared to death for him."

"Well, she should be," Sam said, sending a chill through her bones. "But manipulating him with petty ultimatums isn't going to solve things."

"And what will? Letting him get shot to death as an example for anyone else who decides to cross Givanti?" She felt her face reddening, and her hands began to tremble. She'd never wanted to talk to him about this. She hadn't even wanted to think about it.

"He won't as long as I'm here." Sam's voice was broodingly earnest.

"And what about after? You won't be there forever. After the trial, when they decide to get revenge, is anyone going to be there to protect him then? And how long? Indefinitely? Even a good friend can't take that kind of responsibility."

"I thought you said protecting Sherry wasn't your forte."

"It isn't. Understanding her comes a bit easier, though. She doesn't see an end to this. Do you?"

Sam let out a heavy sigh and scanned the trees. "I wouldn't be here if I didn't."

From the porch, Sherry watched Clint walking around like a man carrying a great burden. Two guards flanked him, obviously lending more stiffness to his demeanor. She fought the urge to go after him, to tell him she was just confused, that she desperately wanted him safe, and that the only thing she was certain of was her love for him. But if she loved him, she had to stop him. And running after him wouldn't do it.

She watched as he threw a rock into the distance, his back rippling beneath his T-shirt as he reared back to throw another. He had been working out in these eight months, she realized. His shoulders seemed much broader than they had before, and she had recognized the new, corded power in his biceps last night. She slid down the wall of the house until she sat on the rotting planks.

Clint dropped to the grass, his back to her, and rubbed his hands roughly through his hair. Her heart melted and left a void. Across the yard, she met Sam's eyes—cold, accusing, dull. *Look what you're doing to him*, they said. And suddenly she knew that Sam was right.

Swallowing back her misgivings, she got up and stepped down the four steps off the porch. She watched him stare out at the trees that surrounded him, his broad shoulders slumped in hopeless defeat. And she knew he was thinking, *There's loss either way, there's no way to win ...*

... Absolutely no way. Clint raked both hands through his hair and dropped his head. Why had he expected Sherry to alleviate some of the pain and dread? Why had he expected her to understand what he had to do? And why did those blasted guards have to breathe down his neck?

Two soft hands closed over his shoulders. Sherry's hands.

He looked up at her, saw the despair and the turmoil in her eyes, and wanted to wipe it away. But he feared she saw it in him as well. A soft sigh escaped his lips as he took her hands. His brows arched in grateful relief, and he moved her hands to his face. She had come to him. She was here. Thank God, she wasn't going to hold back after all.

She stooped on her knees behind him and pressed her mouth to his shoulder. "I love you. And I don't want to lose you again."

"You won't," he assured her. He pulled her around to face him, his eyes looking earnestly into hers. "I'm right here. Let's just take one day at a time."

Sherry shook her head slowly. "I can't think that way," she told him. "I can't live that way."

"But it's just for a little while longer. The trial has already started. Your father will send for me any day now, and I'll go on that stand ..."

"Don't do it, Clint." Her face reddened with the words, and her eyes welled up, breaking Clint's heart and blurring his mind.

"I have to."

Sherry bit her lip and looked over Clint's shoulder. "Oh, can't you get rid of those guards for a minute? Can't we talk without someone hearing every word?" Her voice was straining toward the breaking point, but he knew she wouldn't let herself break until she was in private. She had always been strong that way, but today he didn't want her to have to be strong.

"That barn's private," he whispered. "We could go in there. It isn't the cleanest place in the world, but—"

With a shaky hand, Sherry wiped at her tears. "Will they let us?"

Clint pulled her up and started toward the barn, calling back over his shoulder, "We'll be in the barn. We have to talk. *Alone.*"

The two guards looked at each other, then nodded agreement.

The air smelled of old hay, rusty tools, and mildew, but the privacy was worth it. Sherry turned to Clint, clutching his arms, her eyes desperate and determined. "Clint, I've been thinking. I could get Madeline to help. She could say we were in the house or something, and we could slip out the window and take the camper. If we could get to the airport, I have my credit cards and we could get airline tickets. We'd be long gone before any of them caught up to us."

Clint shook his head slowly, and his hands came up to cup her elbows. "Baby, those people out there are not the bad guys. They're protecting us."

"Just long enough to get what they want out of you!" she argued. "Then they'll leave you at the mercy of anyone who wants you."

"It won't happen that way."

"How do you know? Can you give me guarantees?"

"You know I can't."

"Then come with me!" she shouted, shaking him. "I *can* give guarantees! I guarantee that if we leave we won't have to live like fugitives for the rest of our lives! I guarantee that we won't have to be afraid of someone trying to kill us in our sleep!"

"We'll go away after I testify, if you want. But not now. Not before."

Sherry hugged herself and tucked her chin into her chest, trying desperately not to fall apart. "Clint, I'm begging you," she whispered, though she knew it was futile. "Please."

The word was issued on a choking sob, and her face was crimson with the force of her plea. Clint stepped toward her and took her in his arms, letting her cry against him like an orphaned child facing the destruction of the world.

And as he had several times over the last twenty-four hours, he wondered if he was, indeed, doing the right thing.

⊰⊱

Madeline and Sam stepped over branches and pushed aside bush limbs as they attempted a stroll on the wooded bluff surrounding the camp. Madeline held a twig whose leaves she kept pulling off, letting them flutter to the ground. When Clint and Sherry had disappeared into the barn, Sam had seemed willing to let it go at that, and he had brought her up here "to see what she was made of." Smiling to herself, she reflected how she had passed his "endurance test," if liking the woods was the criterion. "Maybe I'll come back here with my sketchbook when all this is over," she said. "Want to come?"

Sam chuckled and ducked under the limb of a young loblolly pine. "There are other places I'd rather go."

"Like where?" she asked.

"Anywhere but here, or the other place we've been hiding. Home has a nice ring to it." He turned back to her, leaning on the limb that reached between them. Laughter and deep thought fanned out from his eyes.

"Where is home for you?"

"Nowhere, really. When you haven't seen your apartment in months it's a little hard to call it home." As if to change the subject, he looked back toward the camp. "Look at this," he said, his voice lowering to the pitch of a sigh. "We're up so high you can see the whole spread from here."

"If you wanted to, I guess," she said with a shrug. She dropped her bare twig and turned around, waving her hands in an all-encompassing gesture. "The beauty's behind us, though." She pointed to a platform up in a tree. "Is that where they sit when they deer hunt?" She turned back to Sam and saw his pensive gaze on her rather than the deer stand.

"Yeah," Sam said. "Want to go up?"

Madeline bit her smile. "Are you sure it can hold us?"

Ducking back under his branch, Sam gave a soft laugh and took her hand, gesturing with the other. "Only one way to find out."

Never one to turn down a challenge, Madeline started up the ladder, careful not to strain her sore knee. The platform was much stronger than it looked, and she pulled onto it and waited for Sam.

With feline agility, Sam climbed up beside her. In the sunlight, reaching in finger-like rays through the trees, she saw for the first time how tanned he was. His brown hair was brushed with streaks of blond that spoke of much time outdoors.

"So what do you think?" he asked, sitting down next to her. Their arms brushed. Their faces were inches apart, and his breath smelled faintly of coffee, and a warm scent that she had come to know as uniquely his own.

"About what?" His eyes seemed to grow darker the closer they moved to her.

"About the stand. Do you like it?"

She drew in a shallow breath and looked around her. The pine trees created a shelter overhead, a giant, green rooftop that cooled the sun's rays. Beneath them, blueberry bushes shared earth with dogwood, and younger pines rustled among them. "It's beautiful," she whispered. "Just beautiful."

Sam nodded agreement, but his soft gaze told her his opinion that the area's beauty was trapped elsewhere. "I like a woman who knows the value of a place like this."

Madeline wet her lips. "I like a man who likes a woman who knows the value . . ." Her voice trailed off as he wet his own lips and moved slowly closer.

Their eyes embraced for a moment, and she held her breath. He was going to kiss her, and every fiber within her stood at red alert. Her heart did a drumroll, and her stomach did a triple flip.

But he stopped before their lips met. "Did Sherry tell you about our run-in last night?" he asked, almost as if it had some bearing on his intention to kiss her.

She shook her head. "What happened?"

"She thinks I'm a prison warden, and I think she's ungrateful. We were in strong agreement, however, about our mutual dislike of each other. I was sure she'd try to make you see what a miserable jerk I am."

Madeline narrowed her eyes and wondered why Sherry hadn't mentioned it. Probably because it wouldn't have mattered, she mused. Madeline was never easily swayed once she made up her mind about people. "She didn't mention it. Just that you're a cop and you're in as much danger as Clint."

A look close to surprise skittered across his eyes, then settled into relief. He pulled back a fraction to look at her. "Doesn't that make you afraid to be around me?" he asked lightly.

Madeline frowned. It was another test, she thought. It was almost as if he was searching for a reason for her not to get involved with him. And somehow, it mattered to her that she pass this one, too. "Heck no," she said. "If there's going to be any danger, what better person could I be with than a cop? Not that I believe you could hurt a fly."

The flicker of a shadow fell over his expression. Suddenly, he withdrew, and she knew she had said the wrong thing. "Let's get down," he said, his tone reticent. "I need to get back."

The abruptness of his letting the magic drop surprised her, and made her the slightest bit angry. "Well, could you?"

Sam turned around to her at the ladder, his eyes hooded. "What? Hurt a fly? I've never had one pull a gun on me. I don't know." He expelled a quick breath and started down. "How did we get on this subject, anyway?"

Confused, Madeline gave a dejected shrug and followed him down. He seemed struck with something that drove him some mental distance away, and her brief surge of anger dwindled. When she was back on the ground again, she touched his arm. "You know, I didn't mean to—"

"Shhh," Sam's hand came up to silence her, and his brows knitted in an apprehensive frown. "Listen."

She did, but she didn't hear anything.

Sam took a few steps to the edge of the bluff and looked out over the barn. The two guards were playing cards on a broken stump, and nothing looked out of the ordinary.

Madeline gasped when he drew his gun.

"Go back to the camp," he whispered. "Now. Hurry!"

"But what's—"

"Do what I say!" he whispered again.

Madeline started back, looking over her shoulder every few steps to see what Sam was up to. She saw him take off on feet trained to be quiet around the bluff to the clearing behind the barn where Clint and Sherry still were.

And then she saw what had changed his mood. A man sat in a grove of bushes, arm cocked back to throw something at the barn. She opened her mouth to scream, but she heard Sam's voice shout, "FREEZE!" and then a gunshot.

And in the wake of the worst sound she'd ever heard in her life came an even worse one. The sound of an explosion.

Chapter Seventeen

A sound like the end of the world exploded in Sherry's ears, and she screamed. The acrid smell of smoke wafted on the air from some source outside the barn, but Clint still stood before her, his hands trembling as he grabbed her against him in a gesture that spoke of terror and fierce protection. Quickly, he cracked the door open and looked out. Satisfied that no one waited in ambush, he pulled her out behind him.

The patch of grass where they had sat together just moments ago was now a smoking black spot—a scalded landmark reminding them that they waited in the shadow of death. The guards were gathered on the bluff overlooking the barn, squatting over something on the ground.

Sherry saw Madeline running toward the house, arms wrapped around her waist, a look of stifled horror on her face. "Madeline!" she called, but her friend didn't answer. "Madeline! What happened?"

Madeline stopped, but didn't turn to Sherry. "Sam ... shot ..." The words were barely audible, and Clint didn't wait to hear the rest. Vaulting toward the bluff, he pulled Sherry behind him.

"It's Sam," he rasped in a panicky voice as they ran. "Sam was shot!"

But before the words could sink in, a shaky, familiar voice reached their ears singing "Let It Be."

Clint stopped running when he saw Sam standing on the outskirts of the group of men, his face as white as a colorless sky. His hands were shaking as they raked through his hair, but he managed a smile.

"You almost bought the farm, buddy," Sam said.

"Looks like you came close yourself. What happened?"

Sam indicated the man on the ground. "Had a grenade with your name on it. I just diverted his aim a little."

"You shot him?" Sherry's question was hoarse and disbelieving.

Sam assessed her for a moment, his self-deprecating expression silencing her. "Yeah, I shot him," he bit out. "If I hadn't, you wouldn't be here to pass judgment."

Sherry bit back her retort. All she knew was that a man was lying on the ground, probably dead, and Gary Rivers was searching his wallet, without much surprise or concern. She forced herself to look at the face, then gasped in surprise. He was young, probably a teenager, nineteen at the most, and he looked innocent and mischievous and a lot like someone she knew but couldn't place. Tears sprang to her eyes and choked her, and she looked away. "He's so young," she whispered. "Couldn't you have—?"

Sam leaned toward her, his eyes pinning hers. "He was about to throw a grenade at the barn. What do you think I should have done differently? *Talked* it out? Fired a warning shot? Run? I did what the situation called for. I did my job."

"But he's just a kid." She knew it wasn't Sam's fault, and that she owed him her life. But the knowledge didn't make reality any easier to bear.

Gary looked up from the body, his face whiter than Sherry had ever seen it. He flashed the man's driver's license at Clint. "Name's Calloway," he said. "Mark Calloway. Did Paul have a brother?"

Clint shook his head. "I don't know. He never said."

"He did," Sherry said. "He mentioned him to me once."

Gary stood up and handed the wallet to another officer, then looked down at the body, as if he, too, were struck with the youth of the young man.

"He must have come to get revenge for his brother's death," Clint said.

Gary nodded his head slowly. "And failed."

"But how did he find us here?" Sherry looked up at him as the reality of his threat dawned on her.

"Good question," Sam said. "Someone had to tell him. And if he knew, then someone else must too."

"Are you sure he was alone?" Clint's words shot through her like missiles.

"Some of the men are still combing the woods," Gary said. "If there's anyone else out there, they won't get away."

Sherry felt a sudden surge of nausea, and she leaned into Clint, whose arms tightened around her. "Then we have to leave again?" His voice held dread couched in acceptance.

"No choice." Sam patted Clint's shoulder. "The only problem is how to get out of here without being followed. But time is crucial. If we can just keep you out of trouble for the next couple of days, we'll be home free."

Sherry stiffened. Clint was determined to go to trial. And she was still just as determined to keep him from it. Even more so now. "I assume you'll be letting my father know of this latest development. Am I right?"

"Of course," Rivers said. "He has to be kept abreast of—"

"Then I want to speak to him." The words grated out through clenched teeth. "You take me with you when you call and you let me speak to him."

"Sherry." Clint's voice was admonishingly low, and it infuriated Sherry even more. "It won't change anything—"

Her hands were shaking, and her legs barely supported her. "It might! If he knew how we felt about all this—"

"*We* don't feel that way," Clint insisted gently. "You feel that it's a mistake, and I don't. I'm going through with what I started. It's the right thing."

"The right thing? Being killed for the sake of one man? Is that the right thing, Clint?"

Until he reached up to wipe back her tears, she hadn't known she was crying. "Just stand behind me," he whispered. "That's all I ask."

"For what?" she spat out. "So that I can catch you when you're full of bullet holes? So I can see that you have a proper burial? Get Sam to stand behind you! He seems to believe in this lunacy."

She threw a haughty glance toward Sam, almost expecting a saucy retort, but he didn't seem to hear. His eyes were trained on the camp, on the porch of the rickety old house, to the woman sitting on the steps with fear and denial in her face.

"I need you." Clint's words came as a shaky plea.

"Why, Clint?" She jerked away from him. "Have you become numb to the excitement, the adventure, after all these months? Do you need one more element of danger to keep the suspense going?"

"Sherry, don't. You don't mean any of this."

"Oh, I mean it," she cried, looking back at Sam. He wasn't singing anymore, and his face was momentarily unguarded. For a moment, she felt sorry for him. She felt sorry for all of them. She wanted to scream, she wanted to collapse in a heap of tears, she wanted to run as far as her feet would carry her, she wanted to fling herself against Clint and hold him as if it might be their last day together. But all she managed to do was start walking down the bluff, toward the friend who seemed to need help in dealing with what she had just witnessed, and away from the man who needed more help in dealing with what he had witnessed months ago.

When she reached the porch, she leaned against a rotting column and looked down at Madeline. If Madeline would only cry, she thought, she would know what to do for her. It was only this stony facade that she didn't know how to handle. Did she want to be left alone, or did she desperately need her company? "You all right?" she whispered.

Madeline nodded.

"We'll be leaving now," Sherry told her, wiping a shaky finger under her eyes. "Seems like there's no place safe to hide, though."

"Who . . . who was it?"

"Paul Calloway's brother. He was about to throw a grenade on the barn while Clint and I were inside."

Madeline nodded quickly and swallowed. "I saw," she said. "He had reared back to throw it, and Sam said, 'Freeze.' And then there was the shot. So loud that it seemed to go right through me. And for a minute I thought Sam was hit. And then the explosion, and the fire, and I didn't know if he'd gotten you and Clint or not."

"We're fine. Everyone's fine."

Madeline drew a deep, quivery breath. "Why does everyone have to be a hero?"

Sherry couldn't answer. Instead she turned away and looked back toward the bluff.

Chapter Eighteen

Although she knew the possibility existed that they could be blown away in ten seconds flat if the right person managed to follow them in their unmarked, bulletproof station wagons to the waiting plane, Sherry was numb to the fear. Clint's silence and his pensive perusal of the trees whisking by on the edge of the narrow road made her want to scream. Gary Rivers, who drove the car, was equally quiet, and Madeline hadn't quite pulled out of her depression yet. Sam wasn't even singing, she realized, and for the first time, she wished he would. Instead, he watched the windows, as if he expected a passing car to open fire on them all.

They hadn't been driving long when Gary pulled into a rest stop to call Sherry's father. "Come on, Sherry," he said when he climbed out of the car.

Clint's hand clamped over her wrist. "She's not going anywhere with you, Rivers."

"She said she wanted to talk to her father," Gary said.

Clint turned to her. "I don't want you to go. It's too dangerous."

"I'm a cop, remember?" Gary's reminder was directed toward Sherry.

Clint's hold on Sherry's hand tightened.

"Let me go, Clint," she said softly. "I want to talk to my father. It'll be okay. Gary won't let anything happen to me."

Clint's eyes narrowed. "You trust him more than you trust me?"

"It's not a matter of trusting one of you over the other," she said. "I just want to talk to my father."

Clint relaxed his grip, and she got out of the car.

Sherry could feel Clint's eyes on her as they walked toward the small building. She shrugged off Gary's attempt to set his arm on her shoulders.

"What are you so mad at me about?" he asked when they rounded the building, out of sight of the others, and found the pay phone.

"Do you really not know?" she asked. "It hasn't occurred to you that I could feel just the tiniest bit betrayed because you lied to me and let me suffer all those months when you knew the truth?"

"I wasn't the only one, Sherry. I was just doing my job. And your father insisted."

"I'll deal with my father!" she cut in. "Just get him on the phone. I didn't come here to talk to you."

Blowing out a frustrated breath, Gary slipped in a quarter and dialed the number. She listened as he got orders from her father, then explained that she was waiting to talk to him. Then, with an appeasing pat on her shoulder, Gary handed her the phone.

"Hi, honey." Her father's endearment only infuriated her, and she bit her lip.

"Dad, I want you to put a stop to this madness right now. I don't want Clint to testify. I want Breard to find some other way to win your case."

Eric cleared his throat. "Honey, you don't understand. We don't even have a body. All we have is Clint's word. There *is* no case without him."

"Then drop it!" she said. "It's not worth his life. Someone just tried to kill him."

"I hear you were in that barn too." His voice was tighter than before.

"Yes, Dad. Think about that. You've gone to great lengths to protect me for the past eight months. If I get killed right beside Clint, all those lies were wasted." Her face reddened. "All that energy trying to look sympathetic. All the satisfaction for letting me think, again, that I wasn't worthy of being loved! That I was abandoned for the second time in my life, without any explanation at all. If you can't see Clint as a human being, then think about me. Enough people have died, Dad."

"We won't let anyone else die," he said with little conviction.

"You can't stop it as long as this trial is going on!" she rasped. "You're murdering him a little bit at a time! I don't understand how you can do it!"

"You're under a lot of strain, honey. You're nervous, and I don't blame you."

"I'm scared," she said. "More than I've ever been."

"So am I," he admitted. "Especially now that you're there. If I could stop it now, I would in a minute. But I can't."

"All that power," she mocked. She pressed her forehead against the phone mounted on the wall and squeezed her eyes shut. "All that power and you can't save the man I want to marry. It's ironic that justice over one man's life is probably going to cost so many more. Or is it justice you're really after, Dad? Maybe it's not. Maybe it's just a little glory. A little more recognition. A little more power."

"Sherry . . ."

She couldn't bear to hear his denial, or his declaration of his love for her, or his pleading that it was out of his hands. So she hung up the phone and kept her forehead pressed against it. There was no one she could turn to to make Clint stop. No one who could be trusted.

"It'll be all right, Sherry," Gary said. He set his hands on her shoulders and pulled her back against him.

"Get your hands off of me," she warned. "I can't trust you."

"You *can* trust me," he said. He turned her around to face him and bent his head down to hers.

She met his eyes defiantly. "No, I can't. You were the first person I turned to, and you lied to me." She gave a mirthless laugh as the memories came back to her. "You even tried to get things started up between us again. When Clint was fighting for his life!"

Gary's face hardened. "If it weren't for him, we'd still be together. You can't blame me for trying to get back something that he took from me to begin with."

"He didn't take me from you!" she retorted. "It just wasn't working out with us, Gary. We didn't love each other."

"I loved you," he blurted, his face intense. Maybe he really had, she thought, but that didn't excuse things. His hands tightened on her shoulders, and he pulled her closer.

"Let go of me," she said cautiously. "Gary . . ."

"We were good together," he whispered. "We could be again, Sherry. Your father knew it. That's why he let me come. That's why I was one of the only officers he kept informed on what was happening, so I could step in if I had to. He knew that I could protect you better than Clint or any of those others, because of how I feel about you."

"Let go of me." Her voice wobbled. "Gary, it was over for us a long time ago."

"No, it wasn't." His mouth came down on hers, not forcefully, but not gently either. And before she could pull away, she heard running footsteps. Gary let her go as he was slung to the side, and she saw Clint lunge for him, grasping him around the throat, throwing him to the ground and straddling him with death in his eyes.

"Clint, stop!" she shouted, and Sam tore around the corner.

"Jessup! Rivers!" He tried to pull Clint off of him, but met with resistance.

"You scum!" Clint railed. "If I ever catch you touching her again—"

Sam jerked him loose, and Gary scrambled to his feet, blood clotting at the corner of his mouth. "I look forward to seeing you dead, Jessup!" he spat. "And I probably won't have to wait long. Grayson's calling you to the stand tomorrow!"

The angry statement hit Clint like ice water, and he dropped his hands to his sides. Sherry caught her breath and took Clint's arm, but he jerked it from her and started back toward the car, leaving her feeling accused for something she hadn't done.

She and Clint didn't speak during the long ride to the airstrip where the plane waited to take them to their next hiding place, even though Sam was now driving their car and Gary was in another, but she couldn't help wondering what went through his mind. Not doubts about her relationship with Gary, she hoped. And not anger and judgment. He knew her better than that—or he should. But hadn't they both changed enough not to completely trust the other anymore? She shook off the thought and looked out the window at the trees whizzing by again. He needed to be concentrating on staying alive tomorrow, when Gary's cruel premonition of his death would be tested. He needed to try to relax.

Her throat knotted as she watched his fingers dig into his thigh, watched the other hand finger the gold chain at his neck, watched the subtle nervous habit of him shaking his foot, and heard the intermingling of shallow and deep breathing that told her of his frustration and dread. He stared, unseeing, out the windows, shutting out tomorrow, shutting out yesterday. She reached for his hand, but he recoiled and a muscle in his temple twitched, revealing the anger he held in check. A shiver went up her spine as she withdrew her hand and vowed to clear the air as soon as they were alone.

The plane was waiting at another small airstrip out in the middle of nowhere, and Erin was waiting at the door as they all piled on. The flight was short, and as Sam and the others got off of the plane to make sure their cars awaited, Erin came back into the cabin. She saw Sherry sitting more complacently beside Clint, and she smiled. "Are you two speaking again?"

Sherry didn't find it amusing.

"Off and on," Clint said.

Madeline got up and sat on the arm of a chair. "So, Erin ... you said you worked for a commercial airline. How can you just take off any time these people need to go somewhere?"

"The FBI hires me through my airline. I have security clearance."

"Aren't you afraid of having your head blown off?"

Erin looked at Clint, then at Sherry. "Somebody's got to do the tough stuff. I'm not married, I don't have a family, and everybody else does. I'm the most likely choice."

"Doesn't that bother you?"

"Not really. I feel like I'm helping the good guys."

Sherry couldn't help softening the look on her face. She looked over at Clint. He was, indeed, one of the good guys, despite what she had allowed herself to believe.

Sam came back in and ushered them all off. Tucked away in armored cars again, they headed to the new hiding place.

When they reached it, Sherry vaguely noticed that it was on Lake Bisteneau, about an hour's drive from where Clint would be taken to court. She was only dimly aware of the subtle wealth sanded into the grain of the luxurious weekend home on the water. It probably belonged to a friend in a high place. But the new location did nothing to soothe the look of despair in Clint's shadowy eyes, and she intended to set things straight before he even got into the house.

The door slammed behind him when they were all out of the car. Ignoring Sherry, Clint went to the trunk to get his suitcase and started toward the house.

"Clint," she said, catching up to him. "Clint, we have to talk. What happened back there was not my fault. You know it wasn't."

His throat convulsed as he reached the front door, and he opened it and stepped inside. Sherry was getting angry.

"Clint, stop and look at me. We have to talk."

"Not now, Sherry."

Setting his mouth in a tighter, grimmer line, he started up the stairs. He was going to blame her, she realized with alarm and the initial sting of fury. "Clint, I didn't do anything wrong. Don't you dare shut me out!"

Clint flung his suitcase to the top floor, its loud crash resounding throughout the house as he swung around to face her. Color climbed his neck and seeped under the stubble darkening his jaw, and a cord in his neck swelled. He held the banister and leaned toward her. "You think I like playing these games with you, Sherry? You think I like wondering what mood you're going to be in from one minute to the next? Whether you're going to love me or detest me? Whether you're going to support me and stand behind me or fall into some jerk's arms?"

"That's not fair!"

"Fair?" A dry, chilling laugh tumbled out of Clint's throat, his mirthless eyes slashing her heart. And then he turned and started back up the stairs, and retrieved the suitcase that had opened with the impact of its fall. "You're right. It's not fair, Sherry," he said over his shoulder before he disappeared into one of the bedrooms.

Sherry dropped her face against the banister. She wasn't strong enough for this. She was crumbling, and it was affecting him. But she didn't know what to do about it.

He came back to the head of the stairs a moment later, clad in a pair of red jogging shorts and a white tank top that revealed the straining definition in his arms and chest and the stiff set of his broad shoulders. His skin glowed with a bronze hue, but his face was pale, strained, distant. He didn't even acknowledge that she still stood there as he started for the door.

"Are you going to run?" she asked in a flat, metallic voice.

"Obviously."

She swallowed and started up the stairs. "I'll change and run with you."

Setting her mouth in a stiff line, she ran up the stairs and searched the five bedrooms for the one with his suitcase. When she found it, she riffled through it and pulled out a pair of his shorts. *So they're a little big,* she thought, wriggling out of her jeans and slipping the shorts on. They were better than anything Madeline had brought for her.

She glanced out the window and saw that Clint was already beating a trail around the large house, and that most of the cops that had come with them were pacing around the grounds checking its security.

Madeline was coming up when she bolted down the stairs. She stopped and grabbed her friend's arm. "Can I wear your tennis shoes?"

"I'm wearing them," Madeline said.

Sherry rolled her eyes as if the observation was irrelevant. "Madeline, it's important. I have to go run with Clint."

Brushing her fingers through her hair and sweeping it behind her ears, Madeline eyed Sherry's feet. "Well, at least you're wearing socks ..."

"Madeline, please!"

"All right." Expelling a long-suffering sigh, Madeline set down the duffel bags she had carried in and jerked off her shoes.

"Thanks," Sherry said, and slipped them on as fast as she could. Then she rushed out, and waited for Clint to come around before she joined him.

She started to run beside him, though his pace was faster than she was used to. "Clint, think about it," she said. "You know how upset I was today. You know the last thing I wanted was for Gary to touch me."

Clint didn't answer, but he sped up, as if doing so would cause her to fall back. But summoning all the strength she had built up over her years of jogging, she managed to keep his pace, at least for a while.

After several laps without slowing down, however, Sherry realized that Clint was running with fury, with rage, with the need to purge himself of his pain, and the intent to hurt himself worse than anyone else could. His arms and legs were red, as blood pumped furiously through his body.

"Clint, slow down," she panted. "Please. I can't—"

"Then stop, Sherry!" he said between breaths. "Nobody's making you run with me."

"I'm not stopping until you talk to me!" she shouted. "I'll pass out first."

He kept running and she followed, though every muscle in her body rejected another step.

"Clint, I love you." She wiped the perspiration out of her eyes and forced herself to keep up with him. "I'm sorry I hurt you."

He kept pounding the packed dirt, remaining a wall of numbness that she feared she could not penetrate.

Tears escaped her eyes and mingled with the perspiration. "Clint, please. I can't do this much longer."

"You can stop anytime you want to," Clint rasped.

She stumbled, and he slowed a degree and looked over his shoulder. The simple gesture gave her hope and enough strength to catch up to him again.

"Not on your life," she said furiously. "I'm going to keep this up as long as you do, Clint. I'm going to collapse with you!"

"Leave me alone, Sherry!" He bolted ahead of her, picking up speed again, and she saw blood on the heel of his shoe, but still he ran. She followed as fast as she could for several laps, but finally he stumbled and lost his momentum. Seizing the opportunity, she lunged forward. He tried to pick up his speed, breathing furiously, but she reached out and grabbed the back of his T-shirt.

"Stop, Clint," she cried. "Please ..."

He tried to shake free, but she caught his arm. The force made him trip again, slowing him enough for her to throw her arms around his waist. And then, with all the strength she possessed, she flung herself to the ground, pulling him with her.

He caught her before they hit the dirt, then let her go and rolled away from her to his back. His breath came in gasps, and his arms hung idly at his sides. She sat up and looked down at him, tears in her eyes.

"I love you," she grated through her teeth. "I love you no matter what you do to me or yourself. And you can't run from that."

His shoulders quaked, and he sat up and buried his face in her neck and held her, coughing as his lungs screamed for oxygen. The pink of his skin drained to a pallid gray, suddenly matching hers, and she wanted to sit there and comfort him until their breathing settled. But he pulled up and coaxed her to her feet. "Get up, baby," he told her. "Come on, get up. We have to walk."

Wiping at the perspiration on his face with the back of his hand, he draped his other arm across her shoulder and pulled her beside him. They walked at a brisk pace for a lap, then two more, slowing until their pulses were normal. And when their breath settled and their hearts were no longer threatening to resign, he pulled her against him and again dropped his face into her shoulder. "I can't do it without you," he admitted in a forlorn whisper. "Not any of this."

"You won't have to," she returned, in spite of what it would mean. "Not any of it."

Then he pulled her into the house, into one of the back rooms. She sat him on the chair, and carefully worked his jogging shoe off of the injured foot, then the other. One tear dropped onto the bloody spot as she looked at it, but Clint cupped her chin and brought her face to his. His kiss was gentle, grateful, tender. "The foot will heal," he whispered. "The heart needs a little more care."

And Sherry knew that she had no choice but to mend the heart that needed her.

Chapter Nineteen

Pretty night," Madeline said as she came upon Sam. He was sitting on a chair on the porch, guarding the front door.

"Pretty lady," Sam returned, smiling. "But I thought you were avoiding me for dear life after what you saw this morning."

"You were the one who didn't come to dinner," she pointed out softly.

He smiled. "You call slapping a piece of bologna between two slices of bread *dinner*?"

Madeline shrugged. "We've all got to eat."

"Yeah, well. Guess I wasn't hungry."

Madeline sat down on the bench next to him and braced her elbows on her knees. Cupping her chin in her hand, she looked out over the dark water rippling in the breeze. Tree frogs exchanged mating calls in the distance, accompanied by chirping crickets and an occasional splash of an acrobatic fish. Overhead, the stars shone clearly, and the air was cool, lacking the usual southern spring humidity. The atmosphere gave one the deceptive feeling of permanency, and though she knew it was deceptive, Madeline clung to it. Fear was something that erected barriers, and she had no time for those.

"What I saw this morning shook me," she admitted finally. "It made it all real. It made your job real, and that gun you wear, and that enemy I'd been hearing about but hadn't really cared much about."

Sam tipped back his chair, leaned his head back against the wall, and looked at her, the humor in his eyes gone. "You saw me shoot a man. I didn't want you to see that."

Madeline swallowed, but kept her eyes locked with his. "I really didn't think you were capable of such a thing," she said. But in her eyes there was no accusation. Just a deep, gnawing need to understand.

Sam dropped his gaze to the dirt at his feet. "We do what we have to do, Madeline. There's nothing that says we have to like it or feel good about it. I had a gut instinct and I listened to it."

She nodded and sat erect, leaning her own head back. "On one hand, I was awed. If not for you, Clint and Sherry would be dead. You saved their lives single-handedly. You're very good at what you do."

"And on the other hand?"

Though they were only inches apart, that distance seemed much too far. And at the same time, she had never felt closer to or more in tune with anyone. "And on the other hand, I didn't want to believe you had pulled that trigger."

"Why?" His voice came softly, like a caress.

"Guess I wanted to believe you were an innocent. Mysterious, maybe, but pure and untainted."

"But I mean, why did you want to believe that?" he asked. "Even when you thought I was some criminal trying to kidnap you, you didn't really seem afraid of me. It was as if you knew more about me than I had told you, even then."

Madeline looked into those silver eyes that mirrored her confusion and her tenderness, and she thought how obvious it was that he was a good man. If he could only see himself that way, she thought, he would understand her certainty. There would be no question about her faith in his sense of right.

"I had a gut instinct and I listened to it," she replied quietly.

He held her gaze for a segment of forever. "Has it changed?" he asked, finally. "Now am I some tainted, evil man who courts danger?"

She sighed, smiling slightly. "If only you were," she whispered. "If only you were."

Their lips met in tentative offering, and Madeline was awed at the softness of lips that she had been tasting in her fantasies. He shifted in his chair and touched her arm, such a simple gesture, but its tenderness devastated her. Slowly, she parted her lips beneath his. Had she seen the violence and the tenderness in the same man, or was one just an image her heart had conjured up to protect her from the other?

The kiss ended, but Sam did not pull back. He looked at her with eyes that had found the gold hidden away at the end of his rainbow. He pushed her dark curls away from her eyes, and let his fingertips sculpt the crest of her cheekbone and the delicate slant of her jaw. "I don't know why he did it, but I'm glad God sent you here," he whispered.

"So am I," she whispered, startled at the honesty of her emotions. "So am I."

------◆------

Sherry sat alone on the couch, hugging her knees, waiting as Clint showered in his room. She saw the bloody shoe lying on the floor, and wished she had done more for Clint's foot than put a Band-Aid on it. Was that what she had done with his life? Had she cured the immediate symptom of frustration and anger by promising to stand beside him? And what would be the end result? Would he be killed tomorrow because she hadn't succeeded in changing his mind?

So little time, she thought, as tears welled in her eyes. Too little time to waste fighting about something that could not be changed. Clint would go through with this whether she wanted him to or not, because he believed it was right. And how could she be worthy of a man like that if she didn't stand behind him? She took a deep breath and thought about tomorrow. She would go to court with him, and hold onto him until they called him to the stand. And somehow her being there would make him invincible. It had to.

The door opened and Clint came back in, holding a shoe box in his hands. He had showered and shaved, and he looked a hundred percent better than he had earlier. She wondered if it was the shower or her declaration of love that had done him the most good. He sat down next to her, one leg bent under him and the other on the floor.

"What is that?" Sherry asked quietly, referring to the box. He smiled at her and dropped a kiss on her lips. Then he opened the box, revealing a stack of papers covered with his handwriting.

"Your manuscript?" she questioned. "The book you said you wrote?"

He shook his head. "There was no book. I kept thinking there would be. But every time I sat down to write, I thought of all the things I wanted to say to you. And so I did. On paper, I told you everything I felt. It's like a journal. It was my only link to you." He breathed a great sigh and handed the box to her. "In a way, it kept you with me. It kept me sane. I want you to have it now, if you want it."

She took it, smoothing her fingertips across the ink and the page that testified to Clint's love, to the months of separation, to the fear and pain he suffered, and to the fact that he'd kept her in his mind as well as his heart.

"We can't get those eight months back, Sherry, but this might help to fill them in. And the next time we're apart, it will hold us together again."

Somehow it sounded like a good-bye, but she told herself that he needed her to be strong. No more tears. There was too little time left. She would cling to the man who sat before her, and concentrate on the night's reprieve they had been granted. And if the day came for him to be torn away from her again, she would turn gratefully to the soul he had written down and handed her in a cardboard box. Then she would grieve and regret and hate.

But not before. Not before.

———◦———

Late that night, sleep wouldn't come for Sherry. She lay on her side and thought of the man she loved so much who could be snatched from her tomorrow. Had she loved him enough? Had she loved him too much? Should she have held back and continued trying to make him succumb to her wishes? No, she told herself. That would only have made him more frustrated and tense, but it wouldn't have changed his mind. And he needed all his wits about him for what he would face tomorrow.

Tomorrow. Would it be the end of their nightmare, or merely a new chapter? What if Givanti's circle was bigger than they thought? What if it reached farther? What if . . . ?

Closing her eyes, she covered her forehead with her wrist. One thing at a time, she told herself. Just be there while he needs you tomorrow, and believe that there is an end to the terror. Just push through one moment at a time, for tomorrow would come too soon.

The men sat around the breakfast table the next morning sipping their coffee quietly, nibbling at their food with a noticeable lack of appetite. Madeline, pale and drawn, sat across from Sherry next to Sam, who hummed softly. Sherry hadn't known him long, but she had been around him enough to know that his singing often signified his anxiety.

Clint sat with his arm draped across the back of Sherry's chair, his ankle crossed over his knee, in a stance that made him look at ease, but Sherry knew better. She had helped him tie his tie this morning, had seen the distant, too-accepting look in his eyes, and felt the rigid set of his muscles. He had been quiet. Much too quiet.

One by one, the men left the table to go and prepare for the hazardous trip to court. Clint sat still, gazing into his coffee cup. When they were, at last, alone, Sherry set her shaking hand over his. "We'll be all right, Clint," she whispered. "I'll be with you, and—"

"You can't go," Clint cut in, his eyes luminous with dread. "You have to stay here."

Sherry's eyes filled with alarm, and she drew back her hand. "No. I'm going with you."

Clint shook his head firmly. "It's been decided, baby. It's too dangerous. You'll be safer here."

"But I said I'd be with you," she blurted, tears springing to her eyes, tears she had vowed not to cry. "I need to go, Clint. I need to be there. You can't keep me away."

"It's too dangerous."

"That's why I have to go!" she shouted. "If you're in danger, I want to be with you. We can survive it if we're together. And if you don't, I don't want to either!"

Clint caught his breath and pulled her against him, holding her with his eyes squeezed shut, as if it could keep out her terror and reasoning. "I know that feeling," he whispered into her hair. "I do. But your father has left strict orders that you are not to come to the courtroom. And I agree with him."

Sherry was trembling. "That's because my father knows that you'll be killed! If he's willing to let you get killed for his case, then he'll have to let me be too."

Clint pulled her back and took a deep, ragged breath. "I'm sorry, baby."

"No!" Sherry jerked out of his arms and stood up. "They can't make me stay!"

She bolted out of the kitchen. Her eyes wild, she approached each officer she could find, but no one would help her.

Finally, she went to Sam, her eyes pleading. "Sam, you've got to let me come."

Sam shook his head. "I understand why you want to, Sherry. I would, too, in your place. But you have to understand and respect our decision."

"It's not the decision. It's the implication behind it. My father knows he'll be hurt."

She looked at Sam, and set her hands on her hips, struggling with the tears brimming. "I want you to tell me how you can be sure that someone won't blow him up before he even gets into that courtroom."

Sam looked at Clint with eyes that said he *couldn't* be sure. "If he gets blown up, so will I."

"Oh, that's comforting!" she said, throwing up her hands. "And to think I've been so concerned!"

Sam sighed roughly. "I meant that I'm not going to leave his side until he's on the stand. I'm a good cop, Sherry. And Clint's a good friend."

Sherry turned back to Clint, the fight draining from her. "Clint, please ..."

Clint pulled her against his chest and walked her into the vacant living room. "I need your strength, Sherry," he whispered, kissing the top of her head. "I need to know that you're back here waiting for me. That you'll marry me when I get back."

She looked up at him, as if he didn't know how much he was asking. Strength was such a rare commodity for her lately. His black eyes hid a wealth of emotion—more than most people know in a lifetime—and yet he seemed to cope so well.

"You will come back, won't you? And it'll all be over then?" She wouldn't think about afterward. If they could just get through this part ...

"I'll be back," he assured her. "When do you want to get married?"

"We should have done it yesterday," she said. "We should have done it the first day you came back for me. We should have done it eight months ago."

"We can do it the day I come back, if your father can pull some strings."

Her eyes blanched to the color of frost. "I don't want my father to be a part of it."

"He will be a part of it," Clint said. "I want you to forgive him for this. He did the right thing."

"He put your life in danger. He's *still* putting your life in danger."

"He did the best he could, and he will continue to."

She straightened the knot in Clint's tie, and tried not to cry. "Let's not talk about him," she managed to say. "Let's talk about our honeymoon. Where will we go when this nightmare is over?"

"How about home?" he asked. "We could find a house and buy it, and move in and not come out for a few weeks.

I want to hear you laugh again, and I want to see that smile creep back into those beautiful blue eyes."

"Come back to me and you will." Her voice broke with the promise, and a tear escaped to roll down her cheek. "Come back to me, Clint."

"I'll be back."

Someone cleared his throat from the doorway, and they both looked up. Gary Rivers leaned smugly against the jamb, watching them with disdain. "Sorry to interrupt this touching little scene," he said. "But I believe Clint has an appointment."

Slowly, as if he were being called to the execution chamber, Clint let go of Sherry.

"Don't worry about her," Gary said. "I promise to take good care of her."

Clint's eyes whiplashed across the room. "What did you say?"

"You heard me," Gary said, his brown eyes challenging. "While you're in court being a hero, I plan to make sure that nothing happens to Sherry."

Clint's laugh was dry, grating. "You honestly think I'm going to get in a car and ride away, leaving scum like you behind to 'protect' my fiancée? Who's going to protect her from you?"

Gary seemed to balance on the verge of laughter. "Sherry doesn't need protection from me. Her father trusts me."

"Well, I don't." Clint's neck reddened. "And I'm not leaving here without you."

Gary wasn't convinced. "Come on, Jessup. All these months of exile and you expect me to believe you'd give up your little crusade because you don't want me to stay with Sherry?"

"You'd better believe it," Clint bit out.

Sam came to the door, clad in a navy hooded jacket and holding another in his hand. "You ready, pal?"

Clint didn't budge. "I'm not leaving him here with her. If he stays, I stay."

"You could take me with you," Sherry ventured again.

"I'm not taking you," Clint said, "and I'm not leaving him."

Sam looked at Gary, who had lost his smugness. "All right, Rivers. You're going with us. I'll get someone else to stay. Go get one of the jackets and put it on."

"But Grayson—"

"Grayson will understand," Sam said.

Shooting Clint one final, fiery glare, Gary left the room.

"What if he doesn't try to protect you?" Sherry asked. "What if he—"

"He'll do his job," Clint assured her. "I'll be fine."

"He will," Sam said, tossing Clint the jacket he held. "Put it on," he said. "With the hood up. It's the latest style in sniper-proof wear."

"But you're wearing one too. What if they mistake you for me?"

"That's the general idea, pal. And if they see ten of us in the same jacket, we're liable to confuse the pants off of them."

"I'm looking forward to it," Clint said dryly.

Sherry watched them both pull up the hood. "It's a good idea," she said in a shaky voice.

"It was your father's idea," Sam said. "Just like the ambulances."

"Ambulances?"

Sam nodded toward the front door. "Come on. You won't believe this."

Sherry followed them out the door and caught her breath at the sight of ten officers wearing hooded navy jackets, milling around three ambulances.

"With everybody wearing the coats, and not a clue as to which ambulance holds the witness, there's not a whole lot they can do, is there?" Sam said. Then he laid a comforting hand on her arm. "We'll bring him back this way too, Sherry. We'll take care of him."

"Who's going to take care of you?" Madeline asked from the side of the house, where she leaned pensively against the wall.

"I'll take care of myself, pretty lady," Sam said in a softer voice. The wind whipped Madeline's hair across her mouth, and Sam stepped forward to push it back. "You'll be here when I get back?"

She shrugged and attempted a smile. "Where would I go?"

"Good point," he said. His hand lingered on her face, and his eyes softened. "I will be back, you know. I have this gut feeling."

"Hold onto it," she said, but her voice cracked.

The engines cranked to life, signifying that the time had come.

Sherry clung tighter to Clint's arm, but she reached out for Sam's as well. "I haven't been very nice to you," she choked out, tears blurring her eyes. "But you've been good to Clint. Will you ride in the same car with him?"

A poignant smile sauntered across Sam's face. "You bet I will. And I expect to be best man in the wedding when we get back."

Sherry nodded and lowered her eyes. She saw Gary look back at her with a sullen expression, and he got in one of the cars—thankfully not the one Clint was riding in. Clint took her face in gentle hands and kissed her one last time. "I love you, Sherry," he whispered.

"I love you too, Superman," she said, before he turned and dashed into the ambulance.

She and Madeline were left behind with three guards as the ambulances started their procession to Shreveport and the trial.

"Are we all right?" Sherry asked in a tremulous voice as the cars disappeared from sight.

"I hope so," was all Madeline said before going into the house, to bask in her own despondency.

———❖———

Madeline was washing the dishes when Sherry found her in the kitchen, stacking them on a drainer without anything under it to catch the water, but Sherry didn't correct her. The fact that she was doing such a domestic chore at all was a major indication of her state of mind.

A wet cup slipped from her hand and crashed onto the floor. Muttering, Madeline stooped to pick it up, but she turned her back to Sherry when she saw her watching.

It was too late. Sherry had already seen the rare tears forging shiny paths down her friend's face. Swallowing back her own fragile ball of emotion blocking her throat, Sherry pulled out a chair and sat down. "I've been pretty caught up in my own troubles," she said. "I just realized that you're getting attached to Sam, aren't you?"

"Yeah." Madeline gave a soft, unspirited laugh. "Imagine me falling for some guy who carries a gun and doesn't know where—or if—he's going to live from day to day. All this time I've been waiting so patiently for God to send me the right guy. Sam's not really what I expected."

"If anybody could fall for him, you could."

Madeline wiped at her eyes and tossed the shattered remains of the cup into the trash can. "Are you implying that I fall too easily?"

"No. I wasn't even thinking of Gene at the studio, or the Italian circus acrobat, or the paratrooper, or that guy who made like Evel Knievel every time he cranked up his bike." They both forced a smile. "No, I meant that if anybody could handle someone with such an unpredictable occupation, you could. I've never met anybody with such acceptance. Such an ability to take one day at a time. I envy you for it. You put so much value on what you have, and don't even seem to worry about tomorrow."

New tears sprang into Madeline's eyes to replace those she had wiped away, but she blinked them back. "Don't envy me, Sherry. It's a defense mechanism. And it's slipping. Because I'm very worried right now." Her voice cracked with the admission.

Sherry gazed solemnly at her for a moment. "Are you in love with him?"

Madeline swallowed. "All I know is that when I'm with him, I'm shriveling up inside. His eyes make me warm. And when he kisses me . . ."

"He kisses you?" Somehow, Sherry's image of Sam didn't fit that role.

Madeline gave a soft smile. "When he kisses me, I burst all over. And now that he's gone, I ache."

Sherry didn't know what to say, for Madeline had never been quite *that* serious. "How long have you known the guy, anyway? Three days?" Sherry asked.

Madeline shrugged. "It could have been three years."

"Maybe it'll be three more decades," Sherry ventured.

"Or three more minutes," Madeline whispered.

Sherry's face contorted, and she covered her mouth to hold back the onslaught of despair. "Don't, Madeline. I need you to tell me that we'll be all right. That things will be great. I need you to get my mind off of it. You're so good at that."

"I need the same things." The words were spoken on a gasp of restraint, but big tears spilled over her lashes and rolled down her cheeks.

Sherry stood up and set her arm around her friend's shoulder. It was time to return the favor Madeline had granted her for the past eight months. It was time to swallow back her own self-pity, to move past it, and to help her friend through this horror. "Could I interest you in some bologna?" she asked.

Madeline smiled through her tears. "I'm not hungry." She wiped her eyes and pushed her hair back behind her ears.

"They'll be all right," Sherry said, and she tried to believe it. "They're strong, and Sam is the best bodyguard Clint could hope for."

"But bodyguards have been known to stop bullets for the body they're guarding," Madeline said. "And Sam feels a big responsibility to Clint."

"They aren't the only two out there," Sherry went on. "They may be as close as you can come to being heroes, but they aren't stupid."

"No, they aren't stupid," Madeline agreed. She looked at the ceiling, as if tipping her head back could waylay the tears. "I should have brought my camera. I should have gotten a picture of him. I should have taped one of those ridiculous songs he kept singing. I should have ..."

Sherry pulled her against her shoulder and hushed her like a mother hushing a child. It had to be purged, this misery. This was Madeline's purging time. She only hoped she could hold herself together long enough to see her dearest friend through this.

Chapter Twenty

Wes sat in front of the television set in his living room, his eyes transfixed on the news as it unfolded regarding the Givanti trial. Laney stood behind him, rubbing his shoulders. "Honey, don't you need to get to work?"

"No," he said. "I have to see what he's up to."

"He? He who?"

"Eric Grayson," he said coldly.

"Your father."

He took in a huge sigh. "He's not my father. He's just some man whose genes I happen to have." He got up and paced in front of the television. "They're bringing the mystery witness today. Clint will be a sitting duck as he goes into that courtroom, and I'll bet you anything that Sherry will be right there with him."

"There'll be protection for them," Laney said. "Wes, you have to trust your father's office to provide what they need."

"Forget it. Why should he care if my sister's life is in danger? It's not like he has any emotional attachment to her. Easy come, easy go."

"I don't think that's true, Wes. Why don't you call and talk to him, just to give you peace of mind? Find out what he intends to do to protect Sherry? Maybe he'd listen to suggestions."

"I don't want to talk to him."

"Maybe for Sherry's sake, you should anyway. Maybe it's time to swallow all that pride."

"This isn't about pride, Laney," he said, defeated. "It's about history . . . experience. He doesn't have a great track record when it comes to taking care of his own."

"Then go over there . . . be in court . . . make sure that he knows you're watching. Maybe there's something you can do."

Wes stared at her for a moment, turning the idea over in his mind. "You know, I think I will."

He grabbed his keys, and started toward the front door.

"Wes?"

He turned back. "Yeah?"

"I love you. And I'll be praying."

He wilted and came back to her, pulling her into a tight hug. "Thanks. That's what I should have been doing, but I've been in knots over this, worried sick, and I've just . . . I've forgotten to pray about it."

"Well, I haven't." She kissed his lips, then wiped the lipstick from them. "Be careful, Wes."

Wes felt that he walked a little taller as he headed out to his truck.

Chapter Twenty-One

The sound of Sam's lamentably off-key singing tempered the low roar of the ambulance's engine, his slow voice coming across like a dirge rather than a pick-me-up as Clint was used to. He sat with his legs crossed on the stretcher, his head swaying slowly against the wall.

"How much farther?" Clint cut in uneasily. The technician's seat felt like a vibrating slab of concrete, and his heart raced in anticipation of something he couldn't even name.

The driver, adorned in a bulletproof vest with the navy blue hooded jacket over it, glanced back over his shoulder. "About thirty more minutes. So far, so good."

So far, so good. Why did that sound like a countdown to doom? Clint wondered. And why the feeling eating at his gut that something terrible was going to happen—not to him, but to Sherry?

"How well do you know those three cops we left back there?" he asked Sam.

Sam stopped humming. "Enough to know I can trust them. You don't have to worry."

Another moment of silence followed, this time without Sam's singing. Clint watched him glance out the window, his eyes distant and full of thought. "She was really worried, you know," he said finally. "She pretended not to be, but she was."

"Sherry?"

"No, Madeline. It's been a long time since anyone worried about me."

A soft smile tugged at Clint's lips. "Becoming attached to her, are you?"

Instead of the usual quip, a pale shadow intruded on Sam's eyes, and he shrugged. "As much as a man like me can become attached."

His grin faded, and his gaze gravitated back toward the window. "I've gotten attached before. It nearly destroyed two pretty decent people."

"What? Your marriage?"

Sam swallowed and slid his hood off of his head. "Yeah. I watched her turn from a levelheaded, independent, cool woman into a basket case whenever I walked out the door. She was sure that one day I wouldn't come back." He sighed and shifted on the stretcher. "We both got bitter. I felt smothered and guilty, and she got angrier and angrier. The best thing we ever did for each other was call it quits."

Clint watched Sam gaze out the window, watching the trees whirring by.

"Madeline seems different, though." Sam's observation was set on the edge of hope, but couched in caution.

"Sherry says she's had a tough life. Both parents died when she was pretty young. She takes things in stride, and doesn't dwell on things that would break most people."

"And she's beautiful," Sam tacked on. He reached to the oxygen cylinder and tapped it thoughtfully. "That silky, curly hair, and those eyes ..."

Clint couldn't suppress his laughter. "Man, you've got it bad."

Sam cocked a half-grin and leveled a look on his friend that held no denial. "Seen any of her cartoons?"

"Yeah. She's pretty good. She's one of Justin Pierce's top animators." He thought about Madeline, and how they had behaved toward each other, as if they each disapproved of the other's way of caring for the common person they loved. Clint's eyes grew serious. "I get aggravated with her, but she's been good for Sherry. Helped her through a bad time. Sherry has a short fuse, and she explodes emotionally just as quickly as she pulls in the reins. She can't stand to sit still and let things go by without her. That's why it was so hard on her when I left and there was absolutely nothing she could do about it. Madeline's get-on-with-life attitude was helpful to her."

"What do you think?" Sam's smile left his eyes, and a shadow of doubt crept into them. "You think a woman like Madeline could be attracted to a deviate like me?"

Clint grinned. "What do *you* think? Has she run kicking and screaming away from you?"

Sam laughed. "Not since that first day." His laughter died in a sighing expiration, and he looked down at his callused hands. "Matter of fact, she's gotten pretty close to me a time or two. Pretty darn close. I don't know, maybe there is hope."

"I wouldn't be surprised, buddy," Clint assured his friend. "There's always hope."

Hope became the thin thread that pulled Madeline from the quicksand of her depression almost as quickly as she had plunged into it. After washing her face and brushing her hair, she came into the kitchen and informed Sherry that it was time for them to look at the positive side.

"Is there one?"

"Of course." Madeline took a deep breath and began the recitation as if she'd rehearsed it. "The chances of anyone getting through that security barricade to either Clint or Sam are pretty slim. And I trust your dad. He'll make sure that nothing happens to them on the way out, either."

"Give it up, Madeline," Sherry moaned. "I'm furious at my father, and I'm not interested in hearing how good and kind and conscientious he is. He had no right to do what he's done."

Madeline sighed and sat on the table. "All right. We won't talk about it then. Let's just go watch television."

"Television? There's nothing on television in the middle of the day."

Madeline cast her a disbelieving look. "Surely you can't be serious. I realize that you spend most of your waking moments working for your brother, but you can't have completely missed the soaps in all these years."

"I hate to break this to you, but ..."

"Then don't. Some of the greatest stories ever woven are on the soaps. On this one I watch, there's a girl who's a KGB agent, but she has amnesia and thinks she's a hairdresser. Only Russia has a little disk in her tooth, and they record everything she says or does with her CIA husband. Where do you think I get my cartoon gags? Come on, it's great. I'll narrate for you. It'll get your mind off your problems. *No one* can have problems worse than those people." Madeline hopped off of the table, starting toward the living room.

Resigned to letting Madeline's methods of diverting her fears and anxiety help her, Sherry followed her friend out of the kitchen.

Minutes later, Eric Grayson paced in his own kitchen in Shreveport, his hand trembling as he held the telephone. "I don't care what she said!" he shouted to one of the police officers guarding Sherry. "Get my daughter on the telephone immediately or I'll have your badge!"

"I'm sorry, sir. She refuses to talk to you. I tried to—"

"Don't give me *tried!* Tell her I *order* her to get on this phone!"

The young officer muffled the phone with his hand while he relayed the message. Grayson dumped his uneaten breakfast into the garbage disposal and searched the cabinet for an antacid to stop the burning in his stomach. If he could just hear her voice, he could be ensured that she was completely safe. The timing was crucial here, and after a sleepless night going over every angle to assure Clint's safety en route to court, it had finally occurred to him that it wasn't Clint's life that would be in jeopardy today. He was too well guarded, and Givanti's cohorts wouldn't risk the publicity of Clint's death. But what if they managed to get Sherry? What if his daughter were used as the go-between to keep Clint from testifying honestly?

After a moment, the young officer cleared his throat. "Uh ... sir. I gave her the order, and she said she didn't care."

"*Didn't care?*" Grayson bellowed.

The phone was snatched from the officer's hand, and Grayson heard his daughter say, "Give me that!"

Grayson's blood pressure dropped a degree, along with his voice. "Sherry?"

"I have nothing to say to you, so you're wasting your valuable time trying to call me."

"I just wanted to see if you're all right. I've been very worried about you."

"It's Clint you should be worried about," she said. "He's the one you've made into your pawn." Her voice faltered. "Has he made it there yet?"

"Not yet," her father said. "But I don't expect them for twenty minutes or so." He cleared his throat and looked down at the oak grain on his kitchen table. "It's going to be all right, sweetheart, but I want you to be careful."

"If anything happens to him, I'll never forgive you." She caught her breath on a sob. "I'll probably never forgive you, anyway."

Grayson slumped down in his chair and tried to picture the woman who had so easily forgiven him before. "When it's over, I'll come there and we'll talk . . ."

"I have nothing to say to you," she snapped. "You've used the man I love like a toy to satisfy your legal ego, and you've lied to me to do it. Go back to work, Dad. Go make Clint spill his guts. Then bask in the glory of the press and your awed followers. I won't be there."

The phone slammed in Grayson's ear like a clap of thunder that reached straight through to his soul.

───◆───

The telephone was cold beneath Sherry's trembling hand, as cold as the betrayal she felt. Madeline's soap opera wasn't going to do the trick. She needed to think. She needed to be alone.

Pinching the bridge of her nose, she turned back to the officer who had answered the phone. "I want to go out to the pier and catch my breath."

The young man still looked shaken by his run-in with the attorney, but he got his sunglasses. "I'll come with you."

She squelched the urge to scream about her need to be alone. The poor guy looked as if he'd had enough. "If you have to," she said.

Terri Blackstock | 185

"You won't even know I'm there," he said. "Not unless you need me."

Quickly, before Madeline could insist on joining her, too, she darted out the door and made her way to the pier. Treading out to the end of it, she sat down and crossed her feet. Hugging her knees to her chest, she looked out over the water. The sun hadn't climbed very high in the sky, but already the air was sweltering. From somewhere upwind on the still lake, she heard children laughing and the sound of a ski boat farther down. She wondered what it would be like to have nothing to worry about again. Here, in this isolated section on the still water, she could almost pretend she was a lazy socialite out for a tan. So peaceful. So private. One would never know that the end of her world could be lurking just around the corner.

Would they contact her if Clint was hurt en route to court? Or would her father insist on "protecting" her again? A fresh surge of anger shot through her. What would she do if Clint didn't come back to her?

What was she doing? She caught herself and shook her head, as if the violent movement would shake her back to her senses. How could she think about what she would do if he didn't come back? She hadn't given up already. Even when he had disappeared for eight months, she had never given up entirely.

She dropped her head onto her knees, and reached deeply inside herself for the strength to endure what she was facing. If only it would rain. Rain cleansed and soothed and purged. It had always been a great source of comfort to her. She looked up into the sky and issued a silent prayer for strength. The prayer brought back a memory ... a night months after her mother had died, when her father had shown up on her doorstep and announced that he wanted back into hers and Wes's life. She had called Wes to come over, and there had been a terrible fight among them. Wes had wound up leaving.

But she had wanted a relationship with the man she'd so often wondered about, so she had invited her father to stay in her apartment until he could get a hotel room the next day. Far into the night, when she had believed him to be asleep, she had begun to grieve over her mother's death and the life she'd been forced to lead when he'd abandoned them. Caught in a whirlwind of emotions, she had opened her window and sat on the windowsill. It had been raining, and she remembered the whip of lightning in the distance, the rumble of thunder, and the cold, cruel prickles of hard rain upon her skin as it slanted into the window. But she had not been afraid, and she had not closed the window. The storm had drowned out the pain and memories inside her apartment, and she had seen the lightning as flashes of future trying to break into her world and promise her something better. Maybe her father's reappearance in her life was God's provision for the loss of her mother.

She remembered how long she had sat there, how cold she had become, yet the thought of going back in and facing what was happening had been too overwhelming. Perhaps it was the cold that had awakened him, or the sound of thunder through the open window, but he had finally come into her room and asked her to close the window and get into something dry.

She had done as he'd asked, and told him good night. He had struggled to keep back his own tears, and had lectured to her about lightning and pneumonia and falling off the slippery window sill. Something about that paternal concern had touched her, bonded her to him. Then he'd told her how much he loved her, and that he'd spent most of his life as a shell of a man who hadn't had the capacity to love. He'd changed, he said, and he knew it was hard to believe. But he needed for her to give him a chance, even if her brother would not. She had known that night that he really did love her.

Perhaps too much. And that love had led him into lying about the fate of another person she had allowed herself to love.

If only there were a wet windowsill she could sit on today, she thought, and distant lightning glittering on the slanting rain. If only there were some escape from this hell she and Clint were being dragged through. If only she had some guarantees about God's provision this time.

———◆———

Clint closed his eyes and tried to stay calm. They'd be there soon, and there had been no attempts made to stop them. In moments he would be inside the courtroom, waiting to tell everything he'd seen on that night eight months ago. He hoped it was worth it. He hoped Givanti would be locked up for the rest of his life.

He opened his eyes again and saw Sam sitting erect and alert, peering between the front seats out the windshield for some sign of danger. Maybe there wouldn't be any. Maybe Givanti's arms didn't reach far enough to—

"Hold on!" The driver slammed on his brakes and screeched into a slanted halt, barely missing the ambulance in front of them. "What the—?"

"It's a tree." Sam's face turned white at the sight of the fallen tree obstructing their passage. He pulled his gun and held it toward the ceiling as he pulled his hood more closely around his face. "Someone doesn't want us to get through."

"Stay alert, guys," the driver warned.

Sam's eyes were straining up toward the small clay cliffs overlooking I–20. Clint's stomach plummeted. It wasn't the tree that was the problem. It was the fact that they were forced into sitting still.

"Back up!" Sam ordered the driver.

He tried to back up, but the ambulance behind them was too close.

"Get out of this line as fast as you can!" Sam yelled as the driver tried to maneuver between the cars. He did half of a U-turn, backed up, then screeched around and slammed his accelerator to the floor. The other ambulances tried to follow suit, except for the one Gary Rivers drove. Through the back window, Clint saw Rivers with his hood pulled down, getting out and running toward the tree.

"What's he doing?" the driver asked, staring into his rearview mirror.

"Just go! Drive!" Sam shouted.

At that moment the ground erupted in an explosion that left the world behind them in flames and debris and a whirl of smoke from which they had barely escaped. The ambulance skidded off the road, leaving a trail of burnt rubber. Behind them, one of the other ambulances careened into a tree.

"Let's get out of here!" Sam yelled to the driver. "Somebody up there has a rocket-launcher or bazooka aimed right at us!"

The driver pulled the ambulance back onto the road, and behind them, the other ambulance, still functional despite the huge dent in its fender, followed.

"Where's the third car?" Clint asked, peering through the back window.

"Blown to pieces," Sam said. "I don't get it. Why wouldn't Rivers turn around and follow us back? Why would he take down his hood and get out of the car like that?"

Clint was watching the bridge and the cliffs for another sign of attack. "What's the range of those things?" he asked.

"We're out of it," Sam said. "But that doesn't mean there won't be another attack somewhere down the line. Man, this is even bigger than we thought. We've got to get you there, so you can make sure Givanti fries."

Chapter Twenty-Two

"S herry!" Madeline's voice was racked with horror as she screamed her name from the doorway of the house. "Oh, Sherry, hurry! Sherry, come here!"

A moment of panic froze Sherry, but then she pulled herself together and got up to run toward her friend, the bodyguard close on her heels. "What happened? Did some—?"

"I don't know." Madeline's voice trembled. "I was watching television, and the program was interrupted by a special bulletin. There was an explosion on Maincast Road. An ambulance. One man was killed, three wounded."

"What?" Blood drained from Sherry's heart, leaving her dizzy. "No. It wasn't them."

The television sliced across her words as another bulletin came to life, this time from the steps of the courthouse. "We've been told the mystery witness in the Givanti trial was supposed to make his appearance half an hour ago. However, it is rumored that the witness is being transported in an ambulance, which may very well be the one that was in the explosion on Maincast Road. We have no further information at this time, but we will be waiting here for word and will keep you informed. Please stay tuned for further updates."

One of the bodyguards rushed for the telephone and began dialing frantically. Sherry and Madeline crouched together and stared at the television. He was dead, Sherry thought. It had happened, just as she knew it would . . .

The woman on the steps of the courthouse flashed back onto the screen, microphone in her hand, her words tumbling out in a burst of excitement.

". . . ambulance has just arrived . . . witness is unharmed and on his way in . . ."

Sherry clutched her face and gave into the tears racking her. "Oh, thank God. He's not dead!"

The camera switched to the group of navy-blue hooded men, with guns pulled, huddled together around the "witness," rushing for the door. "We understand that the explosion was believed to be an attempt to stop the witness from testifying, and that the attack will not be admissible as evidence in the trial. So the jury will not have the benefit of this information that seems to implicate the defendant." She paused and listened as someone relayed a piece of information to her. "We understand that the men in the burning car were police officers trying to divert the potential attacks, and they succeeded at their own expense. We're told the explosion was caused by a bazooka or rocket launcher from the cliff over the highway, and that the assailant remains at large."

"It wasn't Sam," Madeline choked out. "They were in the other car. Thank God, it wasn't them."

Not yet, a voice inside Sherry despaired. Clint and Sam had made it to court. But would they make it back? How many chances would they have for escape before the lunatics stalking them succeeded in killing them?

Numbly, she got up and went upstairs to the room Clint had slept in last night. It still smelled of shower steam and after-shave, but it seemed so cold here without him. So dark.

Turning on the light, she pivoted slowly, taking inventory of the things he had left. The shirt he had worn yesterday draped over the chair; the worn pair of jeans crumpled on the floor; his old jogging shoes. She picked up the shirt and shrugged into it, burying her face in the collar. Taking a deep, fortifying breath, she inhaled its scent. It smelled like Clint: strong and masculine.

Biting her lip, she went back to her room and got out the box of letters he had written to her. She crawled onto the bed and opened it, needing those letters to get her through the day. They were all she had of him until he came back.

And they all began with "My Sherry." She lifted the top one and tried to read the shaky scrawl.

They tell me the infection's gone, and the scar should heal over soon. But there's nothing they can do for the feeling of emptiness inside me. There's no medication that can heal my spirit. Because I know you're hurting, just as badly as I did when Paul rammed that knife into my side. At least I understood what I was going through. You have no idea.

If you could wait until this is over, I'll come back to you someday. And if there's such a thing as justice, and if God is as kind as I know he is, we'll start our lives over again.

I love you. I wish I could convince your father to deliver this to you, but he won't. I suppose he knows best in these matters, but I hate letting you think that a love like mine could die. Even if I do, my love never will.

Sherry closed her eyes and a tear dropped onto the ink, smearing it. He had believed he would die. He hadn't expected to survive those months. And all the while she was sitting at home feeling sorry for herself for having to return the wedding gifts and cancel the wedding plans. She had thought it was the end of the world. But Clint had known it firsthand.

She picked up another letter, and saw that the handwriting was much clearer.

What would I do without Sam? He listens when I talk about you, and he never acts bored or unsympathetic. I think he probably knows everything about you there is to know, right down to the time you spilt pink lemonade on your head—remember when your purse strap slid down your arm, and you raised it to slide it back up, only you wound up pouring your drink on your head? Sam and I got a good laugh out of that one, just like you and I did when it happened. It was good, because there's so little to laugh about these days.

I hope it's not the same with you. I hope you can still laugh, and enjoy, and love life. I hope your eyes still light up when you go outside in the mornings and see that it's going to be a beautiful day. I hope you still feel that sense of purpose that has always been so unique about you. If I've gotten anything from all of this, it is a more defined sense of purpose. I'm doing the right thing, and if that's the only consolation I ever get from it, it'll have to be enough.

I've taken up jogging and working out to lift my spirits. It gives me a boost. Sam sings. It makes him feel better, and though I'll never admit it to him, it makes me feel better too. As long as there's a song for him to sing and a path for me to jog, and your face in my dreams, I'll get through this. And you will too.

She couldn't help smiling at the uplifting tone of that one. She wiped the tears off her face and went on to the next one.

It's so lonely without you. So quiet. So cold. There are days when I think that just seeing your face would get me through another few months. The thought itself gets me through another day. If only there were some end in sight.

I'll never be comfortable in our love again. When I get back to you, I'm going to see every day with you as the dawning of another chance to affirm what I feel for you. I love you in a dimension removed from all this madness.

Are you still wearing your hair the same? Does your bottom lip still feel like warm, wet satin? Are your eyes still putting the sky to shame? Oh, how I want to hold you. Please, just hold on a little longer. Just a little longer.

"Just a little longer," Sherry whispered, nodding her head. "I'll hold on, Clint. I'll hold on."

Chapter Twenty-Three

Wes was almost to the courthouse when he heard about the explosion on the radio. His face drained of color, and he pressed the accelerator harder and flew faster.

A mob scene with cameras and microphones waited outside the courthouse. Wes double-parked behind another car and got out of his car. He started to run toward the building.

"Wes!"

He turned around and saw Eric Grayson sitting in his BMW, a phone to his ear as he leaned out his open door.

Wes ran toward him, his eyes murderous with accusation. "I heard about the explosion," he said. "Was my sister in it? Was Clint?"

"No," Eric said, cutting off the phone and grabbing his briefcase. "Sherry didn't come, Wes. I wouldn't let them bring her with Clint. She's safe, son. And Clint was in one of the other ambulances. He's already inside."

"I want to go in," Wes said. "I want to hear what this is all about. Why my sister has been dragged into something so deadly."

"All right," Eric said. "I'm sure the courtroom is full, but you can come in with me."

With no time to deny his father's favor, Wes followed him into the side door of the courthouse.

Chapter Twenty-Four

"Did you take the pulse of the man you said was shot?" The defense attorney's acrimonious voice was directed to Clint, though he faced the jury. After hours of drilling testimony, in which Southern analyzed everything he dared to say, Clint was getting angry.

"No, I did not."

"Then how can you know that he was dead?"

"He had a bullet hole in his chest. And I heard Paul *say* he was dead."

"Did you examine the alleged bullet wound?"

Clint smirked and shook his head with disbelief. "No, I did not. Under the circumstances I thought it a little silly to pop out from where I was hiding and ask them to let me examine the body so that my testimony in the murder trial might be flawless."

A soft roar of chuckles passed over the spectators, then died.

"Did you see them bury the body?"

"No, I did not."

"Did you see them throw it into the river?"

"No."

"Did you attend the funeral of this man you say was dead?"

"Of course not."

"Could that be because there wasn't a funeral?"

"I don't know if there was. I was busy recovering from my knife wound at the time and didn't much care."

Southern's back went rigid and he swung around to the judge. "Your honor, I want that last comment stricken from the record. It has no relevance in this case."

The judge nodded gruffly. "Sustained."

But the jury had heard every word.

The defense attorney's eyes leveled on Clint's as he faced him squarely, preparing for a duel. "In other words, Mr. Jessup, this man that you are saying was killed on the night in question could in fact be walking around right now. You really have no evidence at all that he was even harmed."

"Do you consider blood evidence?" Clint's question came through steely lips.

"People bleed, Mr. Jessup. They also heal."

Clint hadn't spent the last eight months in hiding just to have some hyped-up lawyer shoot his story down. He'd seen what he'd seen. "I saw Givanti shoot him!" he blared. "I saw him fall, and I saw blood on the left side of his chest! I heard—"

"Your honor, this witness is out of control—"

"I heard Givanti and Paul say that he was dead," Clint said louder, "and I—"

"Mr. Jessup, if you continue these outbursts—"

"—heard them decide to hide the body, and then I watched them drag him out!"

The attorney's face was raging red, and the judge was banging his gavel, but Clint went on. "If he's not dead, why have so many attempts been made on my life? Why was Gary Rivers killed just hours ago?"

"Mr. Jessup, I'm going to find you in contempt of court if you don't control yourself—"

"Control myself? Your honor, what was I hiding for eight months for if I can't tell the truth? He wants you to think Anderson is still alive. I can't show you a dead body to back up my story, but he can't show me a live one to back up his!"

"Your honor, I'd like to request a short recess." This time it was the prosecuting attorney's voice that cut in. The judge agreed.

Clint dropped back into his chair on the witness stand and held his face in his hands.

———

Clint tapped his fingers on the arm of the chair he sat in, wishing he had something constructive to do with his hands. Something like throttling the defense attorney. When Grayson and Breard had stepped in quietly just moments ago, he had not been sure whether it was anger or delight sparkling in their eyes. He didn't much care.

"I could lecture you on the importance of keeping your cool in the courtroom, Clint," Breard said, "but under the circumstances, I think your outburst has been to our advantage. Especially the part about your recovering from your knife wound."

It wasn't the event that was significant, Clint thought, but the telling of it. "He struck it from the record. It doesn't matter that people have been hurt over this. My knife wound is as insignificant to those people as Gary Rivers's death was."

"Oh, it matters, all right. The jury heard every word, whether it's on the transcript or not."

"But what difference will it make when he comes back in there and makes them believe that Anderson is alive and well and living in Kalamazoo somewhere? I *wish* he hadn't been killed that night! You have no idea how many times I've wished that. If he hadn't been shot, Rivers and Paul and his brother would be alive, and I wouldn't have even had to testify. You've got the drug charges wrapped up without me. But I never counted on having to prove that the guy I saw shot in the chest was really dead when they dragged him out!"

Grayson was calm. "You did a good job this morning telling play-by-play what happened. The jury hasn't forgotten. And honestly, I think what just happened in the courtroom did more to make Southern look bad than you." He picked up a sweating silver pitcher and poured himself a glass of water. "He lost the reins when you stood up and started yelling, and he couldn't get them back. His loss of cool showed a little trace of desperation. I expect him to try to get some witnesses in here to smear your character. His last resort is to convince the jury that your word isn't worth anything."

"Smear my character? How?"

"He'll find a way."

"I don't know how," Clint mumbled. "My life is clean. My crimes seem to be only in the mind. Unless I'm wrong, there's no crime against *wanting* to strangle someone."

"Let's hope you're right," Grayson said, patting Clint's knee with fatherly fondness. "But we'll be prepared just in case."

Clint sat in knots for the rest of the day as he heard friends and acquaintances testifying to his character. It was brought out that he was undependable. Hadn't he quit his job when people depended on him? Hadn't he turned on one of the students in his own youth group?

Grayson's face blazed fire when the defense attorney drew from someone the fact that Clint was engaged to the prosecutor's daughter. In spite of Breard's string of objections, the job had been done, and Clint looked like a man whose very words inspired doubt—an ally of a prosecutor out to get the defendant.

Because this judge had a reputation for squeezing all he could into a court day, especially when the trial was close to an end, the closing statements were delivered that afternoon. And the hopelessness and frustration and tension rising inside him became a volatile mixture while he waited for the jury to be dismissed to decide on the verdict.

"The jury could be out for days," Clint told Grayson in a voice that denoted the calm before the storm. "I'm not going to be kept here. I want to get back to Sherry. She must be out of her mind worrying." He paced back and forth before the black tinted window and tried to dispel the feeling that he was smothering. He needed air, and quiet, and an hour in which this trial didn't hang foremost in his mind. Sam's quiet scrutiny told Clint that he, too, dreaded the verdict.

"Don't you care about the outcome of the trial?" Grayson asked. He sat at his desk, going back over his notes, trying to second-guess the twelve men and women who held this situation in their hands. But Clint had the suspicious feeling that that wasn't Grayson's real concern.

"Of course I do. But it won't surprise me if Givanti gets off. The last eight months of my life have been like something out of the theater of the absurd, anyway. A big farce. Might as well end it accordingly."

"I disagree. I think the jury will bring in a guilty verdict. Meanwhile, I'd like to keep you here."

Clint stopped and pointed a warning finger at Grayson. "You can't make me stay," Clint warned. "I'm going back to Sherry."

Grayson's face reddened, and he thumped his forehead with an index finger and compressed his lips.

"Look, I did what I was supposed to do," Clint continued. "I don't regret it, no matter what comes of it. But I'm not going to put my life on hold any longer."

Grayson got up, shrugged out of his coat, and hung it over his chair. A slash of perspiration beaded over his lip. "I'm just asking you to wait a little longer. Until we can be sure that things have settled down."

"Settled down?" Clint's laugh bordered on hysteria. "Are you kidding me? You think I don't know that Givanti will get revenge? That's why I want to get back to Sherry!"

"*That's* why I want you here!" Grayson bellowed, slamming his hand on his desk. "I'm trying to protect my daughter! I'm trying to protect *you!* Don't be blind, man!"

"I'm not blind! But I want to protect Sherry too. She's probably sitting there thinking the danger's here. But if *I* were Givanti and wanted to get revenge, I wouldn't send my goons to the courthouse to make an example of the witness. I'd teach him a lesson by taking it out on the person who means the most to him. I'd—"

"Exactly what I'm getting at!" Grayson cried. "And the closer you are to her—"

"The more protection I can give her. I have to be there to make sure that she's safe and doesn't get careless. *You* can't be there, and those guards barely even know her."

Sam, who had sat quietly in the corner rubbing his jaw, stood up. "Let him go back," he said. "I won't let anything happen to them. I haven't so far, have I?"

"By the grace of God, no," Grayson admitted. "But I don't like it."

"There *is* no safe place," Sam pointed out dolefully. "Not really. Beef up security some more. Pack our cars full this time. All we really have to do is wait to see if we're right about Givanti's little ring being small. Frankly, I think it is. But while we're waiting for the verdict, there's no use making everyone suffer more."

"But some lunatic is still out there. The one who tried to blow you up on the way here." Grayson's voice broke. "What if—"

"I don't care! I've got to be with her, Eric. You owe that to us!"

Eric Grayson stared at Clint, his eyes misting with doubt and uncertainty. "All right," the man said, sinking down into a chair and looking suddenly much older than his years. "All right. Go ahead. I'll be there as soon as the verdict comes in. For Pete's sake, man, be careful."

"I'll die before I'll let anything happen to Sherry," Clint said.

Grayson looked up at him and managed a smile. "Well, how about if we keep both of you alive? I'd sort of like to have grandchildren."

"You'll get them," Clint promised him, his own dark eyes sparkling at the prospect. "You have my word on that one."

The President of the United States could not have boasted more security than Clint had as they left the courthouse that evening. The men again donning their hooded jackets, this time they had twenty police officers accompanying them in four sedans with tinted windows. On a dark, empty side road they changed from the cars into the trailer of an eighteen-wheeler and finished the journey, catching up to a convoy of unsuspecting truckers with which they blended nicely.

Sam had brought along a transistor radio. When a news bulletin interrupted to say that the jury had just delivered the verdict on the Givanti trial, he quieted everyone.

Twenty men held their breath collectively as the anchor's voice said, "Givanti was found guilty on both charges ..."

A loud cheer of approval sounded throughout the dark trailer, with each man patting another on the back, but Clint was quiet. Givanti had been found guilty because of his testimony, but somehow he didn't feel that the nightmare was over. Somehow it just seemed to be entering a new phase.

Sherry stepped out of the bath and pulled Clint's robe around her. He was on his way back to her, and she wasn't going to think about the fact that he might not make it.

Quietly, she padded into the bedroom and got dressed, then went down and began to busy herself cleaning the house. She wouldn't think about fear or death tonight, she thought. She wouldn't think about the possibility that Givanti would go free. And she wouldn't think about Gary Rivers.

Gary, who had only wanted to protect her. Gary, who had died protecting Clint, after she'd had so little trust in him. Despite his efforts to get her back, in the end, he had given his own life to protect Clint.

It was meant to be, she told herself, lifting her chin. God was in control. She had to keep remembering that.

She wouldn't feel guilty that she hadn't argued for Gary when he'd wanted to stay with her. She wouldn't feel guilty that she had wanted him to go. And—God help her—she wouldn't feel guilty for being safe and alive when so many others had suffered.

She would simply prepare this house to be a haven for the man she loved. He would need it when he came back to her. He would need peace. He would need love. And he would need for her to understand the sorrow and grief and self-incrimination etched on his heart for the rest of his life.

Just as it was etched on hers.

Madeline's shouts interrupted her thoughts. She ran into the room with the television. "What happened?"

"The verdict!" she proclaimed. "Givanti was found guilty! It's all over!"

Sherry smiled, but her smile was less jubilant than Madeline's. It *wasn't* over. Not really. To her, the worst part could be just beginning.

***

"Here they come!" Madeline darted out the door as the headlights of the huge truck bumped down the road toward the house.

Sherry followed her into the night, her heart fluttering. She wouldn't relax, wouldn't be able to allay this cold sweat she was in, wouldn't be able to stop trembling, until she was in Clint's arms again and could *feel* that he was safe.

The door to the trailer was opened, and a loud, cocky voice wafted across the breeze singing "Duke of Earl" off-key. "Duke-duke-duke, duke of Earl, duke-duke, duke of Earl ..." Sam appeared at the doorway to the trailer, dancing like a fifties' teen idol with an imaginary microphone.

When he saw Madeline, he sped up the tempo and hopped down, and took her in his arms to pirouette her and then do a mock, rock 'n' roll waltz across the yard. "Duke-duke, duke of Earl ..."

Madeline's giggle rang across the night, lending a note of unreality to the tragedies that had transpired today. It was as if she believed it was all over ...

Clint came to the door and jumped out, his eyes immediately connecting with hers. Sherry felt the love and relief in his look, and suddenly the events of the day fled her mind as well. He was here. He had come back.

Through the men milling around them, he came to her, and she buried herself in his arms.

"I was so afraid," she choked.

"I was so worried," he breathed.

"You're all right," they said together.

His kiss was ambrosia, warm molten joy, a fragment of heaven. The taste of salt tears brought his head back, and he kissed them away, clutching her like a treasure that he would guard with his life.

"Oh, Clint," she whispered. "Don't ever leave me again. Don't ever let me go. Promise me."

"I promise, baby," he said. "I promise." His eyes narrowed painfully, and he pulled back to look at her. "Sherry, Gary's dead. He—"

Sherry's eyes welled into glittering blue halfmoons, and she set her fingers over his lips. "Don't ... don't say it. I already know." She caught her breath on a soft sob. "Please. Let it just be us. Let's not talk about ..." Her voice trailed off, and she couldn't go on.

Clint scooped her up in his arms and pushed through the men and into the house, oblivious to the crowd and the questions and the cheering. She laid her face against his neck and wept quietly, so grateful for his warmth, his compassion, his strength. He swallowed and sought out the source of the slow, sweet violin concerto that filled the room.

"I found a tape player upstairs," she whispered. "They had Bach."

"Bach." The word was murmured in a cracked voice, and his black eyes shone with a luster that would forever brighten her heart. He set her on the couch and sat down next to her. "And a couple of hours ago I thought it would take months for me to feel peace again."

"For now," she whispered. "We have it for now." In her timorous voice was an unspoken plea not to think about the demons of fear and hazard that lurked only a heartbeat away.

Chapter Twenty-Five

The smell of impending rain feathered up on the breeze, and the water seemed restless. The activity inside had settled as each man found a way to make himself useful, and Madeline suddenly found herself outside alone with Sam— that is, as alone as was possible with twenty guards alert for battle.

Sam had danced her to the bank of the lake, the inky water reflecting the clouds in the sky and the partial moon that cast an eerie glow.

"So when do you get to go home?" she asked tentatively, quietly.

"Soon, I hope. I'll have to go into my apartment with a sandblaster to get rid of the cobwebs."

"Is it in Shreveport?"

"Yep."

"I could help. I'm great with cobwebs. I once helped with some of the animation on *Charlotte's Web*."

"I'd like to see it," Sam said. "Do you do self-portraits?"

Madeline grinned self-consciously and gathered her hair back to keep it from slapping into her face. "A self-portrait seems a little pointless."

"That all depends on whose self it is," he said, matching her grin. "I wouldn't mind having a framed sketch of a pretty face to wake up to every morning."

She couldn't believe she was blushing. "Would you settle for a sketch of Khaki Kangaroo?"

He touched her nose, let his finger glide over its tip and settle on her lips. "I said self-portraits. I want your face on my wall."

Letting her smile fade and her eyes widen, Madeline straightened his collar and looked up into his sterling eyes. "I'll tell you what. I'll give you a snapshot, if you'll give me one of you. That, and a recording of 'Duke of Earl.'"

Sam's fatuous grin was all over his face. "Sure. I can make you a copy from my album."

"No," she said, her voice lowering. "I want *your* voice on the tape."

His smile was incorrigible. "I don't know about that."

"No tape, no picture," she challenged softly.

"I'd rather see the real thing, anyway," he said. His lips lowered to hers, and as he kissed her, Madeline vowed that this attachment would not end in misery.

———◆———

Sherry heard the sound of a car coming up the road, and as if the doom she dreaded had at last arrived, she got up and peered through the curtains. Some of the guards met the car. Even in the darkness she could see her father's large form unfolding from the car. "My dad," she told Clint.

"Go easy on him, Sherry," he whispered. "He's a good man with a tough job. And he loves you."

Sherry leaned back against the wall, dejection in every line of her body. "Yeah, well, I have a few things to say to him about the way he loves," she said with soft scorn. "He had no right to manipulate our lives the way he did."

"He also had no choice. It would have happened whether he had been in charge or not."

"There were better ways, Clint." The judgment was uttered on a weary sigh.

Clint strode toward her and threaded his fingers through her hair. "And what were they? I've asked myself a million times, weren't there better ways? I've never been able to come up with any."

Sherry looked out the window again, and Clint's hand slid to her shoulder. Her father was coming toward the house with the imperial posture of a king returning victoriously from war. She could refuse to talk to him, but she had too much to say. Too much rage to vent, for the war had cost too much. "Well, I have," she said, and started for the door.

Clint followed her.

Eric Grayson's seasoned, handsome face lit up at the sight of his daughter. The light died, however, when she stood before him, bitterness and rage battling for a forum in her eyes.

"Hi, honey."

Sherry propped her elbow on the banister and sent her father a dull, impassive gaze. "You got what you wanted, Dad. I don't think we have anything more to say to each other."

Grayson sighed heavily and reached for her. "Honey, I know you're upset. It's been trying for all of us."

"Has it?" Sherry stepped away from her father's touch. Vicious heat started at her neck and rose to color the rise of her cheekbones. "Did *you* get stabbed? Did anyone try to blow *you* up? Did *you* have to give up eight months of *your* life for a cause?"

"Sherry, you have to under—"

"Did anyone lie to you, and tell you that the person you love most in the world just decided he didn't want you anymore and took off for new horizons?"

"I did what I thought was best. I followed my judgment."

"Well, your judgment stinks!" Her voice hurled hoarsely across the room, knocking the wind from the older man. His face seemed to turn gray under her look.

"Don't you think I paid?"

"No. I think you gained a lot more than we lost. I think you're the hero now. You got your conviction. So what if people had to die for it?"

"A lot more people might have died if I hadn't! Including my daughter!"

She came toward him, her eyes like daggers. "Your daughter *did* die! When she thought the man she was going to marry had abandoned her. When she thought he was a criminal to run from. When she found out that his life might not last another day. I'm *still* dying, Dad! Because I know that whoever tried to blow Clint up in that ambulance today is probably not going to give up until he succeeds. Was your conviction worth it, Dad? Was it?"

"Sherry, stop it!" Clint's order rang out, slicing through her anger. "No one forced me to be a witness. If you have to lash out at someone, lash out at me for seeing what I saw. Lash out at Paul for making a mess of all our lives. Lash out at Givanti for killing Anderson. But don't lash out at your father for being put in the position of having to do his job. If he'd handled it any other way, one or both of us might be dead right now. You know it and I know it!"

Sherry clutched her head. "It's such a mess!" Her voice broke, and she started for the door. "I just want to get away from it. I just want it to end!"

Sherry burst out into the night, leaving the two men behind. She didn't want a moment alone, she realized as she saw Madeline and Sam beside the water and went the other way. She wanted a moment without fear, a moment with laughter, a moment with no bitterness. There was no place to go in this madness. No place where they weren't watched and stalked and threatened. No place without cops and guns and memories.

Clint caught up to her and swung her around to him. "Calm down, baby. Calm down!"

She jerked away from him, intent on heading for the boat house where no one could watch her fall apart. Clint followed her into the musty structure and closed the door behind him. He flicked on the light, a dim yellow lantern attached to a beam on the ceiling, making the room into a graveyard of tall, deep shadows.

She set her foot on one of the boats docked there, bobbing with a calming rhythm that made her lower her voice. "I can't be calm anymore, Clint. I'm so angry. I've never been so angry." She turned around and leaned over a tackle box set on a table against the wall. "I feel used and manipulated and so scared right now. It's his fault, and I can't sit still and listen to how he did the honorable thing."

"What would you have done?" Clint's voice was stern. Sherry breathed a great sigh and pulled up onto the stool beside the table. The water made a lapping noise against the boats, and a soft breeze blew in from the open wall facing the water, ruffling her hair. Behind her was a workbench, covered with tools and fishing poles. Someone actually came to this lake house to find peace and relaxation, she mused. "I'm asking you a question, Sherry. What would you have done if you were the U.S. attorney and your daughter's fiancé came to you with what I saw?"

"I don't know," she said quietly.

"That's too easy, babe. I want you to think about it. I want you to see that you would have done the same thing."

"I wouldn't have."

"Okay, let's see. Your daughter's fiancé comes to you and says he saw a local businessman commit murder. So you contact the police. Would you do that?"

"Yes, I suppose."

"All right. While you're handling things, the fiancé slips out and goes home, even though you told him to stay put. Next thing you know, someone's tried to kill him, and almost succeeded. What are your options? Would you try your hardest to protect him?"

"Of course, but I wouldn't have to lie to my daughter to do it. And I wouldn't—"

"What if you knew that if your daughter knew she'd be worried sick and would try to find him? What if you didn't want anyone to suspect that the fiancé was the witness, because you thought that was his best protection? And if the daughter knew why he'd really left, she'd insist on going with him? Would you deliberately want to set your own daughter up for that kind of danger?"

Sherry dropped her face and covered it with a hand. "No."

"If your father had not done everything he could to protect me, I wouldn't have lived another day. I'm convinced of that!"

Sherry's head shot up. "You still might not, Clint! I'm convinced of that!"

Clint took her hands and made her look at him. "I will. As soon as we can, we'll go somewhere else and start over if you want to."

Sherry dropped her head back and focused on a knot in the raw ceiling, letting her tears roll down her temples.

"Are you telling me you don't mind just leaving our lives behind and—"

"Sherry, if I've learned anything in the past eight months it's that you have to accept things. I don't want to leave Shreveport. I didn't want to before. And I didn't want to leave you. But as long as I have you this time, I'll dig ditches on a cratered planet and live in a pup tent. I don't care."

Sherry slid off the stool and into his secure embrace. He crushed her against him and buried his face in her hair. "I love you, Sherry. There were days when I wanted to die, but I knew that you were still there, and somehow it all seemed worthwhile. I would dream of your eyes and the feel of your hair and the way you smell. Your dad kept me up to date on what you were doing, how you were coping. He brought me pictures of you. A few times, before you moved in with Madeline, I even called you just to hear you say hello. Little things, but they kept me going. They kept me feeling, even when I sometimes just needed to be numb. I have you here now, and I'll do anything I can to keep it that way. Be happy, Sherry. Please, be happy."

Sherry lifted her face to his, all shiny and glowing in the yellow light of the lamp. "I am happy," she whispered. "I am." But mirrored in his eyes she saw her worry, her dread, and knew that he wasn't entirely resolved to its being the end either. "It's just that too many people have died. Gary, and Paul, and his brother. So many lives have been hurt. Neither one of us can ever be the same, and I miss that. I'd give anything if we could go back to being the people we used to be."

Clint kissed her eyelid and brushed his fingers up through her hair. "We're the same people we always were, Sherry. We didn't change to cope with this. We just had to dig a little deeper into ourselves than we ever did before. We'll be all right. If we survived this, we can survive anything." He pulled her toward the door and smiled down at her. "Let's go back and talk to your dad. I think it's time you forgave him. He's suffering too."

Sherry heaved a great sigh. Not certain what she would do when she faced her father again, she wiped at her eyes and reached for the doorknob.

"Not so fast." A voice from the shadows beside the farther boat stopped them, and they both swung around. "Neither of you is going anywhere."

Clint's hand clamped protectively around Sherry's, and he pushed her slowly behind him as he saw the glint of a gun in the man's hand. "Who are you?" he asked, his voice harsh.

The man took another step forward, bringing his features partially into relief—the shaggy brown hair, the bitter set of dry lips, the bearded jaw. "I'm the man whose life you ruined," he whispered. "And I've come to repay the favor."

Sherry felt a surge of nausea mingled with dizziness as she looked into the hard, aged eyes of the young man who had started this whole nightmare.

The dull, lifeless eyes of Paul Calloway.

Chapter Twenty-Six

"I thought you were dead." Clint's voice was no more than a horrified whisper.

"I'm sure you wished it more than once," Paul said, keeping his voice low enough so that no one outside could hear.

"But they found your body."

Paul's frosty smile didn't reach his eyes. "It wasn't my body. It was Zeke's, the only guy I could trust. We were torching the building and leaving my fingerprints and clothes and stuff scattered around to make it look like I burned up there . . ."

"You killed him?"

Rage and remembered terror broke through the dullness in Paul's eyes, giving him a mournful, yet youthful quality that took the edge off the cool sound of his voice. "No, I didn't kill him! He was *helping* me! It was his idea! It's just that the fumes rose too fast, and he lit the fire too soon. I had already gotten out. We didn't know . . ." His voice fell off, and he hardened his expression. "The fire backlashed, and he was burned so bad that they couldn't even identify him. They found some of the stuff I left. Figured it was me."

Clint's nostrils flared in disgust. "Then you got what you wanted, after all."

The gun waved carelessly as Paul's haunted eyes glowered. "I never wanted him to die! We grew up together!" He swallowed back his emotion and his lips stretched like thin bands. "Anyway, don't give me that guilt routine, Jessup. I lost everything because of you. Where's *your* guilt?"

A flicker of pain passed over Clint's eyes, then vanished. "Oh, I had guilt, Paul. But it scarred over, just like my knife wound."

A deep laugh rolled from Paul's throat. "You want to talk about scars, man? I have scars you can't even see, and they all date back to that night."

Sherry was trembling, but Clint's hands were steady as they held her behind him, telling her not to panic, telling her to trust him. "It could have gone the other way. I saw you as a mixed-up kid who'd gotten in over his head. A jury probably would have seen the same thing, until you tried to shut me up."

"It never would have gone to a jury," Paul snapped, shaking his head adamantly. "I'd have been dead before they had even set a court date. All it would have taken was for Givanti to know I'd screwed up."

"Well, he did find out, and you're still here, aren't you?"

Paul steadied his gun, though his hands trembled over it. "Only because he didn't know about it until you came to court. You might say I've kept a low profile the last few months. No one knew except my brother and Zeke."

"Your ... your brother?" Sherry's hoarse exclamation came unbidden. Paul's utterance of it suddenly made the death so much more tragic.

"Yeah, my brother." Paul's lips quivered, and his eyes misted, though he blinked to cover the crack in his hard shell. He swallowed and lowered his gun distractedly. "And you got him too." He looked at the ceiling and raked his free hand through his unkempt hair. "He should have killed you, instead of the other way around. And I should have killed you in that ambulance, instead of Rivers. But nothing went right!" He caught himself, and wiped back the moisture blurring his eyes. "Ironic that Rivers was the only one of you I didn't want. He wasn't even supposed to be there. He was supposed to be *here*."

It took a moment for Paul's words to penetrate, but when they did, Clint's face drained of all its color.

"What?" Clint's question came on an astonished whisper.

Paul nodded his head and slumped his shoulders. "That's right. How do you think I knew that you'd be in ambulances going that route, or that you were hiding here? If you'd done everything the way he said you were going to, you'd be dead now."

Clint clutched Sherry's hand, trying to steady himself against the sudden dawning of cold betrayal. "He helped you?"

"Just to the point of telling me where you could be found. He didn't know what I was gonna do, but I doubt if he cared much. I made my intentions pretty clear."

Clint's face was white, and his dark eyes focused on the shadows. "That's why he got out of the car. He thought if you saw that he was there you'd wait."

"I couldn't wait!" Paul said through his teeth. "I'd waited for eight months."

Fear slipped as shock seeped in, and Sherry's wide blue eyes filled with fresh horror. "Why would Gary help you?" she asked raggedly. "Why?"

"Revenge," Paul said simply, as if it was the most logical emotion in the world. "He hated Clint. He would have killed him himself, but he was too yellow. But he did everything he could to make sure that I did. He had a condition, though. He wanted Sherry left unharmed."

218 | *Blind Trust*

"She wouldn't have been if your brother's attempt hadn't failed. She would have been killed with me!" Clint said.

"So Rivers said." He wiped at the perspiration on his brow with the back of the hand holding the gun. "And I told him that if he wanted her alive, he'd have to protect her himself. I didn't have time to be all that discriminating when my chance came."

Clint's hands tightened around Sherry's, and she felt the power borne of rage coiled up inside him, waiting for the moment to vent itself.

"And I tried," Paul went on. "I should have killed you when you went back to Shreveport, thinking I was dead. I should have blown you away then."

"You? You were the one following Sherry? You sent her that letter?"

"Surprised?" Paul tried to look satisfied, but his expression fell far short. "And I was the one following her, the one your friend managed to lose, until I made contact with Rivers and talked him into helping me. And you thought it was a whole stinkin' crime ring, didn't you? That Givanti's power reached everywhere. But I was the only one who wanted you dead. I was the only one who came after you." He sneered and nodded toward the water, as if Givanti were standing there. "His little group of wimps even took off the minute the verdict came in. Scattered all over, in case they were next. You think any of them cared anything about revenge? They were too worried about saving their hides. I'm the only one who had anything to gain by watching them bury you."

"Like what?" Clint asked. Paul was inching toward them, his gun rising to eye level. "Will it change anything? Haven't we all been through enough trouble?"

"You don't know what trouble is. But you're about to, old pal. You're about to find out."

Clint stiffened, every muscle in his body rigid. Sherry's backbone straightened as well, and she held her breath in defiance of that gun. His fingers bit into her skin when she tried to push around him, desperate to protect the man she loved as he had protected her.

"If you pull that trigger," Clint said, "you won't live to see me hit the ground. I don't have to tell you what kind of security I have out there."

"It would be worth it," Paul said. His eyes glittered under the feeble light, making what he was about to do seem less cruel, less cold. "But it won't happen that way. I got in here before you even got back today, and I'll get out. I'm a good swimmer. I'll be long gone before they get through the door."

He cocked the pistol and took another step closer.

"Don't!" Sherry jerked free of Clint and stepped around him. "Paul, don't! Please!"

"Get out of my way, Sherry," Paul said. "I have nothing against you, but I'll blow you away if you don't move."

Clint's breath was audible now, and his eyes locked with Paul's as if holding his gaze could make him drop his intention. "Sherry, move!" Clint's voice was quietly controlled, but she didn't heed his order. Somehow, she was going to stop this madness, and her only bet was that Paul couldn't shoot her as easily as he could Clint.

"Move, I said!" Paul's arm lashed out and grabbed her wrist. She gasped as he jerked her against him and clamped his free arm over her throat, but the gun remained pointed at Clint's head.

Clint's face went white, and a band of perspiration glistened on his forehead. "Paul, let her go," he whispered. "Let her go, and you can do whatever you want with me. You don't need her."

220 | Blind Trust

"With her, I won't have to swim a couple of miles," Paul said, his eyes dancing at the idea. "I could walk right through those jerks who think they've protected you so well. Man, the prosecutor's daughter could do miracles for me. I could get so far out of here they'd never find me."

Clint swallowed, and a muscle on his temple twitched. He raised his palms slowly, as if to calm a rabid beast. "Don't do it, Paul. This is between you and me. You could dive into that water and swim away right now, and no one would ever know you'd been here. You could even take one of the boats. I'd cover for you."

"You think I'm a moron?" Paul's arm clamped tighter around Sherry's throat, inhibiting her breath, and she closed her eyes. "I didn't come here to talk to you. I came here to watch you bleed. I came here to see you die."

Sherry tried to find her voice. "Paul . . ."

His arm tightened so hard around her throat that a wave of dizziness splashed over her. The veins in her neck battled against the arm acting as a tourniquet, but all she saw was the barrel of that pistol as Paul leveled it between Clint's eyes, and the knuckle of his finger turning white as it began to close over the trigger.

Sam pulled away from Madeline and turned toward the boat house, furrowed lines shading his eyes.

"What's the matter?" she asked.

"They've been in there too long," he said. "I don't like it."

"They're okay. Don't worry so much."

He took a few steps toward the boat house, then looked back at Madeline. "Weren't they fighting?"

"Sounded like it when they went in there."

"Then why is it so quiet now?"

Madeline smiled and wagged her eyebrows. "Maybe they made up. Or killed each other."

Sam didn't acknowledge the reference to their joke the first night they were together. "I'm going to check," Sam said, starting toward the boat house.

Madeline grabbed his arm and stopped him with a wink. "The trial's over, Sam. Now why don't you try to get your mind off work?"

"My mind is never entirely off work." He wrenched his eyes from the boat house and threw up his hands. "Ah, you're probably right. I've gotten too paranoid. The place is crawling with cops. What could possibly happen in there?"

"Just a little romance," she said with utmost confidence. "And absolutely nothing else."

Clint's eyes locked unyieldingly with Paul's as the cold barrel of the Saturday night special touched his forehead. "It won't solve anything, Paul," he whispered.

"It'll solve everything."

"For a minute, maybe. But it won't bring your brother or your friend back. Your brother wouldn't even be dead if he hadn't tried to kill me. I cared about you, Paul. That was my worst mistake. I thought I could help you."

"Help me?" Paul gave a dry, brittle laugh. "Get off the self-righteous act. Man, you loved it. You stumbled on something way above your mundane world, and you saw it as a chance for a cheap thrill."

"You think I put my life on hold for a cheap thrill?" Clint uttered in disgust. "Is that why you got involved?"

Paul looked at the water, rippling in the distance with mocking peace that would never be his again. "Man, I didn't have an old man to put me through college, or a genius IQ that got me scholarships. I found ways to do pretty well, but you disapproved, so you shot it all down. And you're going to pay." The words were uttered matter-of-factly, as if their events had come to a logical, inflexible end.

Clint disregarded the gun and looked into the pained depths of his enemy's pale eyes. "Don't give me the poor kid routine. I've been there, pal. If anybody knows about struggle, I do. Nobody helped me, either. But you knew you could have come to me when things got bad."

"Oh, come off it, man. You were so wrapped up in that fairy-tale wedding of yours, you wouldn't have given my problems a second thought."

"Obviously I did," Clint ground out through stiff lips. "Look what it cost me."

"Your life, man!" Paul said, clamping his arm tighter around Sherry's neck. "And your lady, and everything you ever cared about. Say your prayers! This'll be your last chance."

His knuckle was turning white again, about to squeeze the trigger, and something inside Sherry snapped. Clamping her hands together, she summoned all her might and swung her arms up, knocking Paul's stiff aim skyward.

Instantly, Clint's hands clamped over Paul's wrist, wrestling for the gun above their heads, and Paul lost his hold on Sherry. A cry tore from her throat as strength foiled intention, and she scrambled for the door in horror when she saw both hands clamped over the pistol, muscles straining, cords throbbing, fingers clawing. The gun was descending, regaining its aim on Clint, pointing just over his shoulder, turning toward his head ...

She heard herself scream, and as if in slow motion, she turned back and started toward them in a desperate attempt to stop them.

But suddenly the gun went off, and she was hurled back against the wall in a blinding burst of pain, and she heard Clint scream, "She-e-r-r-y!" And she felt herself falling ... falling ... falling into an abyss of herself, until there was nothing left but blackness and the cruel, cold chill of loss.

Chapter Twenty-Seven

S he-e-e-r-r-y!" Clint's voice rang out like death, skipping over the water and reaching the ears of everyone within a mile. Sherry lay motionless on the floor, a widening ring of blood painting her arm.

The door burst open, and Sam shouted, "Police! Freeze!"

The gun suddenly came free of Paul's hand. Clutching it, Clint grabbed the man's collar and slammed him against the wall, the pistol shaking in his hand. "I'll kill you!"

"Cl . . . Clint!" Sherry's weak voice came like the answer to a prayer, melting his immediate intent. She was not dead. Oh thank God, she was not dead.

He dropped Paul to his knees and rushed to her just as Sam stepped inside, his gun in his hand, the others at his heels. Scooping her up in his arms, he held her helplessly.

Eric Grayson barreled in and fell to his knees beside his daughter. "Oh, my soul! We've got to get her to a hospital!"

Clint nodded blindly. "Take her. Hurry!"

With the help of another officer, Grayson pried Clint's arms loose and gathered her into his arms. When they had darted out of the boat house, Clint stood up and stalked over to Paul, who knelt in a shiver at the guns trained on him. "Get up!" he gritted, holding his gun to the man's temple.

224 | *Blind Trust*

Clint's eyes were as dark as death. He cocked the pistol.

Perspiration dripped from his brow and burned his eyes, and Paul squeezed his eyes shut. He was a kid, still a kid, as mean and vicious as the most hardened criminal. And as scared as a boy faced with a mad dog. He looked at that boy and saw through the hatred and recalled the first day he had met him. He had come to the youth group as a scruffy high school senior, for the sole purpose of getting the attention of a girl he was pursuing. Clint had befriended him to keep him coming. What had happened to him?

Slowly, as if it took every ounce of strength he had left, Clint dropped the gun to his side and stepped out of Sam's way.

Sam dashed forward, but before he reached him, Paul dove between the two boats and began to swim underwater. Quickly, Sam fell to one knee and opened fire.

Someone drove the eighteen-wheeler to the bank, shining its headlights over the rippling surface of the reservoir. And finally they saw Paul, the life gone out of his body.

Clint only stared dully at him as some of the men waded out to bring him back. Paul Calloway was really dead, but somehow the knowledge didn't hold much joy.

Turning his back on the sight, Clint ran back toward the house to find what they had done with Sherry. "Where is she?"

"In the car," Madeline cried. "They're about to take her to the—"

Clint didn't hear the rest. The car was turning around on the grass, about to leave, and Clint dashed after it. "Stop! I'm coming with you!"

The car stopped, and Clint got in. Grayson was holding Sherry in the backseat, and Clint leaned over her as the car lurched forward. "Sherry?" His voice was on the edge of tears, and Sherry opened her eyes.

"Is it over?" she whispered.

He took her hand. "Yes, baby. It's over. It's all over."

Sherry closed her eyes again.

"We'll be all right," Clint said hoarsely, pushing her hair back from her face. "We'll be all right now."

———◆◆———

An hour later, Clint sat helplessly in the hospital waiting room with Wes and Laney, staring at the wall, waiting to hear yet another verdict that would determine the course of the rest of his life. Would Sherry die? Would that be the tragic ending to this tragic production his life had become?

He closed his eyes and thought back to the day he had chased her in his Bronco and run her off the road. Why had he done that? Why hadn't he just left things alone, until he was safe? Why hadn't he been more patient? Why hadn't he known that Paul wasn't really dead? If he'd just left her alone, he wouldn't have had to bring her with him. And her life would never have been in danger.

He searched the farthest corners of his mind and tried to find some clue that she would be all right. She had not completely lost consciousness all the way to the hospital. Maybe that was good. And she had spoken. And just before they wheeled her away in the emergency room, she had smiled at him. He had leaned forward and cupped her face in his hands. Oh, did he dare hope that she would be all right? He looked over his fingertips to the door where they had taken her. If only they had let him stay with her. If only he could be there . . .

The door swung open, and the emergency room doctor came out. Clint, Madeline, Sam, and Sherry's father all stood at the same time, none of them asking anything for fear the answer was not what they wanted to hear.

"She's going to be fine," the doctor said. "The bullet didn't even touch the bone. She also has a slight concussion from hitting her head when she fell. Besides some pretty fierce pain, she's going to be completely well soon. We'd like to keep her for a couple of days for observation, though."

Clint sank onto the vinyl sofa, a sudden surge of emotion racking his body. Covering his face, he sent up a silent prayer of thanks, while the others around him expressed relief in their own ways. She was okay. She was fine. She was safe.

"She wants to see Mr. Jessup," the doctor said. "We've got her on some pain medication, but she's pretty alert."

Clint stood up again. "Can I stay here with her tonight? I don't want to leave her."

"I don't think she'd let you go if you wanted to," the doctor said with a smile. "Come on. I'll take you to her."

Sam laced his fingers through Madeline's hand as he pulled her with him across the hospital parking lot, lit only by yellow circles of light from street lamps overhead. He had been quiet since the incident at the boat house, and now that Sherry was fine, that had not changed.

"Guess it's all over," Madeline said quietly when they reached his car.

"Yeah. Over."

He leaned against the car and looked up into the sky. She followed his eyes and wondered what he saw.

"What's the matter?"

"Nothing."

The dead end hurt her. Was the tiny bit of progress they had made toward a relationship going to fizzle out just like that? She looked down at the grimy pavement beneath her feet and frowned. She guessed it was.

Ironic, she thought. All this time she had been afraid of Sam's getting killed or wounded. She'd almost expected to lose him that way, now that she'd found him. She hadn't counted on losing him to indifference.

Clearing her throat, she turned toward him. "I think I'll go on back in. Maybe they'll let me see Sherry."

Sam nodded, as if he didn't care.

Lifting her chin to keep herself brave, Madeline started to walk away.

"Madeline?" Sam's voice was soft, reluctant, but it stopped her. Slowly, she turned around, bracing herself for an explanation about how it had been nice while it lasted. His eyes were so sad that they wrung her heart and forced her to forgive him even before he sent her on her way. "I don't deserve to have you stay," he whispered, "but I don't want you to go."

His voice teetered on the edge of emotion, and she went back to him, hands jammed in her pockets, heart jamming her throat. "What do you mean you don't deserve it?"

He sighed deeply, and reached for her hand. "I mean that I've been such a failure throughout this whole thing."

"A what?" She took his other hand and gazed at him with disbelief in her expression. "How can you say that? We're alive. We came out of it."

"Not because of anything I did. In fact, if I'd done my job, Sherry wouldn't be up in that hospital bed right now."

"No," Madeline argued. "If you'd done things differently, she'd be dead. And so would Clint. In fact, they would have died in that barn when it exploded the other day."

"One accomplishment does not erase a failure," he said, his eyes full of anguish. "I'm a cop. I shouldn't have let them go into that boat house alone. I should have suspected . . ."

"You and the other twenty cops on the grounds thought it was all right. Are you saying that it's okay for them to make a miscalculation, but it isn't for you?"

228 | Blind Trust

"I was Clint's friend. I was his guard. And until today I was a better cop than those other guys."

"Until me," she said as the real problem became clear to her.

"What?" The question was meant to be innocent, but she sensed that she had hit a nerve. She knew he saw his feelings for her as a new weakness that interfered, and she resented it.

"It all boils down to me. If I hadn't stopped you, you would have gone into the boat house. If you hadn't been with me, you might never have let them go in."

Sam was silent for a moment, then he dropped her hand. "I shouldn't have let my attention be so divided when I was on duty. It almost cost Clint and Sherry their lives."

"And since you're virtually always on duty," she said in a despairing, sullen voice, "I guess that means it's impossible for you to have any kind of relationship. Is that what you're saying?"

"No," he whispered. "I don't think that's what I'm saying."

"Wait a minute. Let me try again," she said, her voice growing louder. "You think you deserve to be punished for not being psychic and not getting to Paul Calloway before he got to Clint and Sherry. So your punishment is to go through life alone, nipping good possibilities for relationships with wonderful women in the bud, is that it?"

"No," he said, swallowing. "I'm not looking for punishment."

"Then what are you looking for?" she snapped furiously.

Suddenly, he smiled. "Someone to tell me it's okay," he whispered. "Someone to hold me and give me focus and tell me I didn't screw up as bad as I think I did."

Madeline inclined her head helplessly, and her shoulders slumped in relief. "You've got it," she whispered. She slid her arms around his waist, and he pulled her tightly against him.

"I think what I was trying to say," he whispered against her hair, "is that since I can't really divide my attentions between romance and work, maybe it's time for me to make a change. Maybe it's time for me to choose."

Madeline felt him slipping away again, and she clung tighter. "I never put much faith in guarantees," she assured him, almost desperately. "I don't need them. Please don't choose between us. I can live with your job."

Sam framed her face and pressed his forehead against hers. "You crazy little thing. You think I wouldn't choose you, don't you?"

Madeline closed her eyes. "You don't have to choose," she whispered again.

"Yes, I do," he whispered. "Because suddenly staying alive seems pretty important to me."

His kiss was like molten joy poured over raw nerves, coaxing her to accept the choice he had already made, coaxing her to believe that he was offering guarantees, coaxing her to rejoice in the sacrifice that resulted in so much reward.

And being alive seemed wondrously precious to Madeline, too.

A little while later, Clint sat on the hospital bed next to Sherry, cradling her against him. They'd have to do surgery if they expected to separate them, he told himself. Because he had no intentions of ever leaving her side again.

The door opened, and Eric Grayson stepped into the softly lit room. Sherry sat up and gave him a grudging look.

With eyes as humble and frightened as she had ever seen them, he entered the room. "How do you feel?" he asked.

"I'm fine."

"Well, I'm not. I'm a little shaken," he admitted. Awkwardly, he pulled up a chair to the bedside and sat down. "I thought I'd lost you." He covered his face and shook his head. "I would never have forgiven myself."

Sherry sat up, and Clint started to get off of the bed. "I'll step outside and—"

"No," Eric said. "Stay. You're part of this family, and you belong here. Besides, I owe you a fierce apology."

"No." Clint held up a hand to stem the regrets. "I did all this for my conscience, not because you—"

"I'm not apologizing for that," Grayson cut in softly. "I'm apologizing for undermining you by sending Gary Rivers to protect Sherry. At the time it seemed as if someone who cared for her would do a better job. It was stupid, and it must have made things so much harder for you. And it turned out to be such a disaster."

Clint looked down at Sherry's palm and stroked his hand across it. "I'll admit I cursed you for that a few times."

"You should have." Grayson shook his head. "I misjudged him terribly. I never suspected—"

Clint reached across Sherry and touched the older man's shoulder. "Enough said. It's over, and I think I can understand your reasoning. No hard feelings."

Grayson released a heavy breath, then looked at his daughter. "And now, my apology to you," he said.

Sherry shook her head. "Don't."

His eyes were pleading. "Sherry, I probably could have handled things better. But I was so desperate to protect you. You were all I had left. Can't you see that?"

"You let me suffer, Dad, and I didn't have to. You kept me away from Clint when I could have been there, helping him through it. You robbed me of my marriage, and let me think I wasn't enough for him, that he got bored . . ."

"I never meant for you to think that, Sherry. I never wanted you to feel that way. I just didn't see another way. I thought the emotional danger was much less significant than the physical danger."

"You were wrong," she said. "Emotional ties are strong, Dad. You've never understood them, not really."

"Yes, I have," he insisted. "I understand them now. I understand that I'd rather be in physical danger, myself, than to suffer the emotional danger of losing you. Honey, I'm asking you to forgive me one more time." His voice broke with the words, and he wilted and dropped his forehead on her mattress. He began to shake with deep, hard sobs, and Sherry's face slowly changed.

She looked up at Clint with tears in her eyes, then back down at her father, hurting and broken. She closed her eyes and wiped the tears from her cheek, and breathed in a sob herself. Slowly, she withdrew her hand from Clint's, and touched her father's head.

He looked up at her, his face twisted and anguished. "You have to believe me, Sherry," he forced out. "Everytime I looked in your eyes after Clint left, it was like a knife being twisted inside me. I prayed that God would intervene so that I could bring Clint back, and when we thought we found Paul's body, I believed that was the answer. Honey, don't cut me out of your life because of this. I want to give you away at your wedding. I want to be a grandfather to your children. They don't have to know that their grandfather is a fool."

"You're not a fool." The words came on a whisper, and she reached out and touched his face. Eric pulled her into a hug that included Clint.

"Does this mean I still get to be your father?" he asked.

She breathed a laugh through her tears. "I guess so. Somebody's got to give me away when I get married."

Eric let her go and wiped the tears on his face. "As soon as I leave here, I'm going for the minister. We have a wedding to plan, and there's no time to waste."

Sherry breathed an enormous sigh and smiled at Clint. "Just give me a license and a ring and a few months of uninterrupted peace with the man I love. And then I'll be back to myself."

"Is that possible?" Clint asked softly. "Will any of us ever be ourselves again?"

"No," Grayson said. "We've all changed. But we're stronger now. None of us will ever take the people we love or the time we have with them for granted again."

Clint's arms tightened around Sherry, reaffirming that strength that filtered into their love, promising never to be torn asunder, never to be mistrusted, never to turn against them again.

After Eric left, a knock sounded on the door, and Clint called, "Come in." Wes's face was pale as he pushed open the door. He took a look at his sister, started to say something, then, overcome, just leaned over and gave her a hug. When he had found his voice, he said, "I'm glad you're okay."

"Yeah, me, too," she said. She gestured for him to pull a chair up to her bed, and as he did so, she said, "I heard you were in court today."

He nodded. "Yeah. He got me in."

She knew he referred to their father, even though he'd never been able to call Eric that.

"Are you two speaking now?"

"Hardly."

"Wes, don't you think it's time?"

Wes's expression was stunned. "How could you say that? The man got you shot. You were almost killed because of him. He cared more about that case than he cared about you!"

"I thought so, too," she said, taking her brother's hand. "But Wes, he meant well. He thought he was doing the right thing. Everything he did was to keep me from getting hurt."

"But it didn't work."

"I'm fine," she said. She thought about the struggles with Paul, the gunshot wound . . . "You know, I can keep a scoresheet of all the things that went wrong, dwell on them and get bitter over them, or I can decide that those things are not going to mess up my life, and move on. He's still our father. He's not perfect, and he makes mistakes. But his heart is right, Wes."

"But he let you hurt for all those months. He had the power to give you some peace about Clint, and he didn't. Then he dragged you right into the fray—"

"That's not true, Wes. I was in it whether any of us liked it or not. Getting shot was more a result of my own rebellion than anything he had done. I shouldn't have gone out of the sight of the bodyguards. I should have been more cooperative."

Wes got up and ambled to the hospital window, looked out, and then turned back to her. His face was a study in emotional turmoil, and she knew where it came from.

"Wes, he's not the same man who left us when we were kids. He's changed, just like Laney changed after the two of you were married. He knows what he did was wrong, and he's repented. God's a God of second chances, Wes."

"But I'm not that good. I can't forgive like God does."

"Then you'd better stay away from the Lord's Prayer."

He looked at her. "What do you mean?"

She smiled. "'Forgive us our trespasses as we forgive those who've trespassed against us'? If you're going to *be* forgiven in the same way *you've* forgiven, that could be trouble."

"That's not what that means," Wes said.

"Yes, it is, Wes, and you know it."

Silence held between them, thick and uncomfortable, and finally, Wes came back to the chair and sank back down. "It's hard, Sherry. Maybe if Mom was still alive, if I could see the two of them make peace, maybe it would be easier. But

234 | Blind Trust

she's not here, and she never had the satisfaction of seeing his repentance."

"But you have, Wes." She slid partially up in bed, intent on making her point. "Remember when Laney was nothing more to you than Amy's birth mother? Remember when she found out Patrice was dead, and that Amy was being raised without a mother? She said, 'Amy has a mother, so she doesn't have to grow up without one.'"

"Yeah, so?"

"It's the same with us. We have family, Wes. We have a father. Your kids have a grandpa—and he's the only one they have. Let him be a part of your life. It won't take anything away from you, Wes. It'll only make your lives richer."

Wes's eyes were wet as he rubbed his hands down his face. "I'll think about it, Sherry. That's the best I can do."

"That's enough for now."

❖

Later, Sherry got up and walked down to the waiting room where so many of her friends had gathered. She saw Madeline and Sam, Wes and Laney and the kids, her father, and even Erin, the pilot.

She hugged them all, giving a special, lingering hug to her friend and roommate. "If a person has to get kidnapped, Madeline, you're the one to do it with."

Madeline laughed. "Actually, it was kind of fun."

"Fun?"

"Well, not the dangerous part. But we met some nice people."

Everyone broke into laughter, and Sherry shot Clint an amused look.

"So I guess you'll be getting married and moving out of my house, now? Leaving me high and dry without a roommate?" Madeline asked.

"I'll miss you," Sherry said with a grin.

"I don't do well alone, you know. I like having people around. I'll probably resort to talking to myself ..."

"You can get another roommate."

"Who?"

Erin, the pilot, stepped forward then, her eyes narrowed as she thought over the possibilities. "Are you really looking for a roommate?"

"Yes, I really am," Madeline said. "Do you know anybody?"

"Well, as a matter of fact ... I *have* a roommate—a flight attendant who's almost never home—and we just got notice that our apartments is being converted into a condo, and neither of us wants to buy. If you could handle two roommates ..."

"Are you kidding? We'd have a ball! I'd love it!"

"Well, neither of us is home that much, but you should probably know that I won't be flying any more covert operations. Commercial flights only."

"Let's do it," Madeline said. "I'll take you right over and show you the house, and if you like it, I'll help you move as soon as Sherry moves out ..."

Sherry gaped at her. "Are you trying to rush me out?"

"Yes!" Madeline said. "You and Clint need to start your new lives, anyway. And they have to find a place to live!"

She watched, laughing, as the two women left with Sam, both of them talking ninety-to-nothing.

When they were gone, she turned back to the others left in the room. Wes and Laney sat awkwardly in one corner— the baby sat in Wes's lap, smiling at all the activity, and Amy leaned against her mother. Across the room, Eric Grayson sat alone, rather awkwardly. He got up, and took a deep breath. "Well, I guess we'll all sleep well tonight. I'll go on home now."

Sherry shot a look to Wes, silently pleading with him to make peace with his father now. Wes sat unmoving, and his gaze drifted to his sneakers.

"I'll see you all later," Eric said, pressing a kiss on his daughter's cheek. Then he started out of the waiting room.

"Dad?" It was Wes's voice, slightly hoarse, and Eric turned back. His face betrayed how moved he'd been that Wes had called him that.

"Yes, son?"

"How'd you like to come have a bite somewhere with us? We haven't eaten yet and . . . well, my kids really need to get to know their grandpa." His eyes misted as he spoke.

Eric stared at him for a moment as his face reddened, and Sherry could see how he struggled with the emotion taking hold of his face. "I'd love to do that," he said.

Laney's smile was huge as she got to her feet and handed Eric his grandson. "Can you say 'Grandpa'?" she asked the baby. He grunted something and smiled at the man who looked so much like his father.

Sherry and Clint walked them all to the elevator, said their good-byes, then stood watching the doors as they closed. "I can't believe that," she whispered.

"Me, either," Clint said. "It was a miracle."

"God is so good."

Clint turned her around. "Do you really believe that? A couple of days ago you had lost your faith . . . you said it was self-betrayal. Do you still believe that, Sherry?"

"No," she said. "I was angry, and lashing out. Thank goodness God is still faithful even when we're faithless."

⁕

In the throes of sleep in her hospital room later that night, Sherry struggled with the colliding images ranting through her mind like faces in a haunted house. Paul's face and the cold, cruel glint of his gun; the dead boy on the bluff; the fire that had been meant to consume her and Clint; the navy hooded jackets; the pain of betrayal that was not really betrayal. But on the heels of the horror came an unyielding Bronco to chase her down and rescue her from her grief. And the horror was gone.

She opened her eyes and Clint—still sitting in the chair beside her bed—smiled down at her. It wasn't all a dream. He was here, and no matter what had transpired before this moment, now was what mattered.

"I love you, Clint," she whispered.

"I love you too, baby," he said, stroking her hand. "Go back to sleep."

"You won't leave?"

"Not until you push me away," he said.

"Then you'll be here a long time, Superman."

"That's my plan," Clint said with a smile as he leaned over to kiss her. "That's been my plan all along."

And, finally, Sherry knew that faith that she had almost abandoned. No longer would it be a flimsy bit of self-betrayal. It would become the backbone of her secure world. A world she had fought for and won. The cornerstone of their little square of paradise.

About the Author

Terri Blackstock is an award-winning novelist who has written for several major publishers including HarperCollins, Dell, Harlequin, and Silhouette. Published under two pseudonyms, her books have sold over 3.5 million copies worldwide.

With her success in secular publishing at its peak, Blackstock had what she calls "a spiritual awakening." A Christian since the age of fourteen, she realized she had not been using her gift as God intended. It was at that point that she recommitted her life to Christ, gave up her secular career, and made the decision to write only books that would point her readers to him.

"I wanted to be able to tell the truth in my stories," she said, "and not just be politically correct. It doesn't matter how many readers I have if I can't tell them what I know about the roots of their problems and the solutions that have literally saved my own life."

Her books are about flawed Christians in crisis and God's provisions for their mistakes and wrong choices. She claims to be extremely qualified to write such books, since she's had years of personal experience.

A native of nowhere, since she was raised in the Air Force, Blackstock makes Mississippi her home. She and her husband are the parents of three children—a blended family which she considers one more of God's provisions.

ENJOY THE NEXT BOOK IN THE SECOND CHANCES SERIES

Broken Wings
Chapter 1

*I*f not for a minor car accident that kept her home, Erin Russell would have been copiloting Flight 94 when it crashed, killing 151 people, including her dear friend and captain, Mick Hammon. News of the crash devastated her, and she hasn't flown since. Rumors are spreading throughout her airline that the crash has sent her over the edge, that fear and grief have paralyzed her, that she may never fly again. Addison Lowe, the National Transportation Safety Board investigator who is trying to determine the cause of the crash, has heard those rumors. Just last night, he even heard her trying to resign entirely, though her boss convinced her to give it some time. Despite her fragile state, Addison still has to grill her about the pilot whose errors may have caused his own death ...

The persistent ringing of the doorbell penetrated Erin's thin, shallow sleep, and she opened her eyes and sat up. Through the haze of grogginess, she realized she had fallen asleep on the couch, wearing her faded jeans and an old sweatshirt. There had been too many ghosts to sleep in the bed. The couch kept her from falling too deeply into sleep from which there was no escape once the dreams started.

The doorbell rang again, and Erin stood up and looked around, prepared to destroy any evidence that she'd slept on the couch. People were already beginning to question her mental state. But then, she was beginning to question it, too.

Pushing back her sleep-tousled hair, she stumbled to the door and opened it. The man she had seen waiting outside Frank's office last night stood before her, clad in an ivory sweater that deepened the rough tan on his seasoned face. "Yes?" she asked.

"Miss Russell?"

"Yes," she said again, irritated.

"I'm Addison Lowe. I was in Mr. Redlo's office last night ... "

"I remember, Mr. Lowe," she cut in, crossing her arms with a decided lack of tolerance. "I hope you found my conversation with my boss interesting."

"I wasn't eavesdropping. I had an appointment."

"Regardless," she said, still blocking the door with her body, "you listened to a private conversation that was none of your business."

"That's where you're wrong, Miss Russell," he said.

"Wrong about your listening? You don't expect me to believe—"

"No," he said. "Wrong about it being any of my business. It's very much my business. It's my job to know when a pilot's stability is waning, though I generally find out after it's too late."

All the murky grogginess in Erin's head vanished, and molten fire rose up in her eyes. "I beg your pardon."

Addison reached for his wallet, handed her a card. "I'm with the National Transportation Safety Board, and I came from Washington to investigate the crash."

"The National Transportation ... " The words faded off into nothingness before they were completely uttered, and a foreboding sense of panic descended. Had she really admitted to being afraid to fly in the presence of a NTSB official? Had he heard everything? She tried not to look as defensive as she felt. "What ... what do you want from me?" she asked.

"I understand you were Mick Hammon's first officer," he said. "I thought maybe you could answer some questions for me."

She glared up at him, weighing one consequence against another. He didn't exactly look menacing. In fact, those dark green eyes sparkled with soul. The normal impulse would be to like him at first sight. But Erin didn't want to like him. Not if he was the one sifting through the remains of Mick Hammon's crash. On the other hand, she asked herself, what choice did she really have?

Sighing loudly, she stepped back from the door to let him in. She was still an employee of Southeast Airlines, after all, and when it came to an investigation, the NTSB might as well be the FBI. She looked around for signs of her emotional state that could quickly be discarded, cluttered clues that she was at her rope's end. "You might have called first," she said, gathering a pile of wadded Kleenex from the coffee table and rushing into the kitchen to throw it away.

"I tried," he said. "The phone was off the hook."

Erin swung around, saw him standing in the kitchen doorway. His green eyes probed mercilessly, seeing far too many things that she wasn't prepared to reveal. Guilty, she glanced at the telephone, lying on its side on the counter. "I guess I forgot to hang it up last night."

"No problem," he said. There was an almost amused twinkle in his eyes, but beneath that twinkle lay something else. Something like ... concern. "I leave mine lying around all the time. Just forget to hang it up."

"All right." She stared coldly at him, resentful of the way he was trying to corner her about something that was none of his business. "I took it off the hook on purpose. I was in a bad mood." Impertinently, she held out her wrists. "Go ahead. Cuff me and haul me in."

The deep laughter that erupted from his throat took her by surprise, and her anger began to diminish by degrees. For the first time she noticed the strong texture of his short black hair, the thick lines of his brows, and the startling contrast of those laughing, smoky emerald eyes. The corners of her rigid mouth softened, and she smiled when he rubbed his mouth, as if the gesture could wipe away his condemning grin.

"Sorry," he said, his laughter dying. "I don't mean to drill you. If you want to leave the phone off the hook, it's your prerogative."

"I appreciate that," she said dryly.

"I'm also sorry I woke you," he added.

She looked down at her wrinkled sweatshirt, at the jeans she'd slept in. Self-consciously, she raised a hand to her tangled hair. "I ... I wasn't asleep. I had just gotten up."

"Had you?" he asked skeptically. The look of amusement vanished from his eyes, replaced by that annoying look of concern. Erin wished that just once in the past two weeks she could have looked in someone's eyes and not seen concern. "Well, whatever ... I realize I haven't come at the best time. But I really need to talk to you before I can go on with my report."

Erin turned to the coffee pot, groped for the can of grains, and mechanically began filling the percolator. "I don't know why you have to talk to me. I wasn't there."

Addison shifted his weight to one hip and leaned on the counter. Subtly, the scent of woodsy aftershave drifted to her senses. "No, you weren't there, but you were usually Hammon's copilot, and, I hear, his closest friend at the airline. I need a lot of background on him if I'm going to come to a fair conclusion about the crash. You can give it to me."

His words served as sparks to ignite her tinder-dry emotions, and Erin swiveled and glared at him across the small kitchen. "Fair conclusion? Are you kidding me? You just want more evidence to nail him. Why not? He isn't here to defend himself, is he? You can say just about anything you want to about him."

"Erin, I'm looking for accurate—"

"You can call me Miss Russell."

"I got your name from your file," he said, all warmth gone from his voice. He quietly assumed an authoritative tone. "And I'll call you whatever you like, Miss Russell. As for your hysterical accusation, I am not trying to 'nail' anyone. I'm trying to do my job and make certain that the cause of that crash is known so that it doesn't happen again."

Silence continued between them for a series of eternities as the smell of perking coffee intruded on vexed senses. Finally,

Erin turned back to it, poured two cups, then grudgingly added the cream and sugar he politely requested. A frown cut deep into her forehead as she handed him a mug then set a spoon in her own and stirred the dark liquid. "I don't . . . I don't want to talk about Mick with you. Or the crash. Or anything else."

Addison sipped the coffee and leveled those poignant eyes on her again.

"You have to," he said quietly. "If you don't, I'll have you subpoenaed, and you'll have to talk about it in front of a board of my superiors. Believe me, you don't want to do that."

She gulped her coffee, scalding her tongue. Frustrated, she set it back down too hard. It sloshed onto the counter, but she scarcely noticed, for she was staring at Addison with scathing eyes. "Well, do you mind if I brush my teeth first? Change clothes? I didn't expect to wake up to an interrogation this morning."

"I'll wait," he said, leaning back against the counter. "Take your time."

Seething, Erin pushed past him and slammed the door as she went into her bedroom.

Broken Wings

Available at Christian bookstores.

(ISBN #: 0-310-20708-8)

GRAND RAPIDS, MICHIGAN 49530

www.zondervan.com

Check out these other great books in the Second Chances Series!

Blind Trust
Softcover 0-310-20710-X

Broken Wings
Softcover 0-310-20708-8

Never-Again Good-Bye
Softcover 0-310-20707-X

When Dreams Cross
Softcover 0-310-20709-6

Pick up a copy today at your favorite bookstore!

ZONDERVAN™

GRAND RAPIDS, MICHIGAN 49530 USA

WWW.ZONDERVAN.COM

Seaside

Seaside is a novella of the heart—poignant, gentle, true, offering an eloquent reminder that life is too precious a gift to be unwrapped in haste.

Sarah Rivers has it all: successful husband, healthy kids, beautiful home, meaningful church work.

Corinne, Sarah's sister, struggles to get by. From Web site development to jewelry sales, none of the pies she has her thumb stuck in contains a plum worth pulling.

No wonder Corinne envies Sarah. What she doesn't know is how jealous Sarah is of her. And what neither of them realizes is how their frantic drive for achievement is speeding them headlong past the things that matter most in life.

So when their mother, Maggie, purchases plane tickets for them to join her in a vacation on the Gulf of Mexico, they almost decline the offer. But circumstances force the issue, and the sisters soon find themselves first thrown together, then ultimately *drawn* together, in one memorable week in a cabin called "Seaside."

As Maggie, a professional photographer, sets out to capture on film the faces and moods of her daughters, more than film develops. A picture emerges of possibilities that come only by slowing down and savoring the simple treasures of the moment. It takes a mother's love and honesty to teach her two daughters a wiser, uncluttered way of life—one that can bring peace to their hearts and healing to their relationship. And though the lesson comes on wings of grief, the sadness is tempered with faith, restoration, and a joy that comes from the hand of God.

Hardcover: 0-310-23318-6

Pick up a copy today at your favorite bookstore!

ZONDERVAN™

GRAND RAPIDS, MICHIGAN 49530 USA

WWW.ZONDERVAN.COM

Best-selling books with Beverly LaHaye

Seasons Under Heaven
Softcover 0-310-23519-7

Showers in Season
Softcover 0-310-24296-7

Times and Seasons
Softcover 0-310-24297-5

Season of Blessing
Hardcover 0-310-23328-3

Pick up a copy today at your favorite bookstore!

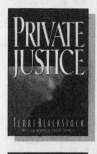
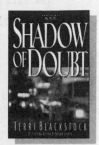
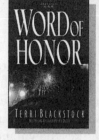

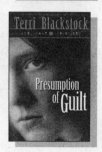
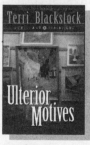
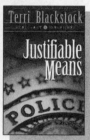

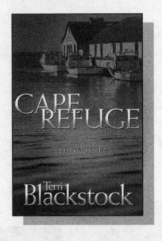

... want to hear from you. Please send your comments about this book to us in care of the address below. Thank you.

ZONDERVAN™

GRAND RAPIDS, MICHIGAN 49530

www.zondervan.com

We ~~so~~ ... Please ~~...~~ this